"YOU REALLY ARE A DANGER JUNKIE, AREN'T YOU, HANK?" SYLVIA SAID CONTEMPTUOUSLY.

"Even in love you have to have that extra little element of excitement. Well, I'm not going to put up with it. I'm leaving now," she told him, breaking free of his grasp.

With a quickness she wouldn't have thought possible he curved his arm around her waist and pulled her toward him again. "If you're looking for pretexts to break off our lovemaking, I'll give you a real one," he said in a voice raspy with anger and frustration.

"Let me go or I'll scream," she whispered hoarsely.

She felt rather than heard his laugh—a movement of hard muscles in his body pressed tightly against hers. "Scream away. It won't do you any good."

"You're despicable," she retorted. "I don't want anything to do with you."

"It's much too late for that," he told her scornfully. "You're stuck with me. Why don't you just admit that? It would make things a great deal easier for both of us."

CANDLELIGHT ECSTASY SUPREMES

77 A WILD AND RECKLESS LOVE, *Tate McKenna*
78 BRIGHT FLAME, DISTANT STAR, *Blair Cameron*
79 HOW MANY TOMORROWS?, *Alison Tyler*
80 STOLEN IDYLL, *Alice Morgan*
81 APHRODITE'S PROMISE, *Anne Silverlock*
82 ANOTHER EDEN, *Dallas Hamlin*
83 PLAYERS IN THE SHADOWS, *Donna Kimel Vitek*
84 AGAINST THE WIND, *Anne Stuart*
85 A LITTLE BIT OF WARMTH, *Jackie Black*
86 HIDDEN CHARMS, *Lee Magner*
87 DOUBLE OR NOTHING, *Lynn Patrick*
88 THE BEST REASON OF ALL, *Emily Elliott*
89 MORE THAN SHE BARGAINED FOR, *Lori Copeland*
90 MAN OF THE HOUR, *Tate McKenna*
91 BENDING THE RULES, *Kathy Alerding*
92 JUST FOR THE ASKING, *Eleanor Woods*
93 ISLAND OF DESIRE, *Antoinette Hale*
94 AN ANGEL'S SHARE, *Heather Graham*
95 DANGEROUS INTERLUDE, *Emily Elliott*
96 CHOICES AND CHANCES, *Linda Vail*
97 SWEETER TOMORROWS, *Kit Daley*
98 MILLION-DOLLAR LOVER, *Blair Cameron*
99 A GLIMMER OF TRUST, *Alison Tyler*
100 TOO CLOSE FOR COMFORT, *Ginger Chambers*

A LUST FOR DANGER

Margaret Malkind

A CANDLELIGHT ECSTASY SUPREME®

Published by
Dell Publishing Co., Inc.,
1 Dag Hammarskjold Plaza
New York, New York 10017

ISBN: 0-440-15118-X

Printed in the United States of America

First printing—December 1985

To Our Readers:

We are pleased and excited by your overwhelmingly positive response to our Candlelight Ecstasy Supremes. Unlike all the other series, the Supremes are filled with more passion, adventure, and intrigue and are obviously the stories you like best.

In months to come we will continue to publish books by many of your favorite authors as well as the very finest work from new authors of romantic fiction. As always, we are striving to present unique, absorbing love stories—the very best love has to offer.

Breathtaking and unforgettable, Ecstasy Supremes follow in the great romantic tradition you've come to expect *only* from Candlelight Ecstasy.

Your suggestions and comments are always welcome. Please let us hear from you.

Sincerely,

The Editors
Candlelight Romances
1 Dag Hammarskjold Plaza
New York, New York 10017

CHAPTER ONE

Sylvia Goddard walked down Caldera Street with the same wariness she used in her own neighborhood in lower Manhattan. She stepped confidently so no watcher would consider her easy prey, stayed away from doorways she could be pulled into, and kept a cautious eye out for the unusual.

The street was a crazy collage of shacks built of every material possible. Tar-paper hovels, roofs of corrugated tin, walls made of billboards with pictures of cowboys lighting up around a campfire, and packing-box houses leaned drunkenly against each other. Here and there an impenetrable maze of passageways and alleys, the location of which could only be guessed at from the street, pierced the dense slum.

In the two months that Sylvia had been teaching modern dance at the university, she had never been in this part of San Lorenzo. Neither, Sylvia guessed, had Elena Vanegas, the dainty, designer-dressed student who had summoned her here.

To the extent that any real antigovernment activity existed in tightly controlled Paraguay, it was here, in the

Caldera district of San Lorenzo. Was Elena "political"? Sylvia wondered. But then why would she have asked Sylvia, an American, to meet her in this dangerous neighborhood?

More to the point, Sylvia thought wryly, why had she come?

Her doubts lasted only a moment. If Elena needed her help, she had it, automatically, no questions asked, because she and Elena were more than just teacher and student. In the short time they had known each other, they had become close friends, linked by their dedication to dance and by their recognition, without pride or arrogance, that both were professionally "good."

Still, as the hot tropical sun beat down on her, Sylvia wished that the young dancer had been more specific about their meeting place. Caldera Street was long, and the afternoon glare, coupled with the fetid odors of overripe fruit on the food stalls and urine-stained walls, was making her head ache.

Then, suddenly, Elena was there—only a few feet in front of her. Sylvia got no more than a glimpse—a swish of a familiar bright-colored skirt and a flash of a pixieish face—but she was sure it was Elena.

Sylvia ran forward eagerly and called, "Elena! Elena!" But the young woman had vanished as quickly as she had appeared. At the same time a rattle of gunfire drummed like scattered pebbles on the hot, shimmering air. Sylvia turned and saw what had made the girl disappear into the nearest odorous alley.

The brutally ugly, monotonous landscape had broken up into a kaleidoscope of people running down the street with a squad of soldiers behind them. Like Elena, the civilians seemed to melt into the shantytown jungle. Then another surge of dull blue uniforms flooded the street, and an armored personnel carrier sealed it off.

Sylvia was stunned. She had heard of street sweeps like

this, but she never thought she could be caught up in such an event.

With quick, sickening apprehension Sylvia realized that being an American wouldn't save her. The government's soldiers had the reputation of shooting first and asking questions afterward. All that waving her dark blue passport would get her was a bullet hole through her picture and maybe one in her heart.

Fear—like a giant mechanical hand—gripped her, squeezing the breath from her body. Instinctively Sylvia darted into a narrow alley of lean-tos and huts. Her heart pounding in her throat, she made her way through a labyrinth of shanties till trembling with terror, she pushed open the creaking wooden door of the last hut and collapsed on the dirt floor.

The earth shook under her. Wildly Sylvia hoped it was an earthquake. In the resulting confusion she might be able to escape. But no sickening sway followed the tremors. The pounding was the tread of soldiers sent in to search the area.

The hut was pitch-dark and stiflingly hot. It didn't seem possible that people lived there. As Sylvia felt around the earth floor to investigate the place, her hand encountered the limp, rough burlap of empty sacks. The hut was evidently a storeroom.

Terrified of making the slightest sound, Sylvia crouched, immobile, on the floor. When her dancer's body began to ache for movement, she cautiously began pacing the hut, moving silently on the balls of her feet. But the exercise created a runnel of sweat down the sides of her safari shirt, already drenched with perspiration.

Sylvia sat down again and put her hands over her ears to shut out the shouts of the soldiers. Instead of abating, her fear had quickened. Solitary confinement in the small dark cell had begun to affect her nerves.

Suddenly the door creaked behind her. Sylvia pressed

her hand to her mouth to silence a scream. Her heart seemed literally to stop as she waited for a rough command in Spanish—or Guaraní, the other Indian language—and the push of cold metal against her spine.

But the door didn't open enough to let in even a sliver of light. Only one person—not a squad of soldiers—had squeezed in. Sylvia held her breath and listened sharply.

It was a man. She could tell by his tread. A big man, she decided, judging from the heaviness of his step. His breathing was ragged. He, too, had been running.

When his voice came, it was almost inaudible. "*¿Quién está?*"

Instinctively Sylvia answered his "Who's there?" in English rather than the Spanish she knew well. "Don't shoot! I'm American."

A low-pitched, savage snarl ripped the darkness. "Shut up, you fool! They're only twenty feet away."

Sylvia felt a sweet tide of relief wash over her. The words were English; his accent was unmistakably American.

Then her heart began a painful rapid tattoo once more. She drew her knees up to her chin and wrapped her arms around them. At best she now had company for her misery. At the worst, what?

Being an American in South America didn't assure a halo. As in any volatile area of the world, there were plenty of unsavory characters of all nationalities looking for an opportunity to make money, to get even with life, to grasp power.

She could hear the steps of the soldiers now, closer than they had been before. More shouts. The sound of someone running, and the pack giving chase. Then a long silence. The man's breathing slowed and became normal. When so much time had passed that Sylvia's eyes closed in nervous exhaustion, he spoke again.

"How long have you been here?"

"I don't know. Hours, I think."

He chuckled, very low. "Couldn't be. It just seems that way."

"What's going on out there?"

"The government's brave soldiers are looking for people," he answered sardonically.

"Oh." Sylvia felt as though she had been struck a blow in the stomach and all the air had been knocked out of her. *Not Elena,* she prayed. *Please don't have it Elena.* "Who?" she asked.

"So-called subversives; anyone they don't like. Dragnets like this strike terror in the hearts of the people, make them think twice about antigovernment activity."

Suddenly the man grabbed her. He clapped a large, strong hand over her mouth. He wound his other arm around her and held her close. Sylvia could feel his heart beating against hers. They began to breathe together in the same rhythm.

Hysteria made her giggly. *Won't the soldiers be surprised,* she thought, *when they burst in here and find a set of Siamese twins?*

Because someone *was* outside. There was a shuffle of feet on the dusty path. Then the door rattled. Terrified, Sylvia buried her face in the stranger's powerful chest, and he tightened his hold. She heard a shout in the distance and an answering yell, very close. Then the door was banged shut, and the footsteps faded in the dust.

The man removed his hands from her, and Sylvia whispered, "Are they leaving?"

"Not yet."

Suddenly, involuntarily Sylvia began to shiver. Independent of her mind or will, her body was responding to the suspense and strain and danger.

"It's going to be all right," the big man assured her, putting both arms around her and pulling her close to him again. The damp cotton of his shirt was cool against her cheek. He smelled, like her, of sweat and strain and maybe fear. He felt unutterably human and dear to her after what seemed like an eternity in that black, stuffy hole.

"We'll get out of this," he whispered. "Don't worry." Slowly, rhythmically his big hands moved up and down her back in gestures of reassurance.

There was another fusillade of shots outside.

The sharp sounds tore at Sylvia's nerves, unraveling the protective, distancing veil her fellow prisoner had woven for her. Without meaning to, she whimpered a little as her courage gave way.

"Shh, it's all right," he whispered. And his strong hands resumed the lulling, stroking motions he had halted for a moment. Gradually the gentle pressure of his hard palms, the nuzzling sensation of his sinewy fingers, the very spread of his hand became the focal point of her feelings. Bit by bit she relaxed as repeatedly they moved up and down her back, pressing her sweat-dampened shirt to her skin. Dreamily she waited for the next slow, horizontal stroking of her slim shoulders, the looked-for thrill when his fingers slowly descended her straight spine, the masculine weight of his hands as they closed over her ribs, folding her in an intimate embrace.

When he paused over the outline of her bra, Sylvia expelled her breath in a sharp little sigh of excitement. She knew he must have heard. Her blood began to race with excitement. What would he do next?

She raised her head. Putting his hand under the long, thick hair that had tumbled down over her shoulders, he pressed her again to his chest. His touch on the bare skin of her neck was electrifying. Sylvia quivered under it like a slender birch swayed by a sudden breeze. Then the firm, soothing hands she thought she already knew so well started something new—a seductive stroking of her nape and throat that enflamed Sylvia's senses.

As he feathered her soft skin, his long fingers reached under her safari shirt. They smoothed themselves along her sleek shoulders with caresses that seemed to reach deep down to her very bones. Sylvia felt a stirring within her as delightful as what was happening outside was horrible. Her body became yielding and pliant, and his slender fingers slipped down toward the first tilting fullness of her small, shapely breasts.

Then a volley of shots outside shattered the short period of bliss. The man holding her started, and his arms stiffened around her.

Sylvia suddenly knew, with the immediacy of insight, that she, Sylvia Goddard, founder and director of the Goddard Dance Group, teacher of modern dance at the University of San Lorenzo, could actually die on a dusty street of tin shacks and shanties. Every trained muscle in her finely tuned body, every organ and cell cried out against this fate. She was made to live and to dance—not to die.

As if begging him for life, Sylvia wound her arms around the big man's neck and raised her face to his. And responding to her need to lay claim to life and perhaps to his own similar need, he bent his head and took her lips with his. He parted their soft surfaces with the tip of his tongue and warmed them with his own living breath. His invading tongue probed deeper and filled her mouth with a sweet-tasting maleness. Lingeringly it explored the warm interior as though it were the last precious territory he'd ever know.

From rapture's farthest edge Sylvia heard a shuffling in the dirt outside. She broke away and laid a finger against his lips in case he hadn't heard it. As they waited, standing close, breath to breath, heart beating to fearful heart, the man outside went back and forth as though undecided what to do. There was a quick scurry of footsteps. Then silence fell on the dust beyond their door.

Their heavy sighs of relief mingled. She sagged a little in his arms, and he tightened his hold.

Suddenly curious to know what he looked like, she ran her fingers over his cheekbones and along his firm, long jaw. Only half-consciously, as though she couldn't help herself, she started tracing his mouth with her finger, dragging it across the lower lip, noting its sensual curve. She had started to trail his upper lip when he caught her roving finger and put it in his mouth for a long, boldly sucking kiss.

Then he pulled her to him and fastened his lips on hers, taking her life and giving it back to her till breathless, they broke apart. They stood like that for a moment, and when he came back to her, she was ready. Ready for his hungry mouth to twist and grind against hers, to want her and demand her.

"Little stranger," he murmured. His large hands spanned her slim sides. She could feel them hard against her ribs. Then, with a sudden slackening of tension, they were soft over her breasts, cupping them, squeezing them gently.

With no fumbling motions, as sure as a cat in the dark, he unbuttoned her safari shirt and undid the belt. He spanned her bare midriff with his large hands, and Sylvia gasped at the feel of them on her warm, smooth skin, at the tough palm and the tensile strength of the long fingers. She reveled in their touch—the touch of another human being, a man facing death with her, a man searching for life with her.

When one hand eased its way upward and with practiced skill released her bra, Sylvia shivered with anticipation. Her small, pretty breasts arched upward, seeking his hands. Then the gentle, sensitive fingers were there, caressing her satiny skin, fondling the high, firm mounds, his thumb lightly circling the pink rosettes. A vital flame ran through her veins like liquid fire.

She needed to celebrate life in the most elemental way. Her hand went to his belt. His breathing became harsh and raspy. He plucked her hand away and pressed her gently to the ground.

For one brief moment Sylvia panicked. It had never even entered her realm of possibilities to make love with a man she didn't know.

"I don't . . ." she started, but the rest of the words were lost in his masterful, lingering kiss. His tender caresses thawed her fears. She trusted him and, for the moment, loved him. Sylvia sensed a poignancy to their lovemaking, a bittersweet acceptance of the limitations of life that made it pure.

Even though the soldiers could burst through the door at any moment, he took his time—perhaps as an act of defiance, perhaps for her sake. He folded her in his arms and kissed her face, salty with sweat. As his lips dropped to her throat, his kisses seemed to melt against her skin. His hot, moist mouth moved insistently downward till it found the pulse that fluttered in the shallow hollow of her throat.

An aching need began to flower inside Sylvia's body. In the dark of the hut she closed her eyes with the sweet, passionate desire growing within her. She sighed contentedly as he laid his face against her breasts and stroked first one nipple and then the other with his stubble-roughened cheeks till they lost their rosebud softness and hardened. A sharp gasp of pleasure escaped her, and with a harsh "Ssh!" he quickly clapped his hand over her mouth.

This abrupt reminder of their situation, coupled with her mounting sexual excitement and the anxiety-filled suspense she had endured for so long, toppled Sylvia's self-control. She sat up and began to cry silently.

"Hush," he said gently, sitting up too. "Don't cry, little stranger." Slowly and deliberately he buttoned her shirt.

Then he cradled her in his arms and rocked back and forth with her. He smoothed her hair off her sweaty brow with the palm of his hand and, with the back, wiped her tear-starred cheeks.

Positioned between his thighs as she now was, Sylvia knew the effort it was costing him to break off their love-making. She was swept by respect for him and gratitude.

Her own wired-up state was gradually returning to normal when suddenly she felt the cords of his muscular arms tighten around her, and her heart jumped sickeningly. But the sounds from outside weren't the usual shouts and gunfire and running footsteps. A harsh grinding of gears rent the new stillness and was followed by the clank-clank of the armored personnel carrier as it moved away.

"I'm going now," he whispered against her cheek. He kissed her gently, imprinting her forehead and cheeks and lips with a tender farewell. Sylvia clung to him, unable to make the quick transition from danger to safety. Or was it losing him that she feared?

He put his hands on her shoulders and held her away from him. "Wait," he commanded, "and if you don't hear any gunfire, leave too." He kissed her lightly again on the lips, and his voice softened to a wistful note. "I love you, little stranger." Then he was gone.

Sylvia sat very still, all her being focused on listening. She couldn't bear it, she thought, if she heard the staccato of guns just when he had gone outside. But the silence lasted till it turned into the high-pitched Spanish of the streets. The women and children, the owners of the little food stalls, the prostitutes the neighborhood was known for had come out. Caldera was safe again.

With still-trembling fingers she arranged her clothing and twisted her thick hair around her head in its usual coronet. Then she got up and left the shack. She retraced her way in the maze of dilapidated shelters till she stepped out into the blinding sunshine of the street again.

The soldiers were gone. It was safe again—for the time being.

And where was Elena now? Sylvia could have sworn the young woman had seen her. Elena, too, must have hidden when the soldiers made their sweep of Caldera Street. Had they gotten her?

Sylvia shuddered at the image of the delicate, ethereal dancer in the hands of those brutal men.

Emotionally drained, she walked along slowly on the cracked asphalt of the street. Her nerves had been stretched to their utmost. Now they were slack and unresponsive. If she had to run for her life, Sylvia wasn't sure at the moment that she could.

Her thoughts reverted with a sense of wonder to what had just happened in the hut. She had almost made love with a man she didn't know and couldn't even see, a man who was a total stranger. Her body was still faintly charged with the electricity of arousal. Her swollen breasts pressed against the thin cotton of her safari shirt. She felt warm and liquid within.

He had been so kind, so gentle. He could have taken her there on the earth floor, but he had chosen to comfort her instead. Yet all the time she had felt the blaze of desire banked within him. His passion had been all the more exciting to her just because it was harnessed and she could only sense its power.

Who was he? What did he look like? She knew only that he was tall and broad-shouldered, that he had strong hands and a long, lean jaw, that his stomach was flat and hard, his mouth sweet.

Sylvia shook her head. She was better off not knowing who he was. She wasn't ashamed of what had happened, but it could be embarrassing to meet him.

Then even he faded from her thoughts. The feeling of

lassitude intensified. She knew what was happening to her. Psychological shock—a reaction to the harrowing sounds of gunfire and of people being hunted, a reaction to terror and fear—was taking over.

It was made worse by the pitiless glare of the late-afternoon sun. Sylvia could feel it burning her fair skin, beating down on her head with a ferocity that was making it ache again.

The blare of an auto horn behind her aroused Sylvia from her numbed state. She turned around and saw a black Mercedes scattering people like chickens.

Only very wealthy people drove Mercedeses, and in case there was any doubt about the status of the man within, a colorful small flag, a personal pennant, flew from the hood. Sylvia stepped quickly aside, then plastered herself against a wall as the car braked beside her.

A heart-stopping moment of terror, of confusion mixed with dread, born of the incident on Caldera Street, gave way to relief. The face peering out the shiny window at her was the round schoolboy countenance of her old friend Carlos Ronderos.

A wan smile crossed Sylvia's lips. *Thank God,* she thought.

Carlos rapped on the chauffeur's glass, and the burly gray-uniformed driver in shiny black boots got out of the car and opened the rear door for Sylvia.

"Sylvia, what a delight to see you!" Carlos said in slightly accented English.

"And *I'm* grateful you came along before I fell over with sunstroke," Sylvia answered emphatically.

Carlos's arms reached out for her, pulling her in. As Sylvia sat down on the plush gray upholstery, Carlos patted her, settling her into place. Sylvia slid across the seat, quietly putting herself out of reach of the pudgy hand on her thigh.

While Carlos gave the chauffeur an order, Sylvia studied his face. His black, shoe-button eyes had gotten smaller as his pale cheeks filled out. The stylish sideburns were new, as was the plump chinline, or was it just that the flesh was pushed up by the starched high collar of his business shirt?

Maybe being back in his own country had changed Carlos, Sylvia thought wryly. Maybe running the far-flung financial empire he had taken over after his father's death had made him think that he could do whatever he wanted and have anything—or anyone—he desired.

Carlos caught Sylvia looking at him and smiled. Then his pleased look turned to one of concern. He reached out and took her hand in his.

"You look completely done in, Sylvia. Has anything happened to you? And what were you doing in this neighborhood?" Carlos asked, frankly curious.

With the swiftness of instinct Sylvia decided it would not be a good idea to mention Elena to Carlos Ronderos. There had been rumors at the university that Ronderos had political as well as financial power. "I got lost and was pinned down in a squalid little shack when I hid from your government's soldiers making a street sweep. They were looking for 'subversives,' I believe." Sylvia loaded the term with irony.

"I'm so sorry! It's terrible that you should have gotten mixed up in such an unpleasant event." It occurred to Sylvia that Carlos was shocked at the wrong thing—not at the raid but at Sylvia's having been caught in it and witnessing it. "But why did you hide if you hadn't done anything wrong?"

"I *hadn't* done anything wrong," Sylvia answered firmly, "but from what I've heard your soldiers don't make distinctions—fine or otherwise."

Carlos curled his fingers around Sylvia's hand. "I could give you all the protection you needed, Sylvia," he said significantly.

"I *have* all the protection I need. I'm a guest in your country, remember."

Sylvia pulled her hand away, and Carlos bowed slightly as if in recognition of this statement.

"How is the teaching going?" he asked urbanely.

Sylvia responded enthusiastically to the change of subject. "Very well! You have a lot of talent in your country. It's been absolutely thrilling for me to work with the dance students at the university."

A smug smile coated Carlos's tallowy features. "Who would have thought, when you were starting your dance group in New York and I was watching you every night instead of studying economics, as my father intended, that I'd end up a person of consequence, shall we say, and you'd be teaching modern dance in San Lorenzo?"

"Who indeed?" Sylvia said dryly. "There must be a moral there somewhere."

Carlos laughed heartily. "The moral is, to forget the puritan ethic and have a good time." He leaned sideways to pat Sylvia's knee again, but she adroitly twisted out of his reach.

"I don't know about *that,*" Sylvia said casually. "If you had obeyed your father, you might have been minister of finance now."

This was the idlest of chatter, Sylvia thought. Once he had married the daughter of the politically powerful General Villacorta, Carlos could have been appointed anything he wanted.

"To return to the subject of dance, Carlos, I'm planning a program for April just before I leave. I hope you'll be able to come see it."

"You don't have to leave then," Carlos said gravely.

"Oh, but I do," Sylvia replied with a laugh. "The Goddard Dance Group has engagements all over the United States for the rest of the year. Mostly, I grant you, in small cities and colleges, but that's all right. In fact, it's great, considering we've been in existence only two years."

Carlos shrugged this information off. "When your engagements are over, bring your dance group here. I'll pay for their transportation, give them good salaries, a nice place to live. You can perform all over *my* country and teach at the university, too, if you like doing that." His rather high voice deepened with emotion. "You know how I feel about you, Sylvia."

"Please, Carlos, let's not talk about that again. I want us to be friends, as we were in New York. And that's all. Even if my feelings for you went beyond friendship—and they don't—I could never become involved with a married man."

"But that is the custom here," Carlos said, laughing. "When in Rome . . ."

"If you mean, when in Paraguay, become a married man's mistress, forget it. I carry my own customs with me wherever I go, and being installed in a fancy apartment on a back street isn't one of them."

Her outburst used up the last spark of energy Sylvia had. She put her head back on the soft upholstery and sighed wearily.

Carlos was immediately solicitous. "Where can I take you, Sylvia?" he asked.

"Home, please. I'm really exhausted."

Carlos rapped on the bulletproof glass in front. He barked an order in Spanish to the chauffeur and sat back in the seat again.

As the Mercedes stopped in front of her stucco bungalow, Sylvia glanced out the window. "It's beginning to rain." After a month in Paraguay she could still be surprised at the speed with which sunshine yielded to needle-sharp, pelting rain.

Carlos chuckled. "Too bad, if it continues, for Emily Adams's garden party tomorrow night." He drew his dark brows together in a puzzled frown. "I know Emily likes to keep up American traditions, but isn't a Washington's Birthday party a little unusual?"

Sylvia laughed. "I think Emily just likes to give parties, and any excuse will do."

Carlos leaned forward eagerly. "Will I see you there, Sylvia?"

"Yes." Sylvia paused. "I'm looking forward to meeting María again too."

"Of course," Carlos said blandly. "My wife has been talking about our little girl's taking dance lessons when she's older. Perhaps you can advise her."

The chauffeur was standing at the door now, waiting for a signal to open it. Sylvia noticed for the first time that he had a flat, squashed-looking nose like a boxer's.

"Thank you for rescuing me." Sylvia smiled politely at Carlos. "And please give my regards to María."

Carlos took her hand and bent his head to kiss it. Sylvia waited for the formal brush of his lips over the back, a bare touching, if that, in the style of those Europeans and Latin Americans who still practiced hand kissing.

But his kiss was a prolonged, moist imprinting of his fleshy pale lips on her smooth skin. Sylvia was repelled and barely managed to withdraw her hand graciously but firmly.

"Thank you again for the ride," she murmured, and put her hand on the door.

Carlos signaled to the chauffeur. The thickset man in the gray uniform opened the car door and held up a large black umbrella. As he escorted Sylvia to her door, a gust of wind whipped her cotton skirt high around her legs.

Sylvia knew Carlos was watching. To her surprise she felt more uncomfortable than she had in the embrace of the stranger.

The rain swirled down the gutters of Caldera Street in a yellow tide bearing mango skins and dog excrement, Popsicle sticks and dirt clods, and miniature funeral barges of curling black tar paper. The wind tore at the political slogans and pictures that papered the walls of the hovels, lifting corners that hadn't been pasted down well and carrying a scrap of leg here and a word or finger there to swell the flooded gutters.

The wind made Hank Weston's loose cotton shirt billow out from his body as he strode up Caldera Street. Then the rain wet it down so that it clung to him like a second skin. He had waited, hidden in a niche between two buildings, to see who the woman was. It wasn't wise, but he had felt that he had to know.

While he waited, it seemed to him that he could still feel her lithe, pliant body under his hands. Her small, exquisitely formed breasts had fitted into his palms as though made for them. Her mouth was the sheerest velvet.

When she had emerged from the maze of shacks and hovels and lean-tos, he had drawn even farther back into the dark crevice and watched her. He had taken note of the small, well-formed head with its coronet of thick golden red hair and of her long, slim neck. He had observed, too, the coltish bare legs, the gracefulness of her walk, the precise way she put her feet down.

She moves like a *dancer!* he had told himself, and he had been surprised at the enormous pleasure this information about her gave him.

He had caught only a glimpse of her profile as she walked away from him. Her nose was short and straight, her jawline cleanly sculpted. Her throat had a lovely swanlike sweep to it.

The combination of pride and vulnerability in her small form seemed poignant to him. He would like to have caught up to her, looked down into her face, and told her who he was.

But that would have been unwise. He was on a job, and one thing he had learned was never to mix women and work.

The red-haired woman had passed, and Hank had been about to step out of his hiding place when a black Mercedes drove by. He couldn't see the man in the back seat, but he recognized the chauffeur from a photo he had once been shown. It was Hank's business to know such things.

As Hank had watched, the woman smiled in the way of someone who recognizes a friend. Then the chauffeur opened the door for her, and she got into the car.

So she was a friend of Carlos Ronderos!

Hank had felt a quick stab of disappointment. Affable, American-educated Ronderos, who had his finger in every business in the country—meat canneries, sugar mills, soybeans, cattle ranches, and cotton—was popular. When he was mentioned as a possible successor to the man who had held power for more than thirty years, it was believed that he would initiate democratic reforms. But Hank had heard stories about Carlos Ronderos that made him question the magnate's public image. It was Hank's business to collect stories like this and pass them on to people who might be interested.

Hank shook his head as his long stride took him out of Caldera Street and onto the avenue that intersected it. The politics of the country were only indirectly his concern. His job at the moment was to find Elena Vanegas.

But it wouldn't hurt to keep an eye on Carlos Ronderos, Hank mused. The socially prominent businessman was sure to be at the Adamses' party tomorrow. If it wasn't rained out! Hank reflected sardonically, taking a damp handkerchief out of his pocket and passing it over his wet face.

The woman might be there too. A longing stirred within him. He had wanted her badly back there in that hut, had wanted her primitively as any man wants a woman, and not so primitively either. Love was the last chance at life, and he had thought to give them both that gift before the blue-uniformed goons banged the door open with their rifle butts.

But hard as it had been for him to do it, it was probably just as well that he had broken off. She had been too unstrung for lovemaking. Moreover, she didn't seem the kind of woman who let herself be loved by a stranger.

Who was she? Hank wondered. And what was she doing on Caldera Street? A sense of incompleteness that was only partly physical bothered him.

But this was one circle that couldn't be closed. Even if the woman were at the party tomorrow or if he met her somewhere else, it would be better if she didn't recognize him. For although he didn't know where the trail he was following would lead, it was doubtful that he could trust any friend of Carlos Ronderos.

Hank Weston pounded his fist into the palm of the other hand like a hammer striking an anvil.

Damn! How could any woman so sensitive and lovely associate with a murdering hypocrite like Ronderos?

Then Hank raised an amused eyebrow. *Is it her ethics you're objecting to or something else?* he asked himself. *Maybe it's the picture of her in Carlos's arms that you can't stand.*

CHAPTER TWO

Sylvia folded her arms behind her head and stared up at the gauzy mosquito netting that draped her bed. The netting swayed slightly in the dawn breeze, but the rain had stopped during the night, and it wouldn't be long before the city became a greenhouse of moist, still tropical heat.

She got out of bed, moved a large floor fan out of the way, and positioned a padded mat in front of the window. She did the yoga positions with which she started each day and followed them with special exercises to keep her dancer's body in condition.

Standing under the tepid shower, Sylvia thought of the man who had held her and kissed her on Caldera Street the day before. Would she know him if they met again? Probably not, Sylvia decided. She'd have nothing to go on except touch—and his voice. But his voice would be different, she told herself. No one spoke normally in the barely audible tones he had used in their hiding place.

As Sylvia coiled her thick tawny hair around her small head, she studied herself in the mirror. If they did meet and recognized each other, would he think she was pretty?

Some men did. Others were put off by the direct, uncompromising gaze of her clear sea green eyes. Her firm mouth and strong chin were further deterrents to men who were looking for women they could dominate.

Sylvia grimaced. Carlos certainly found her attractive. Or was she just a challenge to his obsessive nature?

Suddenly her eyes flashed with amusement. Her mother, catching her only daughter in this moment of self-appraisal, would say, as she often did, "Sylvia, maybe this is the day you'll find your LP, your life's partner."

To tease her mother, Sylvia had occasionally answered, "But I've had a couple of partners, Ma."

Rose Goddard had set her lips, and her own hazel-green eyes had snapped as she answered, "I mean a *husband,* Sylvia."

Sylvia turned away from the mirror. She hadn't found him yet—her LP, her long-playing life's partner. She thought she had—once. But she had been wrong.

Still, a new day was too penny-bright to spoil with unhappy thoughts, and Sylvia hummed an old Beatles tune as she squeezed some oranges for juice and put an egg on to boil.

Her buoyant mood persisted as she walked the few blocks to the university. Looking around her at the bougainvillaea-draped houses and broad, clean streets, Sylvia thought of Caldera Street, not so far away, and she began visualizing a dance that would express the feeling of being alone, trapped in a dark cage like an animal. The dancer would recover her humanness with the entrance of a second, male dancer. Finally, Sylvia thought, she would choreograph movements to show the overwhelming need of the two dancers to affirm the glory of life itself.

Arriving at the beige stucco buildings of the university,

she went directly to the gym reserved for her use as a dance studio. It had been built when the school was new and still small and was set apart from the other buildings by a wall of white-blossomed oleanders. There she found her students, barefoot and in leotards, warming up. Sylvia ran her eyes quickly over the eleven young men and women. No Elena. Sylvia frowned, then put the girl out of her mind. She had work to do here.

Sylvia went to the locker room and changed quickly into a black leotard. She led the class in warm-up exercises and leg stretches, then ran them through a review of the dance she had choreographed and taught them earlier. It had to be perfect before she would let them move on to more advanced work.

Using a drum to keep time for the young dancers, Sylvia watched with green eyes narrowed to keen slits as they soared diagonally across the floor in wide-legged leaps, then executed spinning leaps, single-foot takeoffs, and double-foot landing leaps. She watched for mistakes in the circles, balances, and tilts she had taught them.

She kept her gaze stern, but a glow of satisfaction spread through her. Although the dancers varied in ability, they all were almost faultless in the techniques she had drilled into them. When the dance came to end, they stood before her, their eyes begging mutely for approval, their bodies glistening with their sweat.

"Not bad," Sylvia said, her broad smile belying the faint praise. "Some mistakes, which I'll tell you about in a minute, lots of room for improvement, but not bad."

The students grinned back at her in a mutual explosion of love and respect and recognition of their common endeavor.

Sylvia went among them then, showing each student by her own execution of a movement how to do it.

Later, alone in the studio, Sylvia worked on the dance taking shape in her mind. She would call it "Affirmation," she decided. It would begin with a lot of right-angle movements and tight action designed to suggest individual isolation and end with broad, joyful, expansive movements. It would be a pas de deux, of course, a dance for a man and a woman. And erotic, to show the affirmation of life through passionate love.

At the end of the day, as Sylvia walked home through the almost palpable moist heat, she thought about what she would wear to Emily Adams's party.

Parties were important in San Lorenzo, where there wasn't much to do, and people dressed for them. Although a garden party might seem like an informal affair, Sylvia knew from experience that it probably wouldn't be.

So she chose a long silk one-shoulder dress, tied at the shoulder with a bow. Its peach and gold tropical print set off the apricot of her tanned skin and the reddish gold of her hair. Its form-fitting lines molded the curves of her small breasts and rounded hips. An antique gold torque around her neck and heavy gold bracelets lent the gown a little exoticism.

As a performer Sylvia wasn't afraid of a touch of theatricality. Her evening makeup turned her clear green eyes into dark-fringed shining emeralds and emphasized the high slope of her cheekbones. She arranged her hair in a low chignon instead of its usual coronet and applied a sensuous, uninhibited perfume.

As her cab climbed the hill to the Adamses' house, Sylvia smiled at the dance music and sounds of gaiety spilling downward in the still night air. If Paraguay had been India under the British raj, Sylvia mused, Frank and Emily Adams would have made a perfect viceroy and memsahib.

They had been in San Lorenzo longer than any of the other Americans and, at sixty, were the oldest foreign residents. Frank was head of the largest American company, and Emily Adams was an authority on how to behave, what to wear, and how to treat servants. She also kept score but never rang the bell on the players in the game of love that went on constantly in the foreign colony.

Sylvia had no sooner walked through the open door of the house with a stream of other arriving guests than Emily was at her side. Her chiseled features softened with pleasure when she saw Sylvia. In spite of the thirty years between them there was genuine friendship between the two women.

"You look beautiful in that gown, my dear," Emily whispered. "I'm afraid some of the new people thought Washington's Birthday meant hot dogs and beer and blue jeans. Wouldn't you think 'black tie optional' would give them at least a *clue?* I *have* hung bunting on the tables in honor of the day, however, and there'll be fireworks in the garden later." The patrician Emily Adams winked. "Left over from the Fourth of July. Now," Emily continued briskly, quickly surveying the people in the room and the overflow on the patio, "do you want me to introduce you around a bit or . . ."

Sylvia laughed. "I think I know everyone here—everyone except your newcomers in jeans, that is."

"Not everybody new was that gauche. A very dashing man who says he's the head of something called Americo Import and Export came properly attired."

Sylvia nodded absently and smiled to herself. She had spotted the few offending jeans-clad guests, who looked as though they'd like to crawl under the nearest table and cover themselves with the red, white, and blue bunting hanging there.

"You're a snob, Emily," she said affectionately.

"Of course. How else could I amuse myself in this godforsaken place?" With that Emily Adams floated off in a drapery of green chiffon that softened the ramrod-straight stiffness of her back.

Sylvia was immediately absorbed into a group of people she knew—a teacher at the university and his wife and an English couple. With them was one of the offenders in cowboy boots and jeans, a man in his thirties named Roy, whose beefy face was red with annoyance.

"How did *I* know?" Roy was complaining in a Texas accent. "Where I come from, a garden party means a barbecue. I thought the 'black tie' on the invitation was a joke. On the other hand," he said, running his eyes down Sylvia, "if all the girls looked like you . . ."

"I've been to Emily's parties before," Sylvia explained with a laugh. "Emily stops just short of long white kid gloves."

"I've found that stopping short means missing most of the fun," Roy said, lowering his voice seductively. He reached out to a tray a waiter was presenting to them and took two goblets of pale, bubbling champagne. "I understand that even the Father of our Country, whose birthday we're supposedly celebrating, had a little fun now and then."

Sylvia took the glass he handed her. "Is that the latest gossip?" she asked with round-eyed innocence. She raised the glass to her lips. Glancing over it past Roy's plaid shoulder, she noticed Emily standing near the door with a man. They were watching her. Then Emily murmured something, and even at that distance Sylvia could see the muscles along the man's strong jaw tighten.

They were talking about her, Sylvia guessed. Who was he? Perhaps Emily's favorite, the newcomer who was savvy enough to come in a white dinner jacket, a crisply ruffled pale blue evening shirt, and a midnight blue cummerbund that emphasized the flatness of his stomach.

He was a big man—tall and with burly shoulders. But not clumsy, Sylvia decided. There was a poised alertness, a readiness in his stance to move fast if necessary. His hair was dark; his eyes seemed to be blue. He was not handsome but good-looking in a craggy, very masculine way.

"Who is she?" Hank Weston asked his hostess sharply. "That little redhead over there, the one who holds herself like a dancer."

"She *is* a dancer," Emily answered, beaming at this sartorially correct romantic prospect for her protégée. "She's an American. Her name's Sylvia Goddard, and she teaches modern dance at the university. Would you like me to introduce you to her?"

"Yes. Or rather, no, I won't keep you from your other guests. I'll meet her myself." He gave his hostess a charming smile. And with knowing, amused eyes Emily smiled back and glided away.

Hank continued to stare at Sylvia. He hoped the sharp-eyed Emily Adams hadn't noticed his confusion. He had refused her offer of an introduction because he needed time to think. He hadn't reacted like this—with pounding pulse and fast-scudding heart—to seeing a woman across a room since he was twenty, and that had been fifteen long, women-filled years ago.

And with the usual irony of his life, Hank reflected, this was the one woman forbidden to him. In view of her friendship with Carlos Ronderos, having her recognize him as the man who had been on Caldera Street yesterday could be dangerous.

Then chips of information, like pieces in a jigsaw puzzle, began to come together in his mind. She herself had been on Caldera Street yesterday. And the dossier he had on Elena Vanegas said that the young woman was studying modern dance at the university.

It looked as though he'd have to get to know Sylvia Goddard after all, Hank mused. And when his heart lifted with joy, he smiled wryly. *Fool!* Hank Weston taunted himself.

Sylvia turned away from the stranger's burning gaze.

Roy was asking her to dance. She let him escort her out to the polished hardwood floor laid over the tiled patio and began to move with him to the enticing rhythm of a rumba.

Dancing was as natural to Sylvia as breathing. She followed the intricate variations the Texan led her through with unthinking perfection. She admired Roy's skill, but aside from that, she didn't give her partner a single thought.

Sylvia knew that the big, husky man was watching her. She was not an exhibitionist; nevertheless, the idea pleased her. She *wanted* to be the center of his attention.

As Roy led her back into the house, Sylvia's gaze went compulsively to the spot where the stranger had been standing. He wasn't there, and she felt a twinge of disappointment. Then her eyes picked him up in the crowd. He seemed to be making his way toward her. Was he going to ask her to dance?

"Would you like to go to the buffet?" Roy asked.

Sylvia smiled. "Not just yet, thank you. But another glass of champagne would be welcome."

"Coming right up," Roy answered eagerly. "Wait here, and I'll go to the bar."

Sylvia's heart began to beat high and fast as the stranger drew nearer. Her face felt flushed, and a wave of heat ran through her body. She never responded like this to a man she didn't know. Granted, he was good-looking in a sexy, virile sort of way, but she was hardly a centerfold groupie, Sylvia reminded herself.

Then he was standing before her.

"I'm Hank Weston," he said, unsmiling, his piercing blue eyes fixing her intently.

"Sylvia Goddard," she answered with a polite smile.

"Yes, I know. Emily Adams told me." He was direct almost to the point of rudeness. Sylvia had the impression that he wasn't usually so. "Would you care to dance?"

Sylvia nodded, while her eyes, curious and troubled, searched his. Then, mentally drafting an apology to Roy, she led the way—with a vague feeling of compulsion—back to the polished dance floor she had just left.

The combo had started the slow, sensuous beat of a tango. As Sylvia walked onto the dance floor with the stranger, she hesitated before entering his arms. She had the irrational feeling that something momentous was about to happen to her, and she didn't want it to. Except for Carlos, whom she could see eyeing her even though his wife was by his side, and the problem of the missing Elena, her life was as she wanted it. She definitely was not in the market for adventure or change.

Then Sylvia felt the pressure of his large hand on her bare back. Surprisingly slender fingers in a man of his bulk splayed warmly and firmly across her smooth skin. Her soft breasts and stomach and thighs gave under the push of his hard, muscular frame as he held her close in the sophisticated steps of the tango. His unique, highly masculine, somewhat seductive odor pierced her consciousness.

The surrounding garden, the other dancers, the tinkle of champagne glasses in the background seemed to fall away as they moved in complete unison across the glossy floor. There were just the two of them in a world of throbbing music and bodies pressed close, a world of a man and a woman whose elegant evening clothes were only costumes for what lay beneath.

She ceased to have a separate identity, to be Sylvia Goddard. She was one with this stranger, a single persona dancing in slow, syncopated rhythm to a plaintive love song, a song of kisses and jealousy and heartache.

It was as though they had danced together before—or he had held her before. The feel of his body, of his bones and muscles and sinews, against hers was familiar. And as a dancer Sylvia trusted her kinetic instincts.

Even the contours of his face as they danced cheek to cheek weren't strange to her. She had known strong cheekbones and a long, firm jaw somewhere before—recently.

As she had known burly shoulders and large, sensitive hands and lips salted with sweat.

Suddenly the total experience of Caldera Street flooded over her: the unnerving darkness; the terror of waiting as the soldiers' footsteps passed back and forth outside; the fear of death; then the relief of not being alone, of being comforted by a gently loving man.

Sylvia's flush deepened. She could feel herself reddening even to the tops of the breasts that were crushed against her partner's chest and that his lambent blue eyes were feasting on. She quivered with the force of the longing that tore through her as it had almost ripped her apart when this man caressed her on Caldera Street. And Sylvia Goddard, who never stumbled or fell when she danced, now misstepped and would have tripped if Hank Weston hadn't held her up.

As if this were a signal, he danced her off the parquet floor and out into the shadows of the patio. He took her hand and with the single command "Come!" led her down a gravel path that ended at a jacaranda tree, the tiny lavender-blue blossoms of which scented the air.

"I think we have some unfinished business," Hank said, his voice a bare breath of sound.

The kiss began as gently as the breeze that stirred the jacaranda overhead. His lips, erotically familiar, brushed hers in tiny, superficial sweeps that excited the nerve-rich surfaces and made them tingle deliciously. Then the kiss turned violent in an explosion of pent-up need. His lips ground into hers almost brutally, and she rejoiced in his fervor. This was the kind of caress she wanted from him, to satisfy her own aroused and unsatisfied hunger.

As their lips clung, each to each, the tip of his agile tongue poked at the fullness in the center of her lower lip. The opening made, his tongue slid between her teeth to taste and savor the velvety warmth of her mouth. It teased her with darting, probing, stroking motions that left Sylvia dizzy with desire. Succumbing to her mounting passion, she engaged it in intimate entanglement with her own eager, sinuous tongue.

Her embarrassed flush had paled to the soft blush of a lover. A quiver of anticipation ran through her. Sylvia felt weak with the same need that she knew was consuming him.

But who was he? What did she know about him? Since when did Sylvia Goddard become involved with strangers?

She tried to pull back, but he continued to hold her close. "I want you badly, Sylvia Goddard," he whispered against her lips. "And I know you want me. But now isn't the time for what we both have in mind. Even if I weren't crazy with my need to finish what we started in the hut, I'd still have you in my arms like this in case anyone was watching us. I have to know. Why were you on Caldera Street yesterday?"

Sylvia's thoughts whirled with confusion. Tears of frustration and anger came to her eyes. His arrogance was stupefying. Who did he think he was to boast that he turned her on—whether or not he did was beside the question—and then to claim an ulterior motive? What kind of man was he to forgo the urgency of his arousal, so obvious from the rigid virility pressing the core of her own suppliant desire?

Trying again to break away from him, Sylvia twisted and turned in his arms. But his fingers held her like steel bands.

"Let me go," she whispered harshly.

"Tell me why you were on Caldera Street." One large hand slipped down to curve around her buttocks now, and he molded her closer to him.

It tortured Sylvia to have her body so intimately entwined with his. What kind of control did *he* have when she could hardly withstand the demand made by the loosening of her thighs and the throbbing warmth between them?

Then Hank's tightly held self-control slipped. He had never wanted a woman as badly as he wanted this red-haired dancer. With a strangled, emotional oath he covered her mouth with his own, twisting his lips feverishly against hers.

"Little stranger," he murmured, and he nibbled at the corners of her lips with gentle bites that excited Sylvia into shallow, breathless gasps. He placed his finger on her lips and slowly nudged it forward until they parted for him. He filled her mouth with his tongue again, thrusting deeply inside the soft interior. As he explored the dark territory of her mouth, a torrid chill of primitive, naked desire ran through Sylvia.

The heels of his hands inched up her ribs. Whispering, "Beautiful stranger," he cupped the soft undersides of her breasts; then passed the back of his hand over each nipple, stroking it in back-and-forth motions that made Sylvia close her eyes and sway against him in a delirium of ecstasy.

Abruptly then he let go of her. "No, damn it, this isn't the way."

Her eyes stinging with tears of humiliation and anger, Sylvia lunged at him. "How dare you try to use me, make a fool of me!"

He seized her wrists and held them at the same time that he threw his head back and laughed. "That wouldn't look bad either—if someone were watching." Then he dropped her hands. Placating now, he touched her shoulder, but Sylvia shook his hand off. "Listen," he said, "I'm sorry. I wasn't trying to use you. I got carried away myself. But . . . well, all I can say now is that other people are involved." He paused. "Can we go somewhere and talk?"

"Why should we?" Sylvia asked coldly.

"It concerns Elena Vanegas."

Sylvia was silent for a long time. Her mind was in a tumult of mingled fear and hope. By going with him, she could be either putting Elena in jeopardy or rescuing her from danger. Yet if she didn't act, she would gain nothing. She had to trust Hank Weston. But Sylvia swore she would do so with the utmost caution.

"We could go to my place," she said slowly.

"Sounds good."

"There's a gate at the bottom of the garden. It leads to the street. We can get a cab there."

"Let's do it. Give me your hand; it's dark here."

The simple act of hand-in-hand trust calmed Sylvia. It reminded her of Hank's behavior on Caldera Street. She would be no less wary, Sylvia decided, but for now she would put her hand in his, as silently they traversed the gravel path to the foot of the garden.

Sylvia led the way into the living room, switching on lights and two strategically placed electric fans as she went. "This is the coolest room in the house. I'm renting the place from a professor at the university who's traveling in Europe. It's nice, don't you think?" Sylvia waved her hand at the large areas of polished floor between a few massive pieces of furniture, the good pictures on the walls, and the shelves of books in Spanish, English, and French. "May I get you something? Coffee perhaps? I make it very strong, the local style. Or a cold drink?"

Sylvia stood watching Hank as his vibrant blue eyes

took in windows and doors, the entrances and exits to the room.

"Thanks, no. I had a drink at the party."

Sylvia seated herself in a brown leather chair and invited Hank to sit down.

"I hear you're the head of Americo Import and Export," Sylvia said.

"Did Carlos Ronderos tell you that?"

"Do you know Carlos?" Sylvia asked, surprised.

"No, but you do, don't you?"

Sylvia was taken aback by his aggressive tone. "Is there some reason I shouldn't know Carlos?"

Hank only shrugged.

"He's an old friend, if that's any business of yours."

"He's a member of a power structure that's hardly a beacon of democracy."

"It's not my country, and its politics aren't mine," Sylvia retorted.

Hank repressed the remark that came to his lips. He was going about this all wrong. He was letting his personal feelings—his desire for the beautiful dancer and his jealousy of Ronderos—interfere with the job he had to do.

"Besides," Sylvia pointed out, "I thought we were going to talk about Elena, not Carlos Ronderos."

"Perhaps we can't talk about one without the other," Hank replied.

Sylvia could only stare at him. What did he mean? Was there some link between Carlos and Elena that she didn't know about?

"Do you know where Elena is?" Sylvia asked.

"I'll tell you about Elena if you tell me about Carlos."

Hardly a direct answer, Sylvia thought swiftly. But Hank Weston, as untrustworthy as he was, might be her only chance of finding out what had happened to Elena.

"I met Carlos two years ago at a party in New York. His

father had sent him to the States to study economics, but Carlos was a dance nut. He spent more time at performances than studying."

"So you had dance in common," Hank said.

Sylvia nodded. "I had just started my own dance company. I found Carlos's criticism informed and his ideas innovative. Carlos is one of the few fans I know who can talk intelligently about dance."

"Did you date?" Hank could hear the tightness in his voice as he asked the question.

"A little, but nothing serious. Mostly we were friends until Carlos returned to Paraguay to take over the family's business when his father died."

"And how do *you* come to be in Paraguay, Sylvia?"

Sylvia frowned. Hank's interrogation was getting under her skin. But she had made a bargain, and she would stick to it. "Carlos wrote to me and asked if I'd be interested in teaching some classes in modern dance at the University of San Lorenzo. I saw the offer as a marvelous opportunity to train new talent and to build an audience for modern dance, so I said yes."

Hank's sharp blue eyes fixed her with a knowing look. "There's more to your story than that. I saw the way Carlos was looking at you tonight."

"Carlos wants me to become his mistress," Sylvia said flatly. "I've refused. Numerous times," she continued dryly. "For the sake of our friendship I haven't gotten mad—yet. But frankly, as much as I enjoy the work here, I'll be glad when my classes are over in two months and I can leave."

"Sounds as though Carlos has a thing for dancers," Hank drawled. Sylvia glanced at him sharply. That was perspicacious of him. "Would he have had the same interest in Elena before you came, do you think? Suppose at one time she was more amenable to his demands than you've been, would she have become his mistress?"

Surprised by the idea—she had never thought of a connection between Carlos and Elena—Sylvia said, "I really wouldn't know. Why do you ask?"

"If she had been his mistress, she might not have minded doing certain jobs for him—dirty jobs."

"I haven't known Elena Vanegas very long," Sylvia began slowly, "but I feel that I know her very well, and I would stake my life on the fact that Elena is totally incapable of doing a dirty job, as you put it."

The amused, mocking look in his brilliant blue eyes infuriated Sylvia. She despised people who didn't believe in friendship or love or mutual trust.

Sylvia rose abruptly to walk off her anger. But as she stood at the window and looked out at the distant lights of the city, she could sense his eyes touching her where she knew he wanted his hands to be. She found herself joining his sexual fantasy, letting herself feel the weight of his hands on her buttocks, the splay of his fingers across the smooth skin of her back. Her nipples ached for the moist pull of his lips. Her breasts lifted and swelled and pushed against the silk of her dress.

And he knew, damn him. When she turned, she could see it in his eyes. The world-weary, cynical look was gone. His clear blue eyes had turned smoky with desire, and Sylvia was glad. Let *him* suffer the hellfire of frustration as she had back in Emily Adams's garden.

With a dancer's demure little glide Sylvia walked smugly to the farthest chair from his and sat down.

He got the message and, using a little body language of his own, slouched down in his chair and spread his long legs, resting his heels on the polished floor. The glossy black evening pants fitted smoothly and tightly, making the full arrogance of his masculine offer obvious.

"Wouldn't you call it dirty pool for a woman to set a man up for kidnapping and possibly murder?" he asked coolly.

"Elena would never do that!"

Hank shrugged. "She was the last one to see a certain American journalist alive. According to a friend, he was on his way to meet Elena—they were lovers, by the way—when he disappeared. What do you think of that?"

Sylvia remained silent, considering. Elena had mentioned a boyfriend once or twice, but she had never said who he was. Yet the young woman was usually open and candid with Sylvia. Why would she have been secretive about her American boyfriend?

"Who is this American journalist?" Sylvia asked.

"His name is Peter Burns. He free-lances for various magazines and papers in the States. Do you know him?"

Sylvia shook her head slowly. "I've been here only two months. I still haven't met everyone in the foreign colony. But I assure you Elena couldn't have done what you're suggesting."

"Which brings us back to what *you* were doing on Caldera Street yesterday."

For one wild, panicky moment, Sylvia wondered if she should tell Hank Weston any more than she already had. She didn't trust him and didn't like him. So far as she could tell, he was out to destroy two of her friends, because Carlos was still her friend in spite of his amorous designs on her.

But she was also consumed with curiosity about this man, and she couldn't deny the sexual attraction she felt for him. Every trait she had so far discovered in him seemed to have its opposite. He had been suavely at ease in Emily Adams's home, but Sylvia had sensed, under the debonair evening clothes, a toughness that would have made him equally at home in a waterfront bar or a jungle camp.

And as unlikably cynical as Sylvia found him now, she hadn't forgotten the tenderness he had shown her yesterday. That compassion seemed the one stable point in the shifting kaleidoscope of Hank Weston's complex personality and the quality that prompted her to answer his question.

"Elena is one of my dance students," Sylvia said. "She's my best pupil and shows promise of being a great dancer someday"—Sylvia's voice wavered—"if nothing has happened to her."

"And what do you think *could* have happened to her?" Hank's voice was almost gentle.

"I don't know, but four days ago, for the first time, Elena didn't come to class, and she hasn't been there since. Yesterday I found a note from her in my choreography notebook asking me to meet her on Caldera Street."

"Was she there?" Hank asked eagerly.

"Yes, but she must have been frightened into hiding when the soldiers arrived. I got a glimpse of her. Then she disappeared."

"Did she see you?"

"I think so." Sylvia looked at him sharply. "What's *your* interest in all this?"

"The family of Peter Burns has hired me to find him or, failing that, to find out what happened to him."

" '*Hired*' you?" Sylvia repeated. Why was she shocked? she wondered. What else would she have expected of him—altruism? The thought made her feel like laughing. Yet she was disappointed; she didn't know why. "You're a . . ."

"Paid agent, soldier of fortune, free-lance spy." Let her hear all of it, Hank thought. He didn't want to see disappointment in those shining green-water eyes of hers when they lay side by side and talked about themselves after they had made love. Because they were going to finish what they had started in the hut on Caldera Street. Hank Weston had made up his mind to that.

Sylvia got up again, suddenly agitated. His frankness was shocking. Wasn't he *ashamed* of his profession?

Hank rose, too, and said softly, "I'd like to see that note from Elena." He looked around. "Do you have it here?"

Sylvia shook her head. "It's in my office at school."

"Any idea who put it in your notebook?" Hank asked.

"No! And I won't have you interrogating my students," Sylvia said sharply.

"I won't do anything you don't want me to," Hank said seductively.

He narrowed his eyes, taking in the small, neat head, her long, slender neck, the sexy daintiness of her body.

"But I warn you, Sylvia," he continued in a desire-roughened voice, "I want to take your hair down and see it flow like fire over your bare shoulders. And I want to undo the bow on your shoulder and strip your gown to the waist. I want to touch you all over and kiss you and make love to you. Tell me we want the same things."

She wanted to shout "No!" to him and watch him turn and go to the door. But standing there, looking into his ardent blue eyes and sweeping her glance over his strong, craggy features and powerful, well-proportioned body, Sylvia was consumed by longing for Hank Weston.

Let it be done, she thought as her passion coursed through her, bathing her with liquid heat. *Let us finish what we started yesterday. Then perhaps we can forget each other and have some peace.*

Hank read her answer in her eyes. Their misty greenness, the pupils large and black with excitement, and her lips parting softly in anticipation turned his own arousal into a towering, uncontrollable flame.

He took her in his arms and shivered at the soft, feminine feel of her. Her mouth under his was plump and clinging as a winy grape. He couldn't get enough of her. He had to taste her and lick her and leave nudging little bites on her tender earlobes and the white sweep of her throat and the concave hollow just above her collarbone.

Deftly Hank undid the bow at her shoulder and, plunging his hands inside the dress, peeled it down till it formed a peach and gold petal around her hips. He stepped back and feasted on the beauty of her pearly skin, set off by the golden torque, and the taut ripeness of her straining breasts. And Sylvia's gaze never left his eyes as he looked at her.

Awed, he murmured, "You're like a tree that bears moon apples."

Sylvia's green eyes opened wide. She wouldn't have expected poetry from this man. But then she hadn't expected gentleness from him yesterday either.

"Take your hair down," he commanded softly.

While he watched, she raised her delicately rounded arms and released her chignon into a fiery stream that lapped at her bare shoulders.

After sliding his big hands across her breasts and under her arms, he held her, with his thumbs lightly grazing her nipples. He veiled his face with the copper waterfall and closed his mouth over the tanned golden skin of her shoulder, kissing it, nibbling at its fragrant softness, licking it in exciting sweeps of his velvety tongue.

"My beautiful little stranger. I want you so much. I want your softness, your loveliness."

He lifted her breasts as though they were fruit he was weighing in his hand, hefting each one, holding it, cupping it in his palm. His fingers slid up to the hard little nubs of her nipples. Using just the sensitive tips, he stroked the dainty peaks till Sylvia moaned at the spasm of fiery pleasure which pierced that part of her already taut with longing.

She arched against him, pliant with desire, till her rosy, erect nipples were enfolded in the ruffles of his dress shirt. He put his finger in her mouth and drew it along the inside of her full lower lip and behind her teeth. He painted her lips with it. Then he bent forward and held her in a long, deliciously sticky kiss, stroking her tilted breasts at the same time.

Quickly he slipped the studs out of his dress shirt. With both hands on her slim, bare sides he raised her to him and crushed her breasts against his chest. Sylvia wound her arms around his neck and tucked herself into him. She was mindless with her need for him, ecstatic with the pleasure he was giving her.

"You're exquisite," Hank murmured. "Even in that hovel on Caldera Street I knew you would look like this."

Sylvia laughed at him, a low, rippling musical sound of joy. "You couldn't have. It was pitch-dark there."

Hank chuckled. "Let's just say I knew from experience."

It was like a cold shower. The image of a swashbuckling soldier of fortune and a girl in every seedy tropical capital —with Sylvia Goddard the choice for San Lorenzo—instantly extinguished the flames of passion burning inside her.

Sylvia stepped back and pulled up her dress. "Your shirt studs are on the floor," she said coldly.

His vivid blue eyes impaled her with a furious glance. "You didn't think the white jacket meant I was a virginal bridegroom, did you?"

"I didn't think at all. That was the trouble."

In one quick, dexterous movement he had his studs in his hand and was inserting them in his shirt. "I'll be back tomorrow to see Elena's note." He looked at her meaningfully. "We still have unfinished business."

Sylvia shook her head. "Not even business," she said. "I don't turn my friends over to mercenary spies."

"Friends?" he said ironically. "That's strange company you keep, Sylvia Goddard. A murdering industrial magnate and his helpful mistress."

Her green eyes blazed up. Her anger rose hot and pulsing in her throat. "Carlos may not be Mr. Clean, but he's no murderer. And Elena wouldn't help him if he were. Nor do I think she was ever Carlos's mistress."

"Would you mind if she had been?"

There it was again, Hank thought, his jealousy of anyone else in her life. He wanted this Sylvia Goddard for himself alone.

"Carlos is married," Sylvia said with a contemptuous shrug. "Even here in Paraguay that means something to me."

His eyes were steady on hers, sapphire and emerald burning away at each other. "I'm going to find Peter Burns or find out what happened to him, and you and I are going to finish what we started on Caldera Street, Sylvia."

"Go back to Caldera Street, Hank. That's the place for mercenaries. You'll find what you want *there*—not here."

"You're wrong, Sylvia. What I want is here, and I'm going to take it." His gaze was level, unequivocating, direct. "And you're going to want me to take it."

When he had gone, Sylvia snapped down the blinds and unrolled the gauzy S of mosquito netting over her bed. Her body felt clawed by frustration; her nerves were jangled with more than physical disappointment.

Sylvia turned the lights out and stood by the window, thinking. Hank Weston was a user. He used women's bodies for sex and unsuspecting dupes for information, and he made his living off other people's problems.

Or was he?

The insistent two-note siren of an ambulance alarmed the sleeping night. It evoked images of trouble and sorrow and fear. Sylvia remembered the soldiers and Caldera Street. If ever there had been an opportunity to *use* somebody, it had been there in that squalid, stifling hut. But Hank Weston had refused that opportunity.

CHAPTER THREE

The ringing ripped at the fabric of a dream, seeming at first to be part of it but not fitting into it, destroying with its sharp, drawn-out trill the dream's crazy logic. Sylvia dragged herself awake and reached for the phone.

"Hello?" she mumbled.

"Sylvia! Am I calling too soon?"

"No, it's all right, Emily. It's time for me to get up anyway." Sylvia checked the travel clock on the night-stand by her bed. *Past time,* she thought.

"I waited as long as I could," Emily said half-apologetically.

Sylvia smiled. She could picture Emily watching the clock, tamping down her New England energy till she could politely make a morning phone call, and even then cheating a little on decorum.

"It's fine, Emily," Sylvia assured her. "I've got one eye open, and the other's on the way."

"You sound like a Picasso," the older woman said crisply. "Listen, Frank and I are going out to the cottage to get out of this steam bath for a while. We're having people over for a *fête champêtre,* fancy French for a picnic, tomorrow evening. Can you come?"

"Love to," Sylvia drawled, amused by Emily Adams's directness.

"Good. It's anytime after work—four or fiveish. Bring a suit if you want to go swimming. And we'll all try to stay cool together."

The gentle click of the phone was Emily's good-bye.

With a hurried, guilty look at the clock again Sylvia lifted her green-and-white-striped sleepshirt up over her head and threw it on the bed. She strode into the bathroom and turned on the taps for the shower. The air felt good on her bare skin. Even a short cotton nightgown was too much in this heat.

Before she soaped herself, she lifted her face to the cascade of cool water. As it splashed on her face, wetting her eyelashes, and coursed down her tensed neck to her upward-tilting breasts, Sylvia thought, *I'll stay underwater for hours tomorrow night. I'll become the Loch Ness Monster of Paraguay's Lake Bogado. Emily can keep me there and show me off to her friends*—anything *to be cool.*

When she stepped out of the shower, she dried herself perfunctorily with a large towel, letting the dampness on her body mingle with the warm, humid air for a cooling effect. She paused in the act and glanced at herself in the mirror. A *Picasso?* Uh-uh, an amused interior voice disagreed. A *Degas,* one of those women seemingly caught unaware toweling themselves or binding up their hair or tightening ballet slippers.

Sylvia flashed a lopsided, wryly happy grin into the mirror. "You're a dancer, first, last, and always." And that simplified life a lot, she told herself.

Simplify it more, she added as she went about the business of dressing and breakfast. *Stay away from trouble. Beat Hank Weston to the punch. Have Elena's note delivered to him at his phony business address before he can come here again.*

Getting Elena's note from her choreography notebook at the studio and having it delivered would mean hurrying even more. Sylvia skipped the light housekeeping she did in the morning, when it was relatively cool, and set out for her dance studio earlier than usual. A slight breeze had come up, making it cool enough to walk briskly. The air was fresh and, on the university campus, had the damp, earthy smell of plants newly watered and cultivated.

In the distance a few gardeners in long-sleeved cotton shirts and trousers were hoeing the ornamental flower beds in the main part of the grounds. But not much gardening seemed required in the secluded area of the studio. The oleander hedge and shrubs would require an occasional trimming, Sylvia mused, but to judge from their luxuriant growth, this was done only *very* occasionally.

The main campus was a showplace. Pictures of the traditional Spanish colonial buildings—white stucco with red-tiled roofs—appeared regularly on postcards and calendars and tourist brochures. The campanile, a tall white bell tower in the center of the campus, was nearly always featured and had therefore become the symbol of the university.

Sylvia glanced at it now, wishing its clear, melodious bell that was rung only for special events were used regularly for the changing of classes in place of the nerve-jangling electric system the administration preferred.

She unlocked the door to the studio and stopped on the threshold, taking in the barre, the mirrors, the smooth wooden floor, and the slight lingering smell of sweat, letting the cozy feeling of familiarity flood over her. This bare room or its twin was her home wherever she went, and all the more so in this alien land.

She went to the desk where she kept her class records and paper supplies. It was steel and modern because

Carlos had insisted on ordering only the best for her. Sylvia inserted the short, stubby key in the lock on the center drawer and pulled the wide, shallow drawer open. Her eye swept the contents: her class record book; a sheaf of sharpened wheat-colored pencils bound by a rubber band; a pocket calculator; some loose sheets of white typing paper; colored snapshots of her classes taken at various times by students.

A rush of panic swept through Sylvia. *Her choreography notebook wasn't there.*

Then her alarm ebbed away as she spied the black-and-white-marbled cover at the back of the drawer, where she never put the notebook but might have for all she knew, because she wasn't *that* much a creature of habit.

But the fast-beating heart stayed with her. She had a feeling of dread, a premonition of what would or, more truly, would not be there.

She started to open the notebook slowly, then sped up, turning pages frantically, until finally she held it up by both covers and shook it vigorously. Nothing dropped out. Elena's note was gone.

Sylvia leaned against the desk and stared unseeingly across the gym. It would have been easy for anyone to take it. She frequently lent the studio key to students who wanted to put in extra hours of practice. Anyone could have made a copy of the key and, once inside, could have taken an impression of the desk lock or, she decided with a glance at its simple structure, could even have picked it.

And it could have been done at any time, not just yesterday when Elena's note had mysteriously appeared.

Although the drawer held nothing personal, the thought that someone might have been consistently, deliberately invading her privacy revolted Sylvia. And the suspicion that it might have been one of her own students made her, the victim, feel actually dirty.

In a gesture of defiance she threw the key into the

drawer and slammed it shut. What was the point of locking it?

Sylvia strode across the bare wood floor. It was good she didn't have any classes today. She didn't think she could face people she had, to a man and woman, once trusted and been fond of.

Or *had* it been a student? Sylvia wondered as she walked down the gravel path away from the dance studio. This part of the campus was so isolated that even an outsider could conceivably have entered the old gym without being seen. And unlike the broad avenue in front of the university proper, the street outside was a little cul-de-sac where few cars parked.

Suddenly everything seemed sinister. The snowy white oleander blossoms, so beautiful to look at, were poisonous if eaten. The thick shrubbery surrounding the gym was not just a treat for the eyes but an ideal hiding place for anyone not wishing to be seen.

Sylvia shivered in the hot sun. The blue, cloudless sky looked cruel and pitiless. The humid, enervating heat was a clinging plastic prison there was no escaping.

She was overcome with a rush of homesickness. It was winter in New York. The trees in Central Park would be a Japanese print—shiny black against a pewter sky. The air would be cold and crisp. There would be the creaky sound of snow under her boots. People would move fast, talk fast, talk *her* language.

What was she *doing* in this hellhole? Sylvia bent down and picked up an oleander blossom that had dropped on the path. She tossed it angrily into the shrubbery and wiped her hands with disgust on the sides of her white cotton dress.

Then she made herself relax. She let her shoulders drop. Her furious stride slowed down. She wiped the sweat from her forehead with her bare arm.

You know what you're doing here, she told herself quietly, sternly. *You're teaching dance.*

But when she stepped inside her house, the nervous irritability returned. She didn't have the patience for the housework she had skipped that morning or the personal chores she usually did on the two days she didn't have classes. Her mind kept returning with obsessive monotony to the terrorizing raid on Caldera Street, to the constant, nagging worry about Elena, and to this latest assault on her spirit—the theft of Elena's note.

She wanted to escape from the city with its heat, its sordid poverty, and its oppressive atmosphere. She *had* to escape, she reminded herself wryly, because Hank Weston would be coming for Elena's note and she didn't have it. And if he demanded *her* instead?

The fantastic thought, just an imaginative playing around with ideas, really, made her heart beat trippingly fast. One thing she didn't need at the moment was a third encounter of the close kind with Hank Weston.

Sylvia checked the clock on the mantel. If she hurried, she could still make the midmorning sailing of the river steamer. A day trip upriver and back would cool her off, body and spirit both. Sylvia tossed a white cotton sun hat, a plastic bottle of sunscreen lotion, and a sweater, a symbol of hope for a change in the weather, into a tote bag and left the house.

Hank gave her a block, then turned the ignition on in his rented gray Impala and followed at a discreet distance. His lips curved in a half smile as he watched her walk toward the nearest avenue, where a bus stop and a taxi stand were.

She was mad. He could tell from the way she swung the bleached canvas tote bag she carried and the stiff quickness of her stride, so different from her usual fluid grace.

She had been mad since she left her studio. What had happened there? Hank wondered.

He noted the license number of the cab she got into and followed a little closer. When the cab parked at the steamer ticket office by the river, Hank grinned. Cruising up the river with Sylvia Goddard could make for one hell of a nice day.

He waited for the last warning toot of the old-fashioned steam whistle before buying his ticket. Then he strode up the gangplank, head down so she wouldn't see his face and the smile he wore on it.

Sylvia drummed her fingers impatiently on the wooden railing. Its varnish was long gone; the ship's white paint was freckled with rust; the awning over the upper deck was torn. But seedy as it was, the *Cruz de Malta* spelled escape for a day, and she was eager to be gone.

A few middle-class wives with children came aboard for a day's outing or to visit relatives in one of the upriver towns. There were some *campesinos* in frayed straw hats and bleached cotton shirts and pants, returning to the farm. A couple of salesmen in sweat-stained tropical weaves carried European types of leather briefcases. Sylvia looked them over desultorily.

Suddenly she was jolted into sharper attention. She looked, not believing, then looked again and believed. The big man coming up the gangplank in a few easy strides, looking down at the gray wooden planks, his dark hair aureoled by the sun, was Hank Weston.

Sylvia gripped the railing hard to offset the weak feeling in her knees and the thumping of her heart against her chest.

But by the time he had reached her and said, "Hi," a smile slashing white across his sun-darkened skin, she had pulled herself together.

"Mr. Weston," Sylvia said sardonically. "Going upriver to find Dr. Livingstone, I presume."

"Going upriver on business." Blue eyes alive with humor dared her to call his bluff.

She arched one golden brown eyebrow. "Without a briefcase? All the other salesmen have them."

"I'm not selling . . . or buying."

"Looking?"

He moved closer, bending his head to her, capturing her eyes with the vibrant, electric blue of his own. His lips twitched in a half smile.

"No more," he said softly. "I've found what I want."

Suddenly he stepped back and straightened up, executing both movements so quickly that she half expected him to click his heels like a German officer in an old movie. His mobile features froze in a polite, distant smile. It was as if another man were standing there in front of her.

Sylvia started to glance around.

"Don't," he said, scarcely moving his lips. "You won't see anyone you recognize. And it's better to act as if you don't know we're being watched. So," he said with loud heartiness, "we're to be companions on this little river trip. That will be very pleasant for me. Have you seen our mutual friends Frank and Emily Adams since the party?"

They stood at the railing and chatted about the heat, a film they both had seen, the latest news from the States, while the rusty anchor was hauled in and the steamer set sail up the Paraguay River.

Hank waved his hand at the tattered awning. "We might as well sit down and have a cool drink."

A lunch bar had been set up on the upper deck. After Hank had seated Sylvia in a deck chair, he went to the counter and returned with a bottle of Paraguayan beer for each of them.

"Umm, delicious," Sylvia said, sipping the cold, slightly bitter beer. "Two things I'll miss about Paraguay when I go home—the beef and the beer."

"Not Carlos Ronderos?"

Some imp of perversity, born of resistance to having her feelings examined, led her to say blandly, "We'll write."

"Because you want to hear from him or because you collect Paraguayan stamps?" His eyes were a marble-hard blue now as he searched her face.

"Because I like to go to the mailbox and open it with that darling little key they give you in apartment buildings."

"All right." He grinned. "I'll lay off. Another beer?"

She shook her head. "Not just now, thanks."

"I'll have one. When it's lunchtime, they've got sandwiches."

Sylvia's green eyes crinkled with knowing amusement. "How far away is this town you have business in?"

He smiled back, sharing the joke. "End of the line. In fact, if the guy I want to see isn't there, I may have to come back on this steamer."

"I see." She looked down at her lap with a sly, pleased smile. His aura of masculine assurance was irresistible. With amused disbelief she realized that she'd be spending the day on the deck of the rusty tub, eating beef sandwiches and drinking Paraguayan beer with Hank Weston.

But when he returned from the bar, he was different. He had a formal, distant smile on his face, and pointing ostentatiously to a hole in the canvas above him, he moved his deck chair a few inches away from hers before taking a swig of his beer.

Sylvia started to look around for whoever was watching them. Then, remembering Hank's previous warning, she kept her eyes fixed on him instead.

"What made you become a dancer?" he asked conversationally.

"This may sound silly, but from the time I saw my first

program, I knew dance was what I wanted to do more than anything else. I was just a kid—a teenager, actually—and I had a terrific need not only to express my feelings but to find my own identity."

Sylvia pulled her hatbrim down over her forehead as though seeking privacy even now.

"All teenagers have that need," she continued, "but maybe I had it more than most. I was an only child with two very strong-minded parents"—she laughed—"of opposite minds."

He was listening intently, she noticed, his very blue eyes shining with understanding.

"My father's a painter. Not great, but very good. That's his life, his world. My mother's a housewife who hangs pictures of straw-hatted farm boys fishing from a wooden bridge and plays bridge every Wednesday afternoon.

"I was the wishbone between them. 'Follow your bent, be true to yourself, develop your talent, Sylvia,' my father would say. 'Wear pretty clothes, always look nice, get married, Sylvia,' was my mother's theme song."

"Did you . . . get married?" he asked, tensing up a little as if the answer mattered to him.

Sylvia shook her head. "I chose my father's creed. I poured myself into ballet, then switched to modern dance. But I always wanted to express my own ideas in dance, so when critics began praising my choreography, I decided to start my own company. That was two years ago, and the Goddard Dance Group has done pretty well since then."

He nodded to show he understood. "And no hits, runs, or errors in the romance game," he said, although it was really a question.

Sylvia laughed. "Maybe a few errors. I was engaged once, but when I realized I didn't love him enough, I broke it off. He was a stage designer. We're still friendly. He sends me Christmas cards with sketches of his latest theatrical sets; I send him ballet dancers in tutus." She laughed again. "Maybe next year I'll send him a postcard of Paraguay."

"It's a strange country," Hank said musingly, looking out at the green farmland along the river. "Everything east of the river is fertile and hospitable. But west of the river, the Chaco, the so-called Green Hell of Paraguay, takes over, and that's wild, desolate country—desert in the dry season, bog in the wet, like now."

"Some people do live there, though, don't they?" Sylvia asked.

"A few Indian tribes, a couple of foreign settlements, cattle ranchers, and renegades of various nationalities—and, lately, cocaine laboratories. Bolivia's a major center for the production of coca, the plant from which cocaine is derived, but a crackdown on drug production is going on there. So some of the cattle ranchers in the Chaco are flying the stuff into this country in their own planes."

As the primitive thatch-roof houses and lush tropical foliage of the riverbank went slowly by, a rush of homesickness flooded over Sylvia for the second time that day, and she frowned.

"What's the matter?" he asked quietly.

"Nothing." She shrugged. "Just a little homesick."

"I know the feeling," Hank said dryly. "I grew up in this part of the world. Not Paraguay, although I've been here before, but a couple of other Latin American countries where my father had business interests. I was the gringo or *yanqui* down here, and when I was sent home to school, I was called the spik because I spoke Spanish as fluently as English and wasn't like the other kids."

"Sounds as though you had a tough time."

Hank grinned boyishly. "Not really. Not after I beat anyone up who tried to mess with me—in North *and* South America."

A shadow of compassion for the lonely boy, fighting for acceptance in alien cultures, crossed Sylvia's face.

Watching her through narrowed eyes, Hank smiled in recognition of what she was feeling.

"Afterward, when I grew up," he continued, "I thought maybe it hadn't been that bad a childhood. I learned to take care of myself, not just with my fists but my wits too. A crowd is always stupid; it's the individual who's smart. And the loner especially has to have smarts if he's going to survive."

"You make life sound like guerrilla warfare."

"Sometimes it is, but it's exhilarating, too, to win when the stakes are high."

"A lot of money?" Sylvia asked, thinking of Peter Burns and unable to keep a bitter note out of her voice.

"A man's life," he retorted quickly, stung by her remark and its obvious reference.

His expression changed suddenly. He smiled pleasantly at her, and his tone became vanilla-bland. "We'll be stopping at the next town long enough to get off the boat and walk around a bit. It'll feel good to stretch our legs, won't it?" Sylvia noticed then that a man in a crumpled tan suit had passed close to their deck chairs twice.

The small pier was crowded with villagers come to see the steamer or to sell oranges, lemons, and avocados or manioc bread, carried in a flat basket covered with a large white embroidered napkin, or the gossamerlike Paraguayan lace known as *nanduti,* Guaraní for "spider web."

"It's market day," Hank said with a smile, "undoubtedly the reason we're making a long stop."

They stood at the head of the dusty street and looked along it at the stands with their odd assortment of merchandise: cooking pots alongside toothbrushes; cheap plastic shoes beside old records in faded envelopes; cosmetics and secondhand clothes.

Shawl-wrapped women carrying large black umbrellas

against the sun rode sidesaddle on donkeys. Others carried their purchases home in large round baskets balanced on their heads.

Thirsty customers bought glasses of iced orange juice and lemonade from a stand, shooing the flies away and removing the dead ones, when necessary, before drinking greedily. Another stall sold buns and cakes and the popular *chipá,* rolls flavored with cheese and baked in oil. At another, sausages sizzled in pans of hot oil.

A small fleet of river canoes and rowboats, a few with outboard motors, bobbed at the pier. A sign on a nearby shack advertised that they were for rent.

"Let's go," Hank commanded. He put his hand on Sylvia's arm and steered her away from the dusty street toward the shady path that ran along the river. His touch sent a crackle of excitement through her like static electricity. She felt a sharp twist of desire for him, so intense that she had to let her small white teeth come down hard over her lower lip to quell it.

He caught her fire. She could feel it in the sudden tensing of his muscles, in the hot, slumberous way he looked at her, in his narrowing of the space between them. They were alone beside the wide, slow-moving hazel brown river. In a quick flash of her mind's eye Sylvia saw him pulling her into his arms and kissing her in the deep shade of a leafy tree.

But the moment passed. Abruptly he moved away from her and quickened his pace.

"The man in the tan suit," Sylvia said, seeking an explanation, "is he a spy?"

"It's known as trench coat tan," Hank said jokingly. "They can't stay away from it." That didn't exactly answer her question, Sylvia thought. Then, more seriously, he said, "You were going to show me Elena's note today, remember?"

"It's gone," Sylvia said flatly. "I went to my studio this

morning expressly to get it because I don't have classes today. I was going to *send* it over to your place."

He raised his eyebrows and nodded at this, as if to say, *I know what you're trying, and it won't work.*

"My choreography notebook was still in my desk," Sylvia continued somberly, "but no note—anywhere."

"Access?" Hank asked in a routine, automatic sort of way.

"Easy. I think anyone could enter without being observed. My students particularly. But anyone. The place is pretty isolated."

"I know," Hank said dryly.

"Of course. You followed me, didn't you?" Sylvia's voice was as icy as her green eyes.

Hank murmured something about "protection," but his mocking smile belied the excuse, and Sylvia felt her blood boil at his incursion into her privacy.

"Does your friend Elena know that sweet Carlos is interested in you?" Hank asked.

"Yes," Sylvia answered grudgingly, always reluctant to tell Hank anything about Elena.

"Then she might consider you a rival for his affections. Right?"

Sylvia's laugh splashed out into the still air. "Sure, if either of us cared in that way for Carlos."

Hank shrugged off Sylvia's ridicule. "She's after you for something," he said matter-of-factly.

Her voice laced with contempt, Sylvia answered him. "Do you really think Elena is trying to lure me into some trap so she can have Carlos? We're *friends*, for God's sake! You don't think life's guerrilla warfare, mister. You think it's a *sewer*."

She had stopped, fuming, beside him, her hands balled into small hard fists. Her cheeks flamed with anger, matching her golden red hair in richness. Hank stared, fascinated, into her eyes. Their green had the phosphorescent brightness of a summer storm.

The lines of her small, lithe body seemed to lengthen as she pulled herself up in scorn, and her perfect little breasts heaved with her emotion.

He took a step toward her, and Sylvia knew that this time he would take her in his arms. It was no good, she thought bitterly, putting a social face on their relationship, playing parlor games like Emily Adams and her crowd. The time bomb that had been ticking all day was about to go off. If she didn't do something about it, they would end up in an explosion of passionate need, bodies twisting, hot and luxuriant, like the jungle growth around them.

Forcing coolness into her voice, Sylvia said, "It must be time to go back."

"The steamer will toot when it is."

"I'd rather not take the chance. I wouldn't care to be stuck here till the steamer returns."

Hank grinned. "You wouldn't be alone, and could you think of a better lovers' hideaway?"

"It's a hideaway, all right." Sylvia shrugged. "As for the rest . . ."

His eyes narrowed with secret satisfaction. Love, hate, anger, desire—they all came out of the same bag. And he could play a waiting game. He didn't lack experience in that.

When they got back to the pier, Hank saw the man in the tan suit standing in front of a juice stand. Hank spoke to him and threw a couple of coins on the counter.

"What did you say to him?" Sylvia asked, amazed.

"I told him spying was hard work and to have a lemonade on me."

Hank liked the way she smiled then. It was slow and lazy and full of enjoyment.

"You used Guaraní, the Indian language."

"You don't say."

"So you know it," she continued, vexed by his offputting answer.

"Almost everyone in Paraguay is bilingual in Spanish and Guaraní. After all, ninety-five percent of the population is of this mixed strain. There are a few scattered Indian tribes in the Chaco and a small percentage of white people, and that's pretty much it."

Sylvia only half listened, her mind going down its own track. It all made sense. A daring man who knew the culture and languages of Latin America, a danger buff, a man who liked to use his wits as well as his brawn.

"What made you leave the CIA?" she asked quietly. "Or are you moonlighting, looking for Peter Burns?"

The ship's whistle sounded then. They were standing right under it, and Sylvia jumped at its piercingly sharp blare.

Hank's hand went out as if to protect her; then he quickly let it fall.

"All aboard that's going aboard," he said facetiously.

Sylvia didn't budge. "You haven't answered my question." Somehow it was terribly important to her to hear what he would say.

Hank looked around at the people come to wave goodbye to the steamer, the vendors packing up their unsold wares, the tourists hurrying to the boat.

He waggled his brows comically at her. "Piers have ears."

"Nonsense," she said briskly, hearing herself sound like Emily Adams. "There's no one within twenty feet of us."

"I told you, I'm the lone eagle type. I work best alone."

This man's dangerous for you; leave him alone, Sylvia, a calm, objective interior voice warned her.

But as he looked at her with an expression of quiet, sure possessiveness, her face grew warm. She could feel her lips becoming full, pouting a little and parting, and her body felt heavy and languorous.

The boat whistle tooted again.

He touched her arm and said politely, distantly, in his best shipboard manner, "We really should go aboard."

She turned away from him and started for the gangplank, but not before she had seen in the blue-gray smokiness of his eyes the same erotic current that had just jolted her.

It was evening when they returned to San Lorenzo. As the steamer slowed before dropping anchor at the boat landing, the river breezes died on the still air. The heat seemed to come rushing out of the city like some angry beast impatient for its prey.

Standing on the deck with Hank, stretching her neck and flaring her nostrils for the least stirring of air, Sylvia felt her skin prickle with the steamy heat; her lithe body seemed elephantine with lethargy; her nerves were jangled and irritated.

"This heat turns me into an amoeba, just a blob of protoplasm," she said with a laugh.

"I don't think a San Lorenzo cabby would know what to do if he saw a blob of protoplasm in the back seat of his cab. Why don't you let me drive you home?"

"I promised my driver a return trip. He'll be waiting for me at the boat landing."

"I'll pay him and send him home."

"Very corrupting—to pay a man for work not done."

He moved closer to her so that she smelled the heady aroma of his masculine scent mixed with sweat.

"Very demoralizing—to deprive a man of what he wants."

Sylvia was tempted. Of course, the cabby could be paid and dismissed. But the way Hank Weston made her feel was not something she wanted to encourage in herself.

So she smiled and turned her head to watch the docking of the steamer. And he watched her. The heat had veiled her face with a thin sheen of sweat. It endeared her to him. He didn't know why, any more than he knew why the proud tilt of her small, exquisitely formed head on that long, graceful neck and her well-knit, finely made body were more arousing to him than the flamboyantly gorgeous women he had known in the past.

She turned then and caught him watching her. Her clear green eyes widened and grew serious for a moment. Then she said lightly, "Which of us do you think the man in the tan suit will follow tonight?"

"Sure you don't want to make it easy for him, let him spy on the two of us at the same time?" Hank said, matching her tone. "You might get an award from the IAS, the International Association of Spies."

"Would I have to be present to receive it?"

"Absolutely. Just be sure you take the listening device out of the loving cup they give you."

"Let me know when the IAS gives out wall calendars. That's what I really need," Sylvia said sweetly.

Grinning in acknowledgment of defeat, Hank took Sylvia's arm and escorted her down the gangplank. When they reached the cab, he said tersely, "Is that the same driver you had this morning?"

"Yes, I recognize him."

He put her in the taxi then and lingered for a moment, his expression worried.

"Take care," he finally said.

"If I find Elena's note, I'll get it to you," Sylvia whispered in English.

"Yes," he answered absently, as though he no longer cared about the note, or at least not at that moment.

The cab had hardly pulled away when Hank gunned his own car and followed it.

His face was grim, his long, angular features set in stubborn, unhappy lines. It was a dirty business he was in when the woman he cared for was also the decoy to bring in the game he was hunting—the innocent white goat tethered to lure Elena close enough so that he could find out where Peter was.

God knows, he hadn't arranged the situation. It was already there when Elena tried to meet Sylvia on Caldera Street. Still, Sylvia might someday believe that he had been only using her. She would be wrong. But in the misunderstanding he could lose her.

Hank stopped short in amazement. When had he ever worried about losing a woman before?

CHAPTER FOUR

The street was empty as usual when Sylvia walked to the university the next day. A few parked cars, a little traffic, one or two pedestrians, that was all. Sylvia scanned the faces that passed her on the sidewalk and darted quick, searching glances into the cars.

If someone was watching her, she was going to find him first. The man in the tan suit would be a snap. She'd know his blunt-featured face anywhere. But there might be somebody else. He'd know the route she always took to her dance studio and be waiting for her in a parked car. Or he'd look at her sideways with eyes that seemed disinterested.

But her vigilance turned up no one who seemed more interested in her than he would in any foreign-looking young woman with a springy stride, golden red hair, and morning-clear green eyes. Nevertheless, Sylvia felt a prickling of suspense, of something sinister in the bright sunshine. If she was being watched, it was by somebody more powerful than she was, and for a purpose. A purpose she didn't know.

Suddenly Sylvia felt an overwhelming need for Hank

there at her side. She wanted his rugged, earthy strength and the sheer, self-confident vitality that radiated from him. He made her feel safe.

Safe from everyone but him, Sylvia reflected wryly as a wash of another kind of longing flowed through her. For a moment she recalled the dark, ardent look that had turned his eyes the blue-black of Manhattan's evening winter skies as they walked along the river path yesterday. She let herself feel imaginatively the excitement of being pulled into his strong arms, of having his long, hard body press her soft hollows and curves, his mouth hungrily move against hers.

Then, resolutely, she thrust the fantasy aside. Her job was her talisman. Dance was the reason she was here in San Lorenzo. That was where she would focus her thoughts—not on Hank Weston and his world of undercover agents, spies, and watchers.

Still, as she approached the isolated building housing the dance studio, she peered closely at the thick shrubbery surrounding it. When she unlocked the door, she stopped a moment on the threshold, and her eyes swept the bare gym before she crossed the shiny wooden floor to her desk.

She opened the center drawer and searched again for Elena's note, hoping that somehow she might have missed it before. She pulled the drawer far out and reached her hand behind it, but there was nothing there. Nor did a slim ruler inserted along the sides dislodge a piece of paper.

Don't let the theft of Elena's note affect your attitude toward your students, Sylvia warned herself. *It might not even have been one of them.*

And don't make it a police matter. Sylvia shuddered. She had heard what went on in San Lorenzo's jails.

She took out a pad of paper and carefully drafted the announcement she would make to each of her classes.

As the first group, barefoot and in variously colored leotards stood before her, Sylvia said, "I regret that the studio will no longer be available for work outside class. I realize how much more comfortable its *somewhat* air-conditioned interior is than most of the places available to you"—the joke about the air conditioning was designed to bring a smile to the serious dark eyes fastened on her—"but . . ." Sylvia hesitated. She considered departing from the draft of her speech and mentioning that some things had been missing but decided against it when the image of San Lorenzo's blue-shirted, vicious-looking police came into her mind again. "But I'm afraid I'll be using it myself for a while to work out the steps of a dance I'm choreographing."

Not one of the gracefully poised dancers responded as Sylvia had expected. Instead of enthusiastic curiosity about the dance she had mentioned, excited questions, jokes about being selected to solo in it, her announcement was met with stony silence and a look in the dark eyes of a patient waiting for the truth.

The intimacy of their work together, hour by hour, day after day, gave the young dancers a special insight into each other and into their teacher. *They know I'm lying,* Sylvia thought, and her heart sank. Her students had once repaid her trust with trust. Now they were repaying her suspicion with suspicion.

Sylvia's shoulders sagged under this realization. Her whole being revolted against her behavior. She felt herself becoming a part of a world she abhorred—a world of shadowy motives, covert actions, pervasive distrust; Hank Weston's world.

The thought that Elena might be the danger to her Hank thought she was even flashed through Sylvia's mind. Shaking her head violently in a gesture of self-disgust, Sylvia pushed the thought away. She would not let herself be sucked into the moral swamp of the world around her.

Still, as she taught her classes that day, she kept hoping that one of the dancers would betray by some small sign that he or she was the one who had taken Elena's note. But by the end of the day she had received no hint, and she left the dance studio feeling depressed.

In a hurry now to escape the tropical heat and the miasma of suspicion that clung to the city, Sylvia walked back to her house as quickly as she could. She showered and put on a cool sundress of lime green cotton, which showed her tanned, polished shoulders and slim waist. She slipped her bare feet into flat leather sandals and, throwing a simple white maillot and a beach towel into a tote bag, set out to get the bus that went to Lake Bogado.

The half hour trip to the lake was relaxing and enjoyable. The bus wasn't crowded. The windows were wide open, and as the bus approached the lake, the air became almost cool.

Sylvia felt safer than she had all day. None of the other passengers could conceivably be any other than he or she seemed: a middle-aged businessman returning to his resort cottage from the city; a mother and young daughter with shopping bags from San Lorenzo's leading department store; an old woman dressed in funereal black.

The driver let Sylvia off at the nearest point to the Adamses' cottage. Sylvia dropped her tote bag and raised her face to the cooling breeze from the lake, letting the air flow across her sweat-damp brow. She undid the thick coronet around her head and shook her hair free so that it lay in a thick tawny mass on her shoulders. Then, picking up her tote bag again, she set off across the grassy field that lay between the road and the fringe of cottages around the lake.

Lake Bodago had been a resort for the wealthy and middle classes of San Lorenzo for a long time. Its shores were lined with tropical foliage and trees that went right down to the water. Some of the vacation homes were palatial; others, like the Adamses', were simply comfortable.

Approaching the cottage from the rear, Sylvia heard the high-pitched babble of voices that went with any party. She breathed in the smoky odor of steaks being charbroiled outside and, getting closer, picked up Emily's low-pitched laugh. There was nothing in the backyard but a few swimsuits and towels drying on a line. The party was on the front lawn, facing the lake.

It was a small group, only a handful of couples, close friends of Emily and Frank's, for the most part. Some of the women were in swimsuits, the men in trunks; others wore casual sports clothes as they stood around chatting or sat at umbrella tables on the lawn.

Her eyes found Hank immediately—with all the accuracy of radar, Sylvia thought wryly. Glossy-haired and impeccably dressed in white flannels and a white shirt open at his brown corded neck, he was cooking steaks at an outdoor grill and watching her as she walked across the lawn.

Your heart's pounding because you didn't expect to see him here, Sylvia told herself. *And you picked him out of the crowd because he's taller than anyone else.*

But it wasn't the truth, and she knew it.

They searched each other with their eyes, mutely acknowledging their helplessness against the inevitability, the *necessity* of their being together. The signal was so obvious that Emily Adams, who had been standing beside the grill as Sylvia approached, picked it up.

Sylvia could see Emily's awareness in her shrewd blue eyes as she took a step forward, hands outstretched, and said, "Sylvia, it's a delight to see you." Then, with a sly sidelong glance: "I believe you know Hank Weston."

"Yes, of course," Sylvia answered politely. "We met at your Washington's Birthday party."

"Such a shame you two had to leave before the fireworks." In a low voice for Sylvia's ears alone Emily added, with a look of wide-eyed innocence, "But perhaps you had your own fireworks to go to."

"Hey, how about letting me in on this conversation?" Hank said. "Just because I broil the best steak south of the border—very far south!—doesn't mean I don't like to chat up the ladies once in a while."

"You're burning one of your steaks," Sylvia said matter-of-factly, pointing to a charred piece of beef in the center of the grill.

Hank grinned. "He asked for it well done." Then his expression became serious. "You were late getting here. Did you run into any trouble?"

Sylvia shook her head while Emily glanced from one to the other with a worried look.

"I hope you two aren't involved in something you shouldn't be," the older woman said.

"Not at all," Hank said smoothly. "How did you say you like your steak, Emily?"

"Rare," Emily replied dryly, "and it looks as though I'm already too late. But why don't you let me find somebody else to do the cooking while you get Sylvia a drink? Frank's looking very unhappy because he doesn't have a customer. He's a frustrated bartender, you know."

Hank handed the meat turner to Emily. As he cupped Sylvia's elbow and started to escort her across the grass to the bar set up next to the house, Emily said in a light, conversational tone, "Life's so boring here. If you do run into a bit of excitement, remember, I stand ready to help."

"Emily," Hank said, with a smile on his lips but a very serious look in his eyes, "if I had to rely on anyone in a pinch, it would be you."

Emily smiled at the compliment, but her eyes, too, were serious as they looked into Hank's. Then she broke away and said to Sylvia, "The changing rooms are inside. Yours is marked 'Girls.' "

"Mine's marked 'Boys,' " Hank said with a chuckle. "You're a schoolmistress, Emily."

"I like having the rules laid out ahead of time," Emily retorted as she wandered off, meat turner in hand, to find another cook, and Sylvia and Hank set out across the lawn for the house and the bar.

Frank Adams presided over a linen-draped table holding glasses, an ice bucket, assorted bottles, and dishes of olives, cherries, and sliced limes with the same mild-mannered efficiency with which he was said to run his office.

"Sylvia!" he called out. "So glad you could make it! What can I get you to drink? Something long and cool, I'll bet. Name it, and I've got it," he said proudly.

Sylvia gave Frank her drink order, and when he had placed a tall gin and tonic in her hand, their host turned to Hank. "Another Scotch and water, Hank? I see Emily's got you working. If you're going to cook for us, the least I can do is keep you happy. Although," Adams added, his gray eyes twinkling behind rimless glasses, "you look pretty happy right now."

It was true, Hank thought. Just having that slight, absurdly straight little figure by his side gave him a happiness strangely compounded of excitement and a deep contentment that he had never known before.

He couldn't wait to be alone with her. After he had gotten his drink, Hank cuddled Sylvia's elbow with his large hand and steered her away from the bar, past people he gave her time only to smile at and nod to, and through a stand of trees to the lake.

"How did you get here?" Hank asked.

"There's a bus that goes to Bogado."

"Bus! Good God! Why didn't you ask me to bring you?"

"I didn't know you were coming. Besides, I enjoyed the bus ride. It was cool, and I felt safe."

"I'm taking you home," Hank said firmly. "Has Elena's note turned up?"

"No. I don't know that it was one of my students who took it, but I've told them the studio would not be available after class hours."

"Good idea," Hank said abstractedly. "How about Elena? Has she tried to get in touch with you again?"

"No!" she answered, a shade of defiance in her voice. *Even if she had,* Sylvia thought, *I wouldn't tell you.*

His glance slipped away from hers, his blue eyes narrowed in amusement. She wasn't lying now, but she *would,* to save that friend of hers.

A strip of beach had been created along the part of the lake used for swimming. Colored lights twinkling in the tropical trees made a kind of fairyland of the scene and faintly illuminated not only the water but a raft anchored not far from the shore.

The splashes of a few swimmers and the cries of maids calling children out of the water for supper could be heard. Otherwise, the lake was silent.

"I've thought of nothing all day long but jumping in the lake, with all my clothes on, if necessary," Sylvia said with a laugh.

"Why don't we change now then? A drink, a swim, a steak . . ." His voice trailed off. "A perfect night."

Sylvia sipped at the ice-cold gin and tonic Frank had mixed for her. "Sounds good. I'll take my tote bag to the room Emily marked 'Girls.' "

Hank grinned. "My swim trunks are in 'Boys.' Meet you on common ground in ten minutes?"

"Yes, fine," Sylvia answered. "I'll finish my drink as we walk back to the house."

Sylvia shivered with pleasure as she strode into the lake and felt the cool water cover her legs and thighs. When it lapped gently at the waist of her white maillot, she stopped and glanced at Hank, taking in his broad shoulders and narrow waist, the dark hair on his chest.

His obvious virility had an effect on her. She could sense the slight lift of her breasts under the sleek Lycra of the suit, the tightening here and there of certain muscles. She plunged her wrists into the lake water as if to cool down a sudden fever.

She turned her head away from him, away from those bright diamond blue eyes that scanned the polished shoulders under the narrow straps of her suit, the sun-goldened tops of her breasts with just a hint of white showing above the low-cut neckline, and her rounded, shapely arms.

Staring straight ahead, she could just make out the dark heads and rhythmically lifted shoulders of the swimmers whose splashings she had heard. They were several yards away in the large lake.

"Race you to the float?" Hank asked, his cool, teasing voice holding a challenge that had nothing to do with swimming.

"You're on!" Sylvia replied, and she struck out immediately in a fast crawl.

Hank's powerful shoulders and leg muscles soon propelled him ahead of her, and he was waiting on the raft when she reached it. Tired from the fast, strenuous effort, Sylvia was groping for the edge of the raft when his strong hands reached down into the water for her. He lifted her up and drew her in close to him.

His hands were slick on her wet sides. They curved around her, exciting her so that her limbs felt heavy and languorous in his embrace. She swayed a little toward him, and Hank kissed her while droplets of water from their wet hair made a tiny cascade down their joined faces.

Sylvia reveled in the touch of his lips on hers. They were wet and cool and had the fresh, clean taste of lake water. She felt herself drowning in his kiss, a mermaid who had made the dangerous mistake of loving a mortal. Moving closer, she thrilled to the feel of his chest hair against her bare skin and of his hairy legs, which had locked hers in a tight embrace. She delighted in knowing his whole body, clad only in the briefest of swim trunks.

But this is madness, a warning interior voice said, *the kind of madness born of a tropical night, a virile, handsome man, and a cocktail.*

She moved out of Hank's arms and in a few steps reached the edge of the raft. Calling over her shoulder, "I'm going back," she dived into the water and swam with short, hard strokes to the shore.

She had dried herself and was rough-drying her hair when he came up beside her.

"Here, let me do that," he commanded huskily.

He took the towel from her and, standing close, passed it again and again over her long, thick hair until it fanned out over her bare shoulders in a cascade of red gold.

When he had finished, he made a hood of the towel and used the ends to tilt her face up to his. The simple intimacy of the act, the closeness of his almost nude body, the lulling motions of his hands on her hair made her feel that every intake and exhalation of her breath were charged with an erotic current. She looked up at him with desire-swollen lips, her eyes heavy-lidded and slumberous.

Taking Sylvia's hand, Hank said simply, "Come," and led her away from the beach into the strip of jungle that bordered it.

Their entrance into the thick foliage set off a stirring of night animals, a stealthy patter of feet, the quick whirring of wings. Sylvia felt like a stranger in a mysterious world, a world of lush, steamy growth, of unknown dark shapes, of a power stronger than man's.

A harsh squawking overhead made her jump.

Hank drew her into his arms. "Ssh, darling, it's only a parrot. Look there, you can just see him." He put his hand under her chin and turned her face upward. Sylvia caught a glimpse of brilliant greens and yellows and reds.

Sylvia laughed. "Somehow I don't think this is the place to say, 'Polly want a cracker?' "

"I think *that* Polly might take your finger off. Like this." He reached for her index finger and put it in his mouth, biting down gently on it. Then he kissed it and let her hand drop. "Here, I'm giving it back to you. You might need it when you get home for pointing out your luggage, or hailing a cab, or curling your hair."

He wound a long, gleaming strand of her hair around his finger then and, holding her by it lightly, bent his head to her. His breath was warm against her lips before she felt the gentle pressure of his mouth.

His lips parted against hers. Then his strong white teeth nipped gently at the smooth petals of her lips till like a flower, they opened to his delightful demand. For long, thrilling moments their mouths remained open to each other, exchanging only breath. Waiting. Sylvia thought of bees hovering over a flower. Her own lips felt bee-stung from his kiss, love-swollen, pouting with passion.

Then his tongue, velvety as a bee's wing, pushed past her lips and teeth to claim the sweet nectar of her mouth. He relinquished his hold on her hair and pulled her close to him, almost wrapping his body around her. His long, sure hands smoothed themselves along her back, massaging, stroking, at the same time that his tongue rubbed against hers with an intimacy that made her go weak. Of its own accord her body surged toward his.

Hank slipped his hands under the crossed straps of her maillot. As they rested there, Sylvia was piercingly aware of their hardness and size, their warmth against her lake-cooled skin. Her breasts swelled and pressed against his broad chest. Hank moaned and pressed her intimately closer to him.

Sylvia could feel the strength of his arousal and thrilled to it. Her whole body was pulsing with deliciously erotic sensations. She was lost in her own excitement, in the pull of her body toward his.

When she heard the high-pitched laughter and rapid chatter in Spanish, she wondered how long it had been going on. At first she thought the sounds were far away and seemed close only because of the stillness. But as the voices drew nearer and she could almost distinguish words, she realized that these were the people she had seen swimming in the lake, taking a shortcut back to their cottages through the strip of jungle she and Hank were standing in.

Sylvia pulled herself out of Hank's arms.

"There are people here," she whispered.

His warm breath tickled her ear seductively. "That makes it even more exciting, if that were possible."

Suddenly all the passion within her turned to rage.

"You really are a danger junkie, aren't you, Hank?" she said contemptuously. "Even in love you have to have that extra little element of excitement."

With a quickness she wouldn't have thought possible he curved his arm around her waist and pulled her toward him again. "If you're looking for pretexts to break off our lovemaking, I'll give you a real one," he said in a voice raspy with his own anger and frustration.

Locking her to him with a grip that was both iron-firm and soft as velvet, he plundered her mouth in a swash-buckling, capturing kiss that made Sylvia go limp in his arms. His mouth ground and twisted and pressed against hers. Their teeth touched in the intimacy of the kiss. Then their tongues lay side by side in a kind of truce.

He slid his big hands under the crisscross of her maillot straps and this time slipped them off her shoulders. He palmed her slick, wet breasts while his thighs pressed hers, exciting her into forgetting her anger. He was mastering her anew with his luscious kisses and his clever hands and his near nakedness, Sylvia thought. But she must not let herself be mastered by Hank Weston. A dangerous man to his enemies, what else, in view of her attachment to Elena and Carlos, could he consider her?

"Let me go or I'll scream," she whispered hoarsely.

She felt rather than heard his laugh—a movement of hard muscles in the body warm against hers. "Scream away, little parrot. People will wonder why."

That was true, Sylvia thought wryly. Half the women in the foreign colony of San Lorenzo would be delighted to be in her position.

But he relaxed his grip.

"I told you before, I'll never do anything you don't want me to." He paused. "I won't have to."

"You're despicable," she retorted. "You feed on danger. It's your drug."

"No, you're wrong," he said coolly. "It's my livelihood."

Sylvia uttered a long, angry, frustrated "Oh!" and turned to go back to the cottage. She could hear him laughing softly behind her as she threaded her way through the thick undergrowth.

Then he caught up with her.

"Here now," he said, his voice both rough and gentle, "it'll take you hours if you don't get on the right path."

Angry and upset, Sylvia snapped out, "I don't need your help."

To her surprise he replied seriously, "I hope you never do." Then, shifting conversational gears, he added lightly, "I'm going to cook a steak for both of us. Remember what I said? A drink, a steak, a perfect night?"

"The drink and the steak sound good," Sylvia replied flatly.

"The perfect night will come later."

Sylvia flared up again at the laughing self-assurance in his voice. Among other things wrong with him, Hank Weston had obviously had too many women throw themselves at him. She had no intention of joining *that* parade.

When they separated at the cottage, Hank asked, "How do you like your steak?"

"Rare, but not jungle raw."

"Everything's jungle raw at bottom, Sylvia. You just don't know it yet."

Sylvia was glad to find the "Girls" changing room in the cottage unoccupied. But as she slipped her suit off and stood nude in the center of the floor, she shuddered with the force of the longing that tore through her.

She wanted him to kiss her all over with his eyes and his firm, cool lips. She wanted to feel his strong hands caressing her and his weight on top of her; she wanted him inside her.

Her yearning had nothing to do with "wanting a man." She wanted *Hank.* Hank Weston, mercenary agent, soldier of fortune, free-lance spy. Hank Weston, the man it was dangerous for her to love.

When Sylvia stepped out of the cottage, she hesitated, as though not quite ready to step into the world she saw. The Adamses had illuminated the shrubbery in the garden, creating oases of light surrounded by pools of inky darkness. The white shirts of the men and the light-colored dresses the women had changed into looked ghostly and nostalgic in the dark, as though this were a garden party of another time. The glowing ends of cigarettes waved in the air to punctuate conversation seemed like slow-moving fireflies.

It was a world made up of people who lived in the country but did not belong to it. Yet Frank and Emily Adams and their friends were in Paraguay on a more or less permanent basis, whereas she was truly only temporary.

Sylvia's eyes sought out the other outsider, Hank Weston, and found him coming toward her with a plate in each of his hands.

"I have our steaks," he said simply, quietly. "Emily has invited us to join her and some of the others at that table." He nodded toward a candlelit table set up on the lawn. Emily was there with two other couples, while Frank hosted the second table of guests.

As they crossed the lawn, Hank looked at Sylvia admiringly. "You didn't put your hair up. I like it that way, pouring over your shoulders."

"Of course. All macho men like women barefoot and in leopard skins."

"I don't know about leopard," Hank said with a grin. "But I could get you a jaguar from the Chaco. They're still roaming around there."

"Thanks. I think I'll stick to shoes and my own skin."

"Preferably bare, Miss Goddard."

"Positively clothed, Mr. Weston."

Emily greeted Sylvia and Hank and introduced them to the other people at the table. The conversation, as it often did, revolved about the country's politics.

"The man to watch is Carlos Ronderos," said the bald, large-featured man to Emily's right, an engineer with a large American company. "He's got not his finger but his whole hand in every important business in the country. That's economic power."

"Do you think he'll want political power then?" a woman across from him asked.

The bald man shrugged. "Probably. If you're into power, you want all you can get."

"How do you think he'll set about getting it, Mark?" Emily asked quietly. "Through an election or revolution?"

"He can certainly do it the second way. He's got the money and the influence to raise his own army and his own secret police, if he doesn't already have them."

"How about the drug trade?" one of the other men asked. "Some Latin American politicians finance themselves that way."

"Carlos doesn't need the money," Mark answered. "If he got involved in drugs at all, it would be to preempt some other would-be kingpin from grabbing power."

Sylvia moved restlessly in her seat. Nothing they were saying about Carlos beyond the fact that he was very wealthy was true. She started to speak, but Hank laid a restraining hand on her arm.

She shook off his hand and said, "What some of you may not know is that Carlos spent a number of years in America. I knew him there. I think he has a true respect for democracy, and I doubt very much that he would go in for the kind of abuse associated with secret police."

"You may be right, Sylvia," Emily said soothingly. "Ronderos certainly gives every appearance of being, shall we say, well behaved." She looked around at the others for corroboration. "I understand he pays his employees well and has instituted certain labor reforms."

"Buying future support," the engineer said sourly. "He talks a good game; but actions speak louder than words, and Ronderos is the guy to watch, mark my words."

Emily deftly led the conversation in another direction, the activities of a little theater group in San Lorenzo. But Sylvia didn't join in. She was acutely aware of Hank's body English beside her. He seemed not only to be listening but to be taking in every kind of information possible from the people around the table—intently registering facial expressions, tone of voice, nuances of meaning, listening and remembering, making mental notes.

"I suppose you think what they said about Carlos is true," Sylvia remarked when they were on their way back to San Lorenzo in Hank's car.

"You wouldn't believe *me,*" Hank replied in a faintly bitter tone. "Perhaps you'll believe them."

"It sounded like speculation to me. I know Carlos better."

"You don't know him here in his own environment."

Sylvia was silent for a moment. Hank's remark was shrewd. "I see what you mean, but I still don't think Carlos has changed that much from the man I knew in New York." The dashboard lights made a cozy little world for the two of them, a disarming, trusting world. Sylvia stared thoughtfully at a pale green dial and said aloud what she hadn't meant to. "Except perhaps in one respect."

Hank glanced sharply at her. "He's really after you now—isn't he?—and you're flattered that he loves you."

Sylvia shrugged disdainfully. "Is that love—to *want* a person?"

Hank didn't answer. His long brown hands gripped the wheel, and he stared straight ahead.

Damn the woman. She was complicating his life, making his search for the Vanegas girl difficult, endangering his mission to find Peter Burns.

It was nothing to *want* her. He had *wanted* hundreds of women, and had had them too. And after the way she had responded to him tonight, he was pretty sure he could have her. But would he be satisfied with just that? With another woman the answer would be yes. But with the little dancer he wasn't sure.

Hank moved his hands restlessly. Had she been right when she called him a danger junkie? Would love add just that fillip of excitement, that difference, that change that he wanted?

He looked at her. She had wound her hair around her head again and stared straight ahead at the dark road, her proud little profile earnest and steady.

His lips moved in a smile. Maybe that was the trouble, Hank thought; he always felt like smiling when he was with her.

He put his hand out and clasped hers, and to his surprise she let her small hand lie in his large one for a while. It was a truce, of sorts, in the war they were waging with themselves and against each other.

CHAPTER FIVE

Work was an anodyne. The dance movements Sylvia planned for her students diverted her mind from thoughts of Hank, and the physical execution of them tired her body. Work gave her a respite from the constant strain of worrying about Elena and from the oppressive heat, which now suffused even the dawn with a transparent, shimmering haze.

Legs bare, wearing the simplest, coolest of sundresses, and with her heavy hair off her neck and wound tightly around her small head, Sylvia walked with the least expenditure of energy to her studio the following morning. Even the modicum of air conditioning it offered would be welcome.

If she complained to Carlos, he would undoubtedly arrange for a brand-new air conditioner in the studio, some superduper job to show the modernity of his country and his own personal generosity to favorites.

Sylvia made a grimace of distaste. In spite of her defense of him yesterday, not even for the sake of her hardworking, sweating students did she want to become a "favorite" of Carlos Ronderos.

Hoping even now to see Elena's note there, Sylvia unlocked and pulled open her desk drawer. Everything had been put in neat little piles with her calculator in front. Very neat, Sylvia acknowledged. She might use that arrangement herself from now on.

In fact, Sylvia told herself, looking down into the wide, shallow drawer and drumming her fingers on its metal edge, it looked very much as though whoever had opened the drawer wanted her to know it. Her eyes rested on the pocket calculator. The numbers 57738 shone up at her from the liquid crystal display.

In the sultry heat of the room a chill passed through Sylvia. She hadn't put the numbers there. Who had? And what did they mean?

Taking a sheet of paper and a pencil, Sylvia wrote the numbers down. She tried various combinations of the digits. None of them meant anything to her.

Then she pushed her tongue against her teeth in a little "tsk" of annoyance. She was making a mountain out of a molehill, finding mysteries where none existed.

Pocket calculators weren't that common in this country. The student who had been entertaining himself by opening her desk had probably been having fun with her calculator as well.

Sylvia picked it up and moved to turn the display off, then decided not to. Puzzling over the mysterious numbers again, she turned the calculator around in her hand.

Wavy and oddly formed but still clear, the word BELLS stood out in the display panel.

Sylvia sat staring unthinkingly at the message for a moment. *Bells.* With its churches and schools San Lorenzo was a city of bells. But which church, which school was Elena trying to tell Sylvia to meet her at?

That this was another message from Elena, less traceable than a written one, Sylvia didn't doubt. She did what she was sure Elena had intended and with a flick of her thumb erased the word.

When the clang of the bell for eight o'clock classes rang in the studio, Sylvia jumped. It was almost too opportune, she thought with a smile. Class bells rang all day long, every hour on the hour, at the university.

This was the place Elena had meant. All Sylvia had to do was wait and Elena would come to her.

Sylvia had a warm feeling of gratitude for her students that day. One of them was helping Elena. Which one? Was it Ana, the student who was more acrobat than dancer, more steel-spring bounce than fluid grace? Ana and Elena had been friendly, and when Elena stopped coming to class, Sylvia had asked Ana if she knew why. The girl had been polite but told her nothing, the deep-set dark eyes in the broad-boned Indian face looking back at Sylvia as impassively as they did now.

Arturo, diligent and serious, stubborn about becoming a dancer in spite of his physician father's opposition, was another possibility. He and Elena often paired off for a practice pas de deux. Arturo with his soft brown eyes looked the type who'd crumble cookielike under pressure, but Sylvia suspected that his gentleness came from strength, not weakness. Arturo wouldn't tell Sylvia anything Elena didn't want him to.

She might never know who Elena's accomplice was till that person or Elena herself told her, Sylvia decided. But with a wry smile she acknowledged that the accomplice couldn't help knowing Sylvia had gotten Elena's message because every class-changing bell made her jump. And as the day wore on, the suspense of when and how Elena would appear increased.

Her last class finished at three o'clock. *Elena will come now,* Sylvia told herself. Afraid she would miss her friend if she went to the shower room, Sylvia sat at her desk in her black leotard and, to ease her tension, made notes in her choreography notebook for "Affirmation."

But without the diversion of teaching the heat seemed more than ever oppressive. Figuring it could be no hotter outside than in the studio, Sylvia turned off the unsatisfactory air conditioner and opened the door.

She worked for a while; then, tired by the long day and the heat, she laid her head on her arms and let herself fall asleep. A jumble of harsh, discordant sounds woke her up. She listened for a moment, unsure whether the noises were the tag end of a dream or reality.

But there was no mistaking the commotion of an actual scuffle, followed by the sharp, rattling slide of gravel. She heard Hank's voice in a snarled epithet and another man's frightened squeal.

Sylvia ran outside. Hank was wrestling a man to the ground beside the flowering shrubs. Slight and dark and quick, he slithered like a snake in Hank's grasp.

Using his knees and one hand, Hank pinned the intruder down. He curved the other hand around the man's throat. "What were you doing here?" Hank rapped out. "Who sent you?"

The man twisted from side to side. His eyes rolled with fear, so that the yellowish whites showed. Hank's thumb applied a little pressure. "Talk, you bastard, or I'll choke every bit of life out of you and throw you in the river for the piranhas to eat."

Sylvia suddenly went cold with shock. Somehow the trespasser had managed to free his hand. There was a glint of steel in the bright sunshine. Then the hand reached across Hank's long back and the knife hovered above it.

"Hank!" Sylvia screamed. "He's got a knife."

The paralysis she had fallen into broke instantly. She sprang forward with a dancer's leap and kicked her right leg high in the air to knock the knife out of the man's hand. But Hank was faster.

He seized the knife-holding arm and twisted it till the knife fell with a dull thud on the ground. But the action cost him his grip on his assailant. The man jumped to his feet and zigzagged his way across the grounds and out to the street.

Hank was on his feet at once. He grabbed the knife and ran after the man. Sylvia watched Hank's long legs move in giant, ground-eating steps. When he disappeared from view, she went inside the building, telling herself in the aftermath of shock that this was where she had to be if Elena came.

She didn't sit down at her desk again but leaned against the wall. Her heart thundered in her chest with the terror of the fight. The arc between the gleaming knife and Hank's strong back had been so small; his escape, so narrow.

Then she remembered the look on Hank's face as he held the intruder down. She recalled his snarled threat and the pressure he had applied to the man's carotid, pressure, Sylvia was sure, that he wouldn't have hesitated to increase if he'd found it necessary or expedient.

Her relief at Hank's escape soured inside her as it mingled with revulsion at the violence of his world. No matter how attracted she was to him, she wanted no part of that brutal milieu. No part at all.

A long shadow fell across the threshold. Hank walked in, breathing hard, faltering a little in his step. His white mesh shirt was dark with sweat. Sweat ran into his eyes, and he wiped it away with a sweep of his muscular arm.

He saw Sylvia then. "He got away, disappeared down an alley." Collapsing into her desk chair, he eyed her again. "You saved my life. Thanks."

"He was fast. I almost didn't see the knife in time."

"You were faster." Hank looked at her admiringly. "That was some leap you made."

"You never know when dance lessons will come in handy," Sylvia said wryly. "You were no slouch yourself. Who was he? Do you have any idea?"

Hank grimaced. "Someone watching you—or me."

"Or watching *you* watching *me?*" Sylvia raised her fawn-colored eyebrows disdainfully. "What were you doing outside my studio?"

Hank's breathing had slowed down. His face had lost its strained look. He was his old, coolly assured self again.

"Watching you," he answered with a conspiratorial grin that Sylvia found so appealing she had to turn her head to avoid responding to it.

"The way the cat watches the cheese, waiting for the mouse to come for it? Was I the bait, Hank? Did you think that one day or other Elena would try to see me here?"

Hank didn't answer. He moved his burly shoulder in a huge shrug. A thin trickle of red appeared on his shirt.

"You're hurt!" Sylvia exclaimed. "He cut you."

Hank looked down at his chest. "Probably just grazed me. It should be washed, though."

"There are showers and sinks in the locker room here." Sylvia jerked her head toward the rear of the studio. "And a first-aid cabinet. Come on, I'll help you."

She led the way to the small room to the rear of the studio. When they got there, Hank positioned himself beside a sink and removed his shirt.

Sylvia looked at the wound that ran vertically in front of Hank's shoulder. Hank had been right. It was really no more than a deep scratch, but it was bleeding heavily now.

"Why don't you sit there," she said, indicating a metal stool, "and I'll wash it and apply an antiseptic and a bandage?" She looked sharply at him. "Unless you'd rather see a doctor?"

He grinned at her, a devastating, charming, totally masculine grin. "When I can have a beautiful nurse? I only hope this operation takes a long time."

"Antiseptics sting," she retorted, glancing sideways at him out of amused green eyes as she wet and soaped a clean towel.

"You'd take the sting out of anything," he replied softly.

As she washed his wound, Sylvia said, "*Were* you watching me, Hank, waiting for Elena to show up?"

"Frankly, yes. It's my job to find Peter Burns. I'm sure Elena knows where he is or what has happened to him. Obviously she's been trying to see you but hasn't been able to or has been scared off each time. So I decided to lurk in the bushes today. Ouch, that hurts," he said as Sylvia applied an antiseptic to the scratch.

"I told you," she answered matter-of-factly.

"You're merciless," he said lightly.

"I want you completely well so I can hear the rest of this fascinating story. Here, hold this." She handed Hank a roll of bandages while she unwound the length she wanted and snipped it off.

"Unfortunately I wasn't alone in the shrubbery. Our friend with the knife showed up. Naturally I was interested in knowing who had sent him and why."

"Naturally. Which was why you would have choked the creep to death."

"You're wrong about that, Sylvia," Hank said reproachfully. "I use only as much force as is necessary."

She looked at him then. Her clear green eyes surveyed his bold, sapphire bright blue ones, the sharp planes of his face, that long, lean jaw, and his humorous, expressive mouth.

Standing close to him as she bandaged his wound, touching his smooth, tanned skin, smelling his clean, sweat-drenched body plunged her into that other world of violence they had shared on Caldera Street. The longing she had felt for him then rippled through her again.

But their relationship had grown more complex, taken on complications and the problems of other people's lives. Then there had seemed to be only one other person —Elena. Now Sylvia knew there were five of them—Elena, Peter Burns, Carlos Ronderos, Hank, and herself —pieces scattered at random on a board, and the puzzle was to decide which side of the board some of the chessmen belonged on.

Sylvia became aware then that he was watching her, his eyes sharply quizzical.

"You're still holding a piece of tape in your hand," he said. "Are you going to put it on?"

"It's finished," she said a minute later, handing Hank his shirt. "You're all cleaned up and bandaged."

He stood up then. His bare torso gleaming with sweat, he took a step toward her. But she put her hand out, warding him off, and backed away.

"Tell me about Peter Burns," she said, her back straight, touching the wall, her eyes serious and direct. "I have to know."

He put his shirt on but left it unbuttoned, the bandage very white against his shoulder's tanned skin and the dark chest hair below. He looked down at his long hands, turned up, as though to show he would hide nothing.

"Peter's an old friend. His beat's always been one Latin American country or another. He's fluent in Spanish and Portuguese and studied Latin American affairs in college. We were always bumping into each other down here."

He looked up from his hands then but past her, as though seeing events screened on the wall.

"Pete did more than just report the news. He went looking for it, particularly news of the dirty deeds variety. Because he knew their history, their language, their culture, he had a tremendous amount of empathy with the people of Latin America.

"Pete would get particularly uptight about totalitarian governments with the usual apparatus of staged elections, secret police, terror tactics, torture cellars, and so on. The last word I had from him in a sort of code we had set up for corresponding was that he had been investigating Ronderos. He also told me that he was in love with a woman named Elena."

"There are lots of Elenas here."

"Not Elenas who are dance students at the university. I made the usual inquiries." His sharp gaze returned to her then. "Pete disappears. Vanegas disappears. Vanegas tries to get in touch with you. It's pretty obvious. You're my link to Elena Vanegas, and she's my link to Peter Burns."

"You told me that Peter's family was paying you to find him."

It was very important to Sylvia that he tell her this was untrue. Perhaps she had misunderstood him. Or perhaps he had been joking.

"I'm a pro, Sylvia, and the mark of a professional is that he gets paid. Would I go looking for Peter if I weren't being paid? Is that your next question? The answer is, I might. But the question never came up. Knowing my familiarity with Latin America and my friendship with their son, Pete's parents hired me to find him. The offer came from them. It was an offer it wouldn't have made sense for me to refuse."

There was a certain logic in what Hank said, Sylvia admitted to herself. After all, he was a mercenary, and what else could anyone expect but that he perform his dangerous work for money?

Shoulders drooping, she pushed herself away from the wall and started to leave the room.

He barred her way and put his hands on her arms, stopping her. "Disappointed?" he asked.

His pupils were very dark in his blue eyes, and again Sylvia was reminded of the blue-black of winter skies. There was a hint of pain there too. But mostly his craggy features were set in a look of stubborn pride.

You'll have to take me as I am, he seemed to be saying, *because I'm not going to change.*

"Disappointment presupposes expectations. I had none," Sylvia said in a flat, emotionless voice.

But it was a lie, and he knew it. She flushed deeply and turned away at the triumphant half smile that curved his lips.

"I still have to talk to you," he said softly. He put his hand lightly on her waist and led her back to the dance studio.

Sylvia sat down again at her desk. Hank perched on the edge of it. "Tell me what happened today," he said, looking directly into her eyes. "Why did you stay in your studio so late? Did you receive another message from Elena?"

Sylvia told him about the numbers on her calculator and her deduction that the bells Elena meant were the university's class-changing bells.

"I guess"—she finished in a disappointed tone—"Elena came and, seeing either you or that guy, went away, afraid again to approach me."

"All that makes sense," Hank said. "I would have come to the same conclusions."

"Thanks," Sylvia said sarcastically. "I'm glad I'm in tune with the great detective himself."

He grinned at her, a lopsided, comical grin. "We could make beautiful music together."

"I can think of a few sour notes."

"So can I," Hank answered wryly. "Like your friend Vanegas, our will-o'-the-wisp *femme fatale.*"

"Elena's no *femme fatale,*" Sylvia said hotly. "She's a serious dancer with a lot of talent, who, I suppose, fell in love with your Peter Burns . . ." Her voice trailed off. Why *hadn't* Elena ever mentioned Peter to her? Although they hadn't known each other very long, they were on intimate terms. Elena had shown a great deal of interest in the United States, had asked her numerous questions about how things were done in Sylvia's country. Wouldn't it be natural for her to talk about her American boyfriend?

Pushing into the opening she had left, Hank said, "Did Elena ever mention Pete to you?"

Sylvia shook her head no.

"Why not, do you think?" Hank asked probingly.

"I have no idea."

"But you wonder why, don't you?"

Sylvia shrugged the question away. She wouldn't say anything to increase Hank's suspicion of Elena.

Hank suddenly pounded his fist into the palm of his hand. "Why won't you open your eyes and face facts? Elena never mentioned Peter Burns to you because she planned right from the beginning to lure him into Carlos's hands. That was her job, her mission. And the fewer people who knew about her connection to Peter, the better just in case questions were asked."

"I don't believe that for one minute," Sylvia retorted, jumping to her feet and facing him. "As for facing facts, you're the one who lives in an unreal world of superspies and *femmes fatales,*" she shouted at him. "Not everyone is a betrayer, a double-crosser."

"When will you get it through your thick little skull that you're in danger, that your friend Elena is fingering you as she fingered Peter Burns?"

Hands on her hips, her face flaming with anger, Sylvia spit out the words. "For Carlos? Why would he use Elena? He knows where I live."

Hank looked at her pityingly. "Carlos Ronderos doesn't do anything *openly.*"

"Okay, even if you're right about Elena and Carlos—and I don't believe for a minute that you are—why me? I'm only a dancer. I don't know anything—or anyone—important."

"You know me," Hank said, quiet and serious again.

"So what? You're an American businessman, head of Americo Import and Export, or whatever."

When he didn't answer, she stared at him for a long time, realization dawning gradually in her eyes. She put her hand to her lips. "Oh, Hank. Is your cover blown?"

"I think so," he said curtly. "I'm being followed. That's a sign someone's suspicious of me." Then, seeing her horrified look, he added quickly, "But not necessarily. Down here everyone's a suspicious character, particularly foreigners. It all may just be routine police work."

Hank watched Sylvia as she struggled with this idea, trying to decide whether to accept his attempt to lull her fears.

Her fears for *him!* Hank turned the idea over and over in his mind. He recalled her magnificent dancer's leap and her high kick to hit the knife out of that guy's hand. She might struggle against her feelings, even despise him for being a mercenary, but there was a growing bond between them apart from the powerful attraction they felt for each other.

He ran his hand through his thick dark hair with a feeling of desperation. Not only did he have to find Elena as soon as possible, but he also had to devise a way to protect Sylvia. Because although he might be the *cause* of the danger she was in, he was also her only protection.

When the idea came to him, it was so simple and good that he smiled with pleasure. He wanted to tell her, but she had sat down and was pretending to do some paper work, her face flushed and her lips set in an unyielding line.

She was still angry with him.

Hank bent his head so she couldn't see his smile. He would tell her his plan tomorrow. And what a surprise it would be!

CHAPTER SIX

When her doorbell rang the following morning, Sylvia felt a grinding rush of fear. She never had morning visitors. As she moved slowly toward the door, she checked out the phone on the hall table and an old-fashioned men's black umbrella in a stand.

The sight of Hank in the doorway made her laugh with relief.

Hank volleyed a lighthearted grin back at her. "Glad you're so happy to see me."

"Frankly I expected worse."

"Thanks," he said dryly. "Mind if I come in?"

Sylvia held the door wider, taking in the fresh whiteness of Hank's shirt against his tanned neck, the litheness of his walk as he entered. "To what do I owe the honor of this early visit? Is your shoulder bothering you?"

Hank shook his head. "Nope. I'm moving in." There was a pleasant, bland expression on his strong face. "We're going to become lovers."

"Really!" Sylvia closed the door. "Do I have anything to say about it?"

"Not much," he admitted frankly. "Got any coffee handy?"

"In the kitchen."

Sylvia led the way into the kitchen and poured coffee into two cups. She set them on a round wooden table with a colorful cloth and sat down opposite Hank.

"Sugar? Cream?" Sylvia asked mechanically.

"No, thanks. You'll find once we start living together that I'm an easy man to please."

"That's a discovery I don't expect to make, Mr. Weston." Sylvia glanced at her watch pointedly. "I have to leave for the university in half an hour."

She gestured toward the thin robe she had thrown over her short nightshirt when she heard the doorbell. She meant to indicate that she still had to dress, but she regretted the movement immediately.

She could almost feel the touch of his eyes as they raked her small, full breasts and slim waist and dropped to her long golden thighs exposed by the filmy robe. Against her will her body started to swell and stir, to respond to the promise of mastery in his look, to the allure of his sexual assurance.

Angry with herself and with him, Sylvia rose, clutching her robe. "I think you'd better go, Hank. I really don't have much time."

Hank took a swallow of coffee. "You haven't yet heard why I'm going to move in with you."

"Since you're going to leave, it really won't be necessary, will it?" she pointed out sharply.

"Sit down," he commanded.

Sylvia stuck her lower lip out mutinously. She didn't like being given orders. But his blue eyes were steady and coolly confident. It would be silly, Sylvia told herself, to make an issue of such a trivial thing. And she sat down at the table again.

"I don't know exactly what's going on, but when I find

a guy with a knife lurking outside your studio, as I did yesterday, I figure it's time to take protective steps."

"Like dialing nine-one-one?" Sylvia asked sweetly, still angry with him.

"Don't be funny," he growled. "Like you and I pretending to be lovers. That way we can be together most of the time. That should decrease the likelihood of an 'accident' happening to either one of us."

Sylvia laughed shortly without amusement. "You just want to be here if Elena comes."

"I want to be here if Elena comes and sets you up for something," Hank retorted, flushing with anger at her attack on his motives.

Sylvia stood up, scraping the chair back noisily in her agitation. She went to the sink and stood against it, as if wanting support for the argument she foresaw.

"You know what I think, Hank? I think you've been in undercover work so long that you don't know how normal people behave. I think you're paranoid, and for some reason your delusions have fastened on my friends Elena and Carlos."

With the air of a man trying to be patient, Hank said, "You mean, it's a delusion of mine that Peter disappeared into thin air, that Elena keeps leaving you cryptic messages, that a guy with a knife was hiding outside your studio?"

Sylvia looked at him, at his intelligent, expressive face, at his clear blue eyes calmly sure of what he said, and her gaze dropped. What if he were right? She had not only her own life to account for but his, if her presence could protect him. And Elena's too, she thought.

The poignancy of her friend's repeated efforts to contact her, efforts that no doubt were launched in hope and resulted in disappointment, struck Sylvia forcibly. *She had to be here when Elena tried again.*

Sylvia raised her head and looked directly at Hank. "All right. I'll go for it. You can move in anytime you like."

He nodded. "I'll get my things later."

As Sylvia showed him the rooms he hadn't seen, including his bedroom and bath, Hank studied her. She hadn't put her hair up yet, and her small face looked lost, almost childlike, in that mass of reddish gold hair.

She was pale, too, so that a few freckles on the bridge of her nose showed. He liked her that way, almost a little plain, stripped of her workday and social personas. It was like having her all to himself.

"I suppose you'll want a key to the front door," she said when they had finished their tour of the house.

Hank shrugged. "Under the circumstances . . ."

"I understand," she said coolly. "I have a couple of spares. I'll give you one."

When she went off to get him a key, Hank thrust his hands in his pockets and looked down at the floor. Was she unhappy about his plan? For the life of him he couldn't tell. It was a good idea; he was convinced of that. But he didn't want to make her miserable either.

As she dropped a key into his outstretched palm, he shot his hand out quickly and captured her wrist.

She stood there passively, looking up at him like some captive about to be abused by a man with the power to do it.

"If you don't want to go through with this plan, you don't have to," he said roughly. "I know how you feel about me. We'll take our chances separately, that's all."

She put her hand out and with precise deliberation removed his fingers from her wrist.

"You don't have to manacle me. I'm doing this of my own free will. The house is big enough for us never to see each other if we're careful. And that's the way I plan to be."

"That's all right with me," Hank shot back. "But we're

going to have to put on an act outside, when we're with people." His cobalt blue eyes bore into her green ones. "I want everything laid out in the open at the beginning."

Even as he said it, Hank laughed at himself. *Nothing* between them was open. Everything that was important lay in her smoldering green eyes, in the throaty tones of their voices, in the way they had just moved apart.

One or the other of them was bound to snap under the tension. But in the meantime, living together, they would be fairly safe.

"Well?" Hank demanded. "Do you agree, we put on an act outside?"

"I agree," Sylvia said neutrally.

Hank nodded, satisfied. He had learned a long time ago to play the hand you had, not the one you wanted.

During the next few weeks, when a party every night was the rule, Sylvia and Hank arrived together, danced slow dances cheek to cheek, looked deep into each other's eyes, and went home together—often early, as though they couldn't wait. It was a very convincing act, Sylvia thought.

It was obvious the foreign colony of San Lorenzo believed that the little American who taught dance at the university and the tall, well-built head of the import-export company were lovers. The news added a dash of spice to the parties at which they all knew one another, knew all about one another, and had reached the point where they didn't dare know more.

One evening during a dinner party, when Sylvia had gone to a bedroom to touch up her makeup, she looked up from the mirror to find Emily watching her, an amused glint in her eyes.

"I thought I would put more lipstick on. I think I've eaten it all off," Sylvia said, laughing.

"You look lovely as always, Sylvia. Hank can't keep his eyes off you. I mean, he *really* can't."

Sylvia looked sideways at the older woman, her glance sharply questioning. She had expected Emily Adams to be particularly interested in her rumored love affair with Hank and even pleased since Emily had played matchmaker to the two of them. But this was the first reference Emily had made to it.

"You and Hank aren't really lovers, are you?" Emily continued.

"Why do you ask?" Sylvia demanded, feeling suddenly both nervous and embarrassed.

"Oh, my dear, lovers don't prowl around each other like two hungry tigers the way you and Hank do. They look sleek and contented and just a little drowsy. I know. Frank and I did the unheard-of in our day. We lived together, as the saying goes, before we married."

"*You* were a free soul," Sylvia said teasingly.

"That's actually what I was or thought I was. I was going to save the world through social work, and Frank was going to reveal its shortcomings in his plays. And we weren't going to constrain our love in the straitjacket of marriage."

Sylvia faced the older woman, her face alive with curiosity. Emily had never talked about her past. "What happened?"

Emily's face softened. "I became pregnant. Now we had a responsibility. We got married when I was three months along. Frank gave up playwriting—he hadn't sold a play or had one produced, needless to say—and took a job with a big corporation. And when Catherine—Catherine with a *C*—was born, I quit my job to stay home and take care of her. That was the thing to do then," Emily explained. She chuckled with philosophical amusement. "As it turned out, Frank had more executive ability than literary talent, so we did better financially than we would have if he had stuck to the theater and I to social work."

"Didn't you regret giving up your ambitions?"

"I don't think so," Emily said briskly. "There were two more children after Catherine. It's quite an undertaking, you know, to take care of three children, to put food on the table, buy clothes, send them to college. We thought it a worthwhile one," she added gravely.

"Oh, I'm sure it was," Sylvia quickly agreed.

"However, I haven't related this little vignette, fascinating as it is, for egotistical reasons. What I was getting at is that I know from personal experience how lovers look, and you and Hank don't have that look."

"How many others would have noticed, do you think?" Sylvia asked, suddenly worried.

"No one," Emily replied soothingly. "Don't forget, I know you both and . . . I'm unusually perspicacious." She smirked humorously to take the edge off any suggestion of conceit in her remark.

But Sylvia nodded her serious agreement. "You are, Emily. You really are perceptive."

Their hostess entered the bedroom then with a "Well, here you are, Sylvia. Hank has been worried about you. I wish *I* could get a man to worry like that about *me.*"

Ignoring the other woman for the moment, Emily addressed herself to Sylvia's remark. "When you've lived in a foreign colony as long as I have—"

"Whatever do you mean, Emily?" their hostess interrupted sharply. "We're not foreign to *each other. They*—the Paraguayans—are the foreigners."

Emily and Sylvia looked at each other and smiled and left the room together.

On the way home from the party Sylvia recalled what Emily Adams had said: that she and Hank didn't possess the relaxed contentment of lovers, that they were too hungry for each other. It was never more true than now, she thought as they spun along the road, enclosed in the tight little world created by the lighted dashboard of Hank's two-seater and the darkness outside. Seated close to Hank, Sylvia was overwhelmingly aware of his lean, sinewy thigh next to hers. She found herself staring at his long brown hands and wishing that one of them would leave the wheel and touch her. She could smell his clean, distinctive scent and thrilled to it as she hoped her perfume was stirring him to wild thoughts.

She could sense the tension in his muscles. His lean profile looked grim and set in the dim light. As he moved the gearshift, his hand came within an inch of her thigh, and she could feel him flinch.

The city seemed even hotter and steamier than usual. Above the hills heat lightning flung long white streamers across the sky. In the unmoving air the palm trees that lined the middle-class streets were inert and still.

"Wait here," Hank ordered brusquely as he opened the front door with the key she had given him. He returned a few minutes later. "No night visitors. You can come in."

Entering the house, she accidentally brushed against him. The contact jolted her senses into immediate desire, and she heard his quick intake of breath.

His voice sharp and irritable, he said, "It's too damn hot to sleep. How about a nightcap?"

Play it safe, Sylvia warned herself. *Stay away from him.*

Forcing a yawn, she said languidly, "Thanks, but I think I'll go right to bed."

"My room's cooler."

"Is that part of the game plan?" She could hear her voice rising. "Chapter Four of the *Manual for Free-Lance Spies and Mercenaries?* Move in with the decoy, pretending you want to protect her. If she gets restless before your quarry shows up, keep her happy in bed." She was hitting the high notes of hysteria now. "Is that it? Is that how it goes?"

She stopped, trembling. *God, she really was out of control.* But she couldn't help it. The clinging heat had rubbed her nerves raw. The sordidness of the city beat at her spirit. The sense of being spied on kept her constantly on edge.

But most of all it was Hank. Every line of his long body seemed to be engraved on her consciousness; every movement, each change of expression in his brilliant blue eyes were etched in her brain. She wanted to go to bed with him, to have him possess her, to possess *him,* to be free of him once and for all.

"I was going to *exchange* rooms with you, not share a bed," Hank retorted. "You're not a decoy, Sylvia," he said sternly. "I'm here to protect you—from yourself if necessary," he muttered, turning aside.

"I'm an adult, Hank," Sylvia protested, seething with anger, "and have been for a long time. I don't need to be protected from myself."

"You do if you can't see through your friends Elena and Carlos," Hank said wearily. He went to the buffet and took a bottle of Scotch off the shelf. "You sure you don't want a drink?"

"I'm sure."

He poured a generous amount into a glass and flung himself into a chair. Stretching his long legs out in front of him, he stared morosely down at his highly polished black shoes.

It wasn't turning out well. He had kept them safe by moving in with her, but she was beginning to hate him. She could hardly look at him or bear to be near him. Even her naturally fluid movements had become staccato with tension.

As for him—and Hank laughed to himself without humor—he needed her more than ever. Living intimately with her, he felt his senses constantly aroused by her delicate beauty, the exquisite grace of her movements, her vivid, sensitive face.

And nothing had turned up. There had been no more messages from Elena. And Sylvia had been right, of course. She was, in a way, a decoy—a highly protected decoy.

Suddenly he was tired of the whole business. He'd find Elena on his own, damn it. And get Carlos too.

"Look," he said, "I'll get out. I don't want to make you this miserable."

Her eyes flashed proudly, and he thought with admiration that they really were the bright, rich green of emeralds. "I'm not a quitter, Hank. I can stick this out as long as you can. But I warn you, you may think you're protecting *me* against Elena and Carlos, but I have every intention of protecting them against *you.*"

He had a hard time not showing his joy. She had given him the answer he wished for. She was sticking it out because she wanted to.

"And who's going to protect us from each other, Sylvia?" he asked softly, knowingly.

They stood for a long minute, staring at each other. Hank's tanned face glistened with sweat. One dark eyebrow flicked quizzically upward. Under that mocking, questioning look, Sylvia remembered what he had said weeks ago in this room, that what he wanted was here and that when the time came, she would want him to take it.

She felt as if she were pushing against some invisible barrier, as if they both were straining toward each other but were being kept apart by an unseen wall.

You can't love a man who's out to get your friends, who uses you as a decoy, a scolding interior voice screamed at her. *You can't!*

Masking frustration and regret with a quick flash of anger, she said curtly, "Good night, Hank," and left the room.

In the morning Sylvia set out for the university on foot, as she had been accustomed to doing before Hank insisted on driving her. But a persistent tooting of a horn beside her made her stop.

"Going my way?" Hank asked with a grin.

"Actually, no," Sylvia said coldly.

"You're lucky it's me and not a kidnap car. Hop in. It's really not safe for you to walk alone."

"I think it's perfectly safe. Why don't you just go on to that phony office of yours and leave me alone?"

Hank's expression became serious; his voice, hard. "Do you want me to jump out and put you in the car?"

"That won't be necessary." Sylvia yanked the door open and slid in next to him, her lower lip protruding in a mutinous pout.

Hank took one look at her and suppressed a smile. As he shifted gears, he said jokingly, "See? We're just like a nice married couple, with me dropping you off at your job before I go to mine." Shifting again, he glanced slyly at Sylvia. "Of course, one indispensable ingredient of our hypothetical marriage is missing."

"And it'll stay missing," Sylvia retorted.

"You mean, you think of marriage as basically just a car pool?"

"I don't think of marriage at all," Sylvia snapped back. "At least not in the present context."

Hank raised his eyebrows. He never thought of marriage either. At least he never had before.

The invitations they received to San Lorenzo's frequent parties were issued to both of them now, but when Sylvia saw the creamy thick embossed card inviting her alone to the home of Carlos and María Ronderos, she decided to leave it at that.

"No way," Hank said with conviction, shaking his head. The invitation had arrived in the mail early in the morning while they were still drinking their coffee. "You're not going to Carlos's alone. I'm going with you."

"You're not invited," Sylvia pointed out.

Hank grinned. "That's because Carlos doesn't know what a great guy I am. This way he'll find out."

"Do you always go where you're not wanted?"

"Sometimes I'm asked to stay," Hank said slyly. His marauding eyes roved over her close-fitting French-cut T-shirt. Then he grimaced and turned his head sharply away.

"Something wrong?" she asked, genuinely curious.

"I think I'm ready for a hair shirt and ashes," Hank said wryly.

Sylvia bent her head. A flush heated her skin and spread through her. She was a hot, rushing fountain of flame, a storm of wild and obsessive need. She should have sent him away when he'd offered to go, Sylvia thought bitterly. Her longing for him was ripping her apart.

She had to get away from the torture of being with him and wanting him. Carlos's party would give her a respite of at least a few hours.

Forcing a calmness she didn't feel, Sylvia said, "Seriously, Hank, I don't think you should go to Carlos's party. I—I'm not sure he knows about us."

"Don't kid yourself. He knows *all* about us." Hank looked at her curiously. "Does it bother you?"

Did she really care for Carlos? Hank wondered. Was such a thing possible—that she could be attracted to a slimy type like Ronderos? But love had no logic. If she wasn't at least somewhat interested in the man, why did she object to Hank's going to the party?

"Not at all," Sylvia answered. "It doesn't seem to bother Carlos either. If anything, he's coming on to me stronger than ever." She leaned forward and tapped the invitation. "But I'd feel awkward arriving with an uninvited guest."

"Then get me invited. Call up and ask his wife."

And in the end, that's what she did.

Sylvia dressed for the party with particular care. Many wealthy and influential people would be there, and she wanted to look her best. So she chose her one truly expensive evening outfit, a sleekly cut green silk chiffon woven with gold lamé. She swept her hair up into a thick chignon and, leaving her long, graceful neck bare, wore only pendant earrings and a thick gold bracelet for jewelry.

Sylvia was sitting at the vanity in her bedroom, finishing her makeup, when Hank knocked at the door.

"Come in," she called out liltingly, happy with her appearance and glad to be going to a party.

Hank entered and stopped short as Sylvia rose and faced him. "You look very beautiful," he said in an erotically low, sultry tone. The sophisticated dress with its tantalizing glimpses of her exquisite body, her exotic hairstyle, the potent, sensuous perfume she was using for the first time—all made him mad with longing for her. He wanted to lock her tight in his arms, to feel every part of her beautifully articulated body against his, to kiss her in ways that would make her intoxicated with love—his love.

He took a few steps toward her. Then he stopped, brought to a halt by the thought that she might have gone to this much trouble for another man. "Carlos will be pleased," he said bitterly.

"I don't dress to please Carlos," Sylvia retorted.

"No? Who do you dress for then?" he asked, hoping against hope for an answer that would make him happy.

"I dress for myself," Sylvia said shortly. "I would have worn these clothes no matter which party I was going to or who my escort was."

That wasn't quite true, Sylvia admitted to herself. She

had dressed tonight just to see that awed, admiring light in Hank's eyes as he entered her room, to hear the amorous tone of his voice. But what right did Hank have to be jealous of her?

Every right, an interior voice answered. *He's the man you want to give yourself to.*

"Obviously you'd prefer going to this party without any escort at all," Hank said.

"So Carlos can get me into a nice dark bedroom upstairs, Hank? Don't forget, Carlos is married."

"Tell that to Carlos," Hank said caustically.

She started to sweep out of the room, but he halted her at the door. "Your wrap, madame," he said sarcastically with a deep bow. He took the matching chiffon stole from a chair and draped it around her shoulders. His hands lingered. She could feel their strength heavy on her fragile flesh. She stood for a moment savoring the sensation. Then, knowing if she stayed a second longer, it would be too late, she abruptly broke away.

He swore softly. They left the house and drove in silence to the home of Carlos Ronderos.

As Hank brought the car to a halt on a gravel driveway, he blew his breath out in a low whistle. "I don't believe this!"

"We're talking French château here," Sylvia said dryly.

They sat looking at the three-story brick and stone building with chimneys, a slate-covered mansard roof, and dormer windows.

"You're right. It's a genuine French château, for God's sake. Carlos must have brought it to Paraguay, stone by stone."

"He's even managed a lawn and trees." Sylvia laughed. "Everything but sheep grazing on the grounds."

"Tell him, and I'm sure he'll supply them." Hank's voice became tight and constrained. "You've been here before?"

"Of course," Sylvia said matter-of-factly, refusing to be put on the defensive about Carlos again. "María, Carlos's wife, invited me to dinner when I arrived in San Lorenzo."

Two white-jacketed boys sprang forward to take the car. Hank continued to comment on the architecture of the house as he and Sylvia walked to the front door, but he was speaking automatically, more to be seen talking than for an answer. Sylvia noticed that his eyes were everywhere, flicking over the other arriving guests, touching on the tough-looking men by the door, picking up a loiterer on the side of the house.

"Can't you ever give it a rest, Hank?" Sylvia said.

"Armed guards," he said under his breath. "Lots of them."

"Of course, there are armed guards. Carlos is a very wealthy man. He could be kidnapped and held for ransom."

"It couldn't happen to a nicer feller," Hank said jokingly. As they entered the house, he slipped his hand around her waist and passed his lips across her bare nape. "That perfume of yours is driving me wild."

Sylvia's eyes met Carlos's shoe-button black ones as he stood in the grand entrance hall greeting his guests. His eyes were expressionless as he watched Hank. Only a slight flaring of his nostrils showed how he felt. With a stirring of hope it occurred to Sylvia that the charade she and Hank would play that night might discourage Carlos from continuing to pursue her.

Sylvia greeted María Ronderos, a sweet-faced young woman who had been carefully dressed by a famous designer to disguise her plump, already matronly figure, and presented Hank to her host and hostess. After a few polite words Sylvia and Hank proceeded down the long, narrow salon with its magnificent crystal chandelier and richly painted ceiling to the lavish buffet table at the rear.

The choice of foods was as French as the house itself. There were belon oysters, lobster prepared Provençal style with tomatoes and garlic, asparagus with sauce Maltaise, classic French salads, rack of lamb en croute, a smoked salmon soufflé, a roast of beef, and a table of desserts.

Waiters circulated with bottles of Dom Pérignon champagne. The wines were the finest from French vineyards.

"This is the life," Hank said with a grin as he led Sylvia to an empty table.

"Why no South American dishes, do you think?"

"Because your friend Carlos is a snob." He suddenly grabbed her wrist. "Frown! That couple is heading toward our table."

Sylvia laughed at the lowering expression Hank assumed. "You look positively ferocious."

"That's the way I wanted to look. Good, they've gone away." Holding his champagne glass, he entwined his arm with Sylvia's, and looking deep into each other's eyes, they drank from the other's glass.

When the band started to play a samba, Hank led Sylvia out to the floor. Sweeping her into his arms, he moved adroitly with her to the softly sensuous Latin beat. He glanced down at her face, glowing with the pleasure of the dance; then his eyes dropped lower to the delicate shell-like curves of her breasts. His arm tightened involuntarily, drawing her closer. He bent his head over her perfumed hair and inhaled the warm woman smell of her skin.

He turned suddenly, pulling her against him, trapping her in the steel band of his arm. She tried to free herself, but his grip was too strong.

"Aren't you going a little too far with this?" Sylvia asked.

"Not half as far as I'd like to go." He held her away

from him for a moment. His look was boldly quizzical. "I thought you were enjoying it."

Sylvia's long lashes touched her cheeks. She'd be damned if she'd let Hank see just how much she *was* enjoying it. Enjoying moving with him in perfect, hypnotic harmony, loving the familiar virile scent of him spiced up with some new aftershave, thrilling to the pressure of his long, hard body against her soft contours.

She spread her fingers on the white dinner jacket that stretched across his shoulders, sensing the muscle beneath. With a sigh she laid her cheek against his shoulder and slid her hand up around his neck.

Hank brushed his lips across her ear. "I want to hold you like this forever, Sylvia."

She shivered a little.

"What is it, darling?" Hank looked down into Sylvia's face.

"I don't like the way Carlos is watching us."

"To hell with Carlos. I've got you, and that's all I care about."

He pulled her in even closer to him and tightened his arms around her protectively. Sylvia buried her face against Hank's burly shoulder. Maybe if she didn't look at that white face and those hate-pinched features, she could make Carlos go away.

She heard him first, the sharp tap of his heels on the polished parquet.

"May I?" he asked Hank.

Slowly Hank released his hold on her. Reluctantly, with a feeling of foreboding, Sylvia let herself be taken into Carlos's arms.

"This is like old times—isn't it, Sylvia—when we used to go discoing in New York."

"Only once or twice, Carlos," Sylvia said, forcing a twinkle in her eyes. "As I remember anyway."

He pulled her in close to him. "You are making a mistake, Sylvia," he whispered against her cheek. "That man is not for you. He is just an ordinary fellow. You are a sensitive, creative person. You need someone who would satisfy you differently, in ways that would match your desires."

Sylvia's eyes sought desperately for Hank. Her consideration for Carlos, based on their former friendship, was giving way to revulsion. She didn't think she could stand being in his arms another minute. The feel of his lips on her skin nauseated her.

"I think it's my turn again, Carlos," Hank's deep baritone announced.

Sylvia smiled politely at Carlos while Hank took her into his arms. But as she caught Hank's triumphant look, she also saw the expression on the other man's features.

His face was marked with loathing. The black eyes glinted with hatred. Did he guess how she had just felt about him? Sylvia wondered. But no, it was Hank he was looking at.

Then the malevolent gleam left the shoe-button eyes. They became masked, inscrutable again. The tight face relaxed in a formal smile, and with a bow to Sylvia he left the dance floor.

"What did Carlos have to say?" Hank asked as they were on their way home again.

"That you weren't the man for me, that you couldn't satisfy a creative, sensitive woman like me."

Hank glanced sideways at Sylvia and grinned. "Care to put that theory to the test?"

"I don't think so," she answered dryly. "He's very jealous of you, Hank."

"Yeah, I know."

"Well, if he's as bad as *you* think he is, mightn't he be dangerous?"

Hank shrugged. "I'm not afraid of Carlos Ronderos."

"You don't think we should call off this charade of pretending to be lovers?"

Hank glanced at her with exaggerated surprise. "Just when it's getting good?"

"Come on, Hank, be serious. Emily sees through us, and Carlos is practically beside himself with jealousy. Isn't it time to cancel the act?"

"You mean, you think it's time to fish or cut bait?" he asked slyly.

She tossed her head, and he found himself wishing that the chignon would fall and release her glorious hair over her shoulders. He could see the flush that had started in her face creep down to the first soft swell of her breasts above the low V of her gown.

He loved to see her get angry, to watch her turn from ice to fire in a matter of minutes. He didn't want this trip to her house to end, didn't want to lose the excitement of having her beside him. He didn't want her to sleep in a separate bed. He didn't want her anywhere but with him.

Hank hit the leather steering wheel hard with his palm, so that Sylvia looked at him, surprised.

Great! he thought. It would be just great to feel like that if he were a nine-to-five guy in a downtown office with his eye on a little lifetime house in the suburbs.

He struck the steering wheel again.

But it wasn't great for Hank Weston, free-lance spy and foreign mercenary.

CHAPTER SEVEN

The heat wave continued. Even people who had always lived in the city said they had never known such a hot summer. The frequent rains were too brief to cool the air for long. When the rain stopped, the wet foliage was an acidic-looking green, with an unnatural, almost phosphorescent glow to it.

Mildew appeared everywhere. Sylvia's shoes turned green overnight, and the professor's books developed black spots.

Lizards scuttled with dry, clicking sounds up and down the walls. Fat amber-colored cockroaches, waving feathery antennae, lumbered heavily across the bathroom floors.

One morning Sylvia shook a huge, hairy tarantula out of a shoe in her closet and screamed for Hank.

He was there in a second.

"What is it, Sylvia?" His voice was low, taut, controlled.

She had a glimpse of what he would be like in a real emergency, the kind he was waiting for.

Pressing herself against the wall, she pointed to the enormous black spider.

Hank laughed. "Wow! That's the biggest I've ever seen. No wonder you screamed."

Sylvia moved away while Hank killed the spider. She heard him behind her and turned around.

"You're trembling," he said tenderly, putting his arms around her.

Accustomed to living together, they now wore as few clothes as possible in the house. Hank was bare to the waist and had on only a pair of torn cutoffs. Sylvia wore a thin cotton halter and shorts.

She wasn't trembling—the idea was ridiculous—and she started to say so, but the touch of his bare skin against hers sent shivers rippling through her. His thick chest hair was a silky virile mass under her cheek. His large hands swept up and down her back in soothing movements. As Sylvia arched her back, falling under the sway of his erotic massage, she felt his fingers hesitate at the halter tie around her neck.

Abruptly, as though fearing if she waited, she might not be able to do it, Sylvia put her hands flat against Hank's chest and pushed herself back and out of his arms.

"I'm all right now," she said firmly.

The encounter bothered Sylvia for days. There was a picture on a wall calendar in the kitchen of the Iguaçu Falls, a spectacular 210-foot cascade that lay on the border between Brazil and Argentina. Sylvia saw herself catapulted, in that old cliché, toward the head of such a waterfall, the suspense rising as her frail boat drew closer and closer to the dangerous torrent.

For the first time she faced the issue of whether she and Hank could have a life together. And with unflinching honesty she told herself that they probably couldn't.

She could never live in his world of violence and suspicion and treachery. And he didn't seem ready to give it up.

Besides, there was always that "apartness" in him, that

aura of being a loner. Could such a man ever truly love a woman?

She didn't know. And that was the worst state of all to be in. Fish or cut bait, Hank had said, joking. But the old saying had its serious side. She would have to make a decision soon—either to live completely apart from Hank and not see him or to become further involved.

In the meantime, she hedged by agreeing to give some of her students private lessons in the evening in her studio at the university. But the first night she started to leave the house, Hank stopped her.

"That dance studio of yours isn't safe in the daytime, much less at night. Don't go, Sylvia. Call your students and tell them you can't do it."

His interference, his assumption that he knew what was right for her annoyed Sylvia.

"I'm to tell my students that Big Daddy won't let me? Is that the idea?"

"You can put it any way you want," Hank said seriously. "But you're not going there, not tonight or any other night."

Sylvia thrust her chin out defiantly and pressed her lips together in a thin line. It was unthinkable to let somebody else dictate her behavior. She had always prided herself on taking responsibility for her own life and accepting whatever consequences were the result of her actions.

Yet—a small, secret voice inside her said—Hank was right. The isolated dance studio would not be safe at night. She had realized that herself but had brushed the thought aside in her compulsion to escape her torturing desire for Hank.

"The boy and girl I was going to coach tonight don't have phones. I won't be able to reach them to cancel the lesson."

"I'll go with you tonight."

"Thank you, Hank," Sylvia said sincerely. "I appreciate

your thoughtfulness." She paused as another thought occurred to her. "Or is it just that you don't want anything to happen to your decoy?"

Hank grinned at her. "You're a lot prettier than a wooden duck. Let's go."

The two students were waiting in front of the door to the dance studio. Sylvia felt a pang of regret. If it hadn't been for the theft of Elena's note, she would have given them the key. This way, Sylvia thought, glancing toward the bushes, they might even have become the victims of a crime.

Sylvia introduced Hank to Judit Mendieta and Raimundo Canata. Then the three dancers left the studio to change into practice clothes.

Left alone, Hank walked quickly around the room, taking in everything in one glance. It was a bare gymnasium, nothing more.

He unlocked the desk drawer with a twist of wire he kept for that purpose. But there was nothing in it of significance: no message on the calculator; no scrap of paper in the choreography notebook; no note from Elena anywhere in the drawer.

Hank closed the drawer quietly and stood, hands jammed into his chino pockets, thinking. There might never be another note from Elena. She might have given up in her effort to contact Sylvia, or Carlos might have told her to stop.

There wasn't time for him to wait passively to see if Elena would surface again. Too much time had already elapsed, considering the conditions Peter might be held in. He would have to go out looking for Elena himself.

He would start tonight after he had gotten Sylvia safely back to the house. Meanwhile, he thought, as the trio came out of the dressing rooms, he would enjoy an evening of modern dance.

Raimundo had brown curly hair and a dreamy, sensitive look. His partner, Judit, had a sharper edge, her features aquiline and immobile, carved from dark wood.

But it was Sylvia whom Hank couldn't keep his eyes from. She had let her hair down so that it fell in a shower over her shoulders. Her small face and exquisitely long neck, "a dancer's neck," seemed exceptionally lovely above the black jersey practice clothes she had put on.

"Judit and Raimundo are having trouble with their lifts, so we're going to work on those first," she explained, a little shyly, it seemed to him. Was she pleased that he was there, watching her at her work? He thought she was.

As for him, he was utterly engrossed by every one of her movements as she showed Judit how to redistribute her weight so that when Raimundo lifted her into the air, the act would seem effortless. He watched expressions change on her vivid, mobile face like clouds scudding across the sky and let her soft voice wash over him as she patiently explained over and over what she wanted the dancers to do.

She captivated him, held all his attention, was a magnet for his fantasies. Should he let himself fall in love with her? What a garden of delights *that* would be! Hank's whole being glowed at the thought, as if he had just entered a warm, well-lighted house.

Then, grimly, he shook his head. There could be no garden or house for him, real or imaginary. Sylvia was right. He *was* a danger junkie. He needed to prove himself through danger, to know that he could outwit, outfight, and outthink any opponent. He had to win—*always*—in the toughest game there was.

Once you started loving a woman, you became afraid. You worried about what would happen to her if you didn't come back, about losing your life now that you had her and were happy. And once you started being afraid, you were no good at his profession. You had to have cool nerves and not care too much about getting killed.

Hank raised his eyebrows and smiled ruefully. It had been easy up until now to love 'em and leave 'em. But not with this one, the little red-haired dancer.

"What are you smiling at?" Sylvia said teasingly, coming up to the desk where Hank was sitting. Her fair, lightly tanned skin was pearled with sweat. Her eyes had the slightly glazed look that comes with fatigue. "The lesson is over," she went on, not waiting for his answer. "Did you enjoy it?"

"Yes, very much."

Sylvia laughed. "I don't think you were really watching. You were lost in your own thoughts."

"You were watching me then," Hank said, pleased by her confession.

"Some of the time," Sylvia answered frankly. "I'm sorry I couldn't explain more of the things we were doing. It might have made the lesson more interesting to you."

"*Everything* you do is interesting to me." He ran his eyes over her grave, delicate face, noting the mauve shadows under her eyes and the look of intense concentration that still hadn't left her. His glance drifted to the curved arcs of her breasts under the clinging black jersey and continued downward in a look whose sensuality encompassed everything about her.

Sylvia shivered under his gaze. A blatantly sexy look could be bantered away, but this was different. Hank was serious, intent on an idea in his own mind, an idea that was a twin to her own.

"I'd better shower and change," she said quickly. "I won't be long."

Hank watched her walk to the rear of the gym, her movements lithe and graceful. Her straight back and poised head somehow made her seem poignantly vulnerable.

On the way back to the house he asked her, "Were there any places in San Lorenzo where you and Elena frequently went together? Coffeehouses, discos, cafés?"

"So you can go there and look for Elena? Is that what you want to know for?"

"You're right on target," Hank drawled. "I can't wait forever for our little firefly to light again, and in the meantime, I've got a friend who's in trouble. So, were there any favorite places you two frequented?"

"No. And if there were . . ."

"I know, you wouldn't tell me."

Hank smiled to himself. She was loyal, courageous, and, he thought wearily, stubborn.

Maybe some of what he thought showed because Sylvia added, "Actually we never went anywhere together. Elena was always too busy. Now I realize it was Peter Burns she was occupied with."

Peter! That was his clue. Where did Peter and Elena go to be together? It wasn't Pete's small hotel or Elena's boardinghouse. He had already investigated both and left a pile of guaranis with the respective owners to be informed if either returned. Other sources, who were equally glad to have a few guarani notes squeezed into their hands, were also unproductive. It was as though Peter Burns and Elena Vanegas had disappeared into thin air. But now he felt a mild surge of hope.

When they reached the house, Hank searched it quickly and efficiently.

"It's clear," he told her. "I'm going now."

She stood foursquare to him, her chin stuck out belligerently. "To look for Elena?"

"To see what I can find." On impulse, then, he reached down and kissed her on the cheek.

"Am I supposed to wave and say *'Vaya con Dios'* as you vault into the saddle?" Sylvia said wryly.

Hank grinned. "Something like that."

But she stood at the door anyway and said, "Take care."

And he looked back at her and answered, "I will. Lock the door and don't go out. Okay?"

"Right." She turned and went inside and locked the door.

He sat in the car, hands on the steering wheel, and stared blankly through the windshield. He hadn't the slightest idea where to start looking for the young dancer. Then he asked himself where *he* would go if he wanted to hide out in San Lorenzo. After a few minutes, he grinned and with a crisp click turned the key in the ignition.

What better place to hide or meet than the warren of shanties and twisting alleys that was Caldera Street? Nobody *there*, in that hotbed of discontent, would report an American man and a Paraguayan woman to the authorities.

Maybe, Hank thought further, Caldera Street was where Elena lived now. Perhaps that was why she had asked Sylvia to meet her there. Maybe she hadn't fled into the Caldera Street slum at random when she saw the soldiers, as Sylvia thought, but had gone to her own fragile shelter.

If the steamy heat made living almost unbearable in Sylvia's middle-class neighborhood, it turned Caldera Street into a packing-box hell. Street signs weren't necessary. One could smell Caldera Street blocks away. There was no electricity. A few oil lamps burned here and there inside the shanties, and Hank shuddered at the fire hazard. But most of the residents of Caldera Street were outside, where the air was a little cooler.

The men dealt out hand after hand of greasy, dog-eared cards while the women sewed by the flickering light of oil lamps. And the children played street games.

Occasionally a prostitute led a customer into the dark labyrinth of sordid hovels, but the card games and gossip continued without a glance or remark.

Hank took all this in as he walked up and down the street, describing Peter and Elena, asking if anyone had seen them. But all he got were silent headshakes and hurried noes.

These people had their own "disappeareds." They didn't need Hank's to worry about.

He would try again tomorrow, Hank thought. If not here, then somewhere else.

Sylvia was still up when he got back. Had she been waiting for him? The thought heated his blood with a warm, thrilling glow.

"Any luck in your hunting?" she asked.

Hank shook his head. "I'll try again tomorrow."

Sylvia tilted her head defiantly and looked directly into Hank's eyes. "I hope you don't find her."

"You'd be better off hoping that I do."

With her face turned up to his like that, she was alluringly beautiful. Her eyes took on gold lights from a nearby lamp. Her mouth was temptingly soft. A breeze that stirred the curtains at the window rippled through her hair.

"You're wrong about Elena—and about Carlos, too, although I grant you he's the less likable of the two."

Hank took a step toward her as if mesmerized. "No," he murmured, "I'm right about them and right about you, about what we've meant to each other ever since Caldera Street, about what we mean to each other now."

He was so close that his breath warmed her face, fanning her senses into renewed desire for him. If she just lifted her mouth to his, she would feel his strong arms around her, his firm muscular body pressed against hers. She wanted him so badly; it would be so easy.

So hard, a rueful interior voice reminded her. So hard for Elena and maybe even for Carlos. So hard for herself, when he said, as he had to someday, "I'm leaving you" and was gone.

"No, Hank!" she shouted as a dam to the tide of longing swept over her. "We *don't* mean anything to each other. Caldera Street was an accident—a one-time thing." Not trusting herself to stay or to say more, she turned to go. "Good night. And good hunting tomorrow," she added sarcastically.

Hank went back to Caldera Street the next day. He knew he'd be recognized. He wanted to be. That would show the people who had said no to his questions the night before that he meant business.

But hours of searching and questioning yielded nothing but the same slow headshakes and blank looks from walled-off dark eyes.

Remembering then what Sylvia had told him of Elena's background, that her parents were wealthy members of San Lorenzo's middle class, Hank's mind flicked to the palm tree-fringed country club on the outskirts of the city. From the sordid to the sublime, he thought with a grin, walking to his car, which he had prudently parked away from Caldera Street.

The image of a cool drink and shade made him gun his motor, and the sound ripped through the heavy air like a machine gun tearing through sludge. Hank toyed with the idea of picking Sylvia up. They could sit at an umbrella table by the pool, sipping iced beer, and swim together as they had at the lake. Afterward . . .

Hank shook his head. She wouldn't go with him. Not to spy on Elena. And he drove past the university and onto the road that led out of the city.

By the time Hank reached El Club de Las Palmas, the shadows were long on its green velvet golf course, invisible behind a concrete-block wall until one reached the club's driveway and the white-uniformed guard. He would have to bluff to get in. The big bluff, like the big lie, was always the most likely to succeed. The country club wasn't far from Carlos's French château; it was the sort of place Carlos would belong to.

Hank grinned at the thought of using Carlos in this way.

"I'm here as a guest of Senor Ronderos," he told the guard in an offhand, slightly insolent manner.

"Your name, senor?"

"Carlyle, Chambers Carlyle."

As the guard drew a stubby finger down a list of names, Hank leaned out the car window. "There it is." He pointed to a scrawl a third of the way down. "You missed it," he said pleasantly, "because someone put the 'Carlyle' first. The name's Chambers Carlyle, not Carlyle Chambers."

A puzzled frown creased the guard's forehead. How strange these gringo names were. If they used the names of the saints, like civilized people, a person could tell right away which name was which.

Hank glanced impatiently at his watch, put the car in gear, and called out an insouciant thanks.

"*Sí,* Senor Chambers," the guard answered hurriedly, and waved him forward.

I should sign Carlos's name to all my drinks chits, too, Hank thought, smiling with satisfaction.

He left his car in the parking lot before the largest of the Spanish colonial-style buildings. In addition to the usual white stucco walls and red-tiled roofs, this one had thick pillars at the front door and tall, gabled windows. As Hank expected, it was the clubhouse.

It was dark and cool inside. The furniture was ponderous. Leather chairs crouched on the tiled floor like elephants waiting to be mounted.

Hank sauntered to the reception counter and smiled at the pretty, dark-haired young woman behind it. He pulled out his Americo company business card and held it out for her to read.

"I have a business appointment with a Senorita Vanegas here. Unfortunately I've forgotten her first name." Hank flashed a charming, conspiratorial grin at the clerk. "You know how it is, in America we always use first names. People expect it of us. If I could just glance at your club register. Or if you would do it for me . . ."

"I will look for you, senor."

The clerk reached under the counter and pulled out a book handsomely bound in black leather.

"Senorita Vanegas's first name is Elena, senor," the clerk said.

"And yours?" Hank asked, leaning familiarly over the counter.

The woman laughed, showing small white teeth and the tip of a smooth pink tongue. "It is Constanza."

"Not constant to a husband, I hope," Hank said, glancing down at her ring finger.

She giggled. "No, senor. No husband. No fiancé." She waited expectantly.

"Well, we'll have to do something about your love life," Hank said gallantly. He glanced at his watch. "In the meantime, I'm afraid Elena is late. Have you seen her today?"

"Not for many days. But Senor and Senora Vanegas come every evening to play bridge. They are the ones who have the membership. Senorita Vanegas has a guest card because of her parents."

Hank smiled perfunctorily to indicate that all this was old news to him. "Will you tell her please when she comes that I'll be out on the patio?" He gestured unnecessarily toward the French doors that opened out onto the paradise he had promised himself—a sparkling blue pool and umbrella tables.

Only a few people were in the pool, and even fewer at the tables. Hank ordered a bottle of Paraguayan beer and nursed it while he thought what to do next. Elena hadn't been on Caldera Street; she hadn't come to the club; she hadn't shown up at the university or at the student rooming house she seemingly preferred to her wealthy parents' home.

There were hundreds of places she could be hiding, but if she were working for Carlos, the most obvious one would be a place Carlos had contrived for her, perhaps the place where he was holding Peter a prisoner.

To find out would require bearding the lion in his own den, and to do that, he'd need time to lay a groundwork and to find people to work for him.

Hank slapped a couple of guaranis on the table for the beer and swept the patio with his eyes before getting up and leaving. In that little group of people dressed in swimsuits and tennis whites one figure stood out like a brownie in a bunch of snow fairies.

The man in the crumpled tan suit was at an umbrella table near the French doors, and this time he wasn't alone. A bruiser in a mocha polyester suit and a panama fedora with a brown feather stuck in the brim was with him. His eyes matched his black polished shoes. They looked right through Hank as if he were the invisible man, but Hank knew the panama hat dude wouldn't forget him. He was the enforcer, the robot who followed orders. Tan Suit had just fingered Hank for him.

Hank unfolded his long, lanky frame from the chair and started for the door. On impulse maybe or testing him, the dude stuck out his foot so Hank would trip over it. Hank stopped and gave him a hard look. His fists were clenched and his body was tense, ready to spring. After a long stare-down the dude curled his lip in a sneer and pulled his foot back.

Round One for our side, Hank thought as he got into the car and drove off.

It was night when he reached San Lorenzo. He drove directly to the house and unlocked the door with the key Sylvia had given him. He stopped just inside. Something was wrong. The house was dark and silent.

He went from room to room, sidling noiselessly along the walls, listening, then throwing the light switch on quickly. Every room was empty.

With a thumping heart he returned to his starting point, the kitchen. The house blazed with lights now. He went through it again, methodically looking for bloodstains, overturned furniture, ripped curtains, anything he might have missed before, anything that would show a struggle, an attack, a possible kidnapping.

Then, when he reached the kitchen again, he shut his eyes in relief and gripped the back of a chair to steady himself. There was a note on the floor. It had evidently fluttered from the table when he opened the front door: "Hank. I don't want you to worry about me. I've gone away for a few days. Sylvia."

Gone away where? He looked out the window. Left at night when they both had agreed it was risky to go out alone?

Hank read the note again. It was so brief and to the point that it could have been dictated. Someone could have entered through a rear door she had left unlocked, held a gun to her head, and forced her to write the note. There would have been no struggle, no chance for one.

Elena could have come for her. There would have been no need of a gun then. Sylvia would have gone willingly, eagerly with Elena.

Or Sylvia might have gone to her friend Emily Adams. Telling himself that was the more likely possibility, determinedly pushing all others out of his mind, Hank tore out of the house and threw himself into his car.

He was going up the hill to the Adamses' a few minutes later, his heart hammering in his chest now that he was close to having his fears confirmed or dismissed.

Emily and Frank were having their predinner cocktails. Frank took one look at him and silently got up and poured two fingers of Scotch into a glass. He put it in Hank's hand and sat down to his own Scotch and water again.

"Have you seen Sylvia?" Hank asked abruptly, his blue eyes wild with fear.

Emily hesitated, opened her mouth to speak, then closed it firmly again.

"You've got to tell him, hon," Frank said quietly.

"I gave my word."

"Where is she, Emily?" Hank said tersely, almost threateningly. "We're talking safety here."

"I told you the cottage is no place for a young woman to be alone," Frank said complainingly.

"That isn't the kind of safety you have in mind, is it, Hank?" Emily searched Hank's face with her own sharp blue eyes. "Even if she had stayed in the city, you would have been worried about her."

Hank ignored the question. "I know where she is now. The next question is why she went to the cottage. Did she tell you?"

"She said to escape the heat."

Hank could see in Emily's clever eyes that she realized as well as he why Sylvia had left the city, had left *him.*

"I'm going there." Hank looked from one to the other, as if daring them to stop him. But there was no reply, and he turned on his heel and left.

He drove quickly through the dark countryside on nearly empty roads. The Adamses' cottage had a vacant, closed-up look. Not a light showed anywhere except in the distance, where the colored lights glowed in the trees near the lake.

Hank sat in the car for a while, watching and listening. Nothing. He got out and approached the cottage cautiously, his heart beating fast with fear of what he might find.

He knocked and waited. And continued to wait. When she came to the door, her eyes were soft with sleep. Her face had the gentle curves of a child's.

"You're all right," he said sharply.

Sylvia opened the door wide. "Of course. Did Emily tell you I was here?"

"The information came mostly from Frank."

"Naturally. Emily wouldn't break her word."

He looked at her as she preceded him into the living room. She had a ridiculous shortie sleepshirt on, and for some reason that enraged him. She was so vulnerable to anything, staying here all alone.

"You broke your promise not to go out at night alone. What did you do, take the night bus here?" he asked sarcastically.

Sylvia struggled to sort out her feelings. Finding Hank at her front door had seemed at first like part of a dream—the happy ending; because she had no sooner arrived at the cottage than she missed him. She had gone to bed to make the night pass quickly. The next day, she had figured, would be better. She would see that she could live without Hank. She would swim in the cool lake, write some letters, read a book, relax and rest.

But now she was angry with him for having once again interfered with her freedom of action.

"If I took the bus, walked, or swam here, it's none of your business, Hank."

"Why? Why did you come here?" His eyes swept the cottage. "Just to escape the heat?"

"Are you looking for Elena?" she asked bitterly. "Is

that why you came because you thought your decoy might have finally produced results?"

"I came because you can't run away from me." He looked at her, and his heartbeat quickened at the enchanting softness of her sleep-drenched face and the quick rise and fall of her breasts under the thin cotton shift. He turned away, and there was a resigned, almost bitter note in his voice. "Because I can't run away from you."

He had said it, Sylvia thought. It was finally out there before them. The something they couldn't touch or talk about or examine. The something that could have only one result.

Suddenly she felt gloriously light and free, all suspicion, all fear, all distrust gone. Her heart soared within her. *She could love him now and he could love her.* Her body leaned toward his of its own accord, her lips parted with breathless waiting.

Hank groaned and swooped her into his arms, his kisses a shower of storm-tossed blossoms on her upturned face.

"Oh, my God, Sylvia, it's been so long."

She closed her eyes and tilted her head back, laying herself bare to his cool, sweet lips as a dry land seeks the rain. She felt as if his arms were holding her up, that she was dying a little and being reborn in his embrace.

His lips twisted and ground against hers. He covered her mouth with his half-opened one and united them with the stream of warm air he breathed into her parted lips.

He was bringing her to life, to a state of glorious, sensuously loving bliss. Avid for all of him, she sought and took his velvety tongue into her mouth. Then, giddy with happiness, she teased him with playful advances and retreats.

His big hands were molding her shift to her now, passing restlessly down her back, curving over her firm little derriere, stroking the backs of her thighs. All the while his kisses dropped lower and lower on her pliant, arched neck.

He pushed the thin straps off her shoulders with his lips and strung kisses like pearls across her polished flesh. His hands lifted her breasts, heating her skin through the thin cotton gown, and held them like alabaster bowls, ruby-stoned.

Slowly he lowered her gown farther. It fell to her feet, and she stood, gracefully proud, in front of him. He looked down at her, his blue eyes blazing with desire.

"You're so beautiful, Sylvia. So very beautiful," he said huskily.

He plunged his face into the valley between her breasts. Sylvia trembled at the delicious roughness of his cheek against her soft, yielding flesh and pressed her face into the curve of his strong neck.

Hank groaned with the joy of her, with the unutterable delight of finally having her in his arms. He had never known a woman so delicately beautiful, so finely made, so soft and lithe at the same time. At times, as he caressed her, he felt as if he'd go out of his mind if he didn't have her right away. But they had waited so long that he couldn't let go of these tantalizingly sweet moments either.

And although her response was as warm as any man could ask for, he wanted her to desire him as he desired her, to quiver with him on that knife-edge of longing that was part ecstasy, part agony.

Her fingers began to work the buttons of his shirt. When he slipped it off, Sylvia folded her arms around him, rejoicing in the silkiness of his skin and his well-muscled chest covered with brown hair. With trembling, hasty fingers she undid his belt. And when he stood naked before her, she sighed at the beauty of him, at the inverted triangle made by his broad shoulders and narrow hips. She passed her hands down his slim waist and along his strong, muscular thighs and felt him shudder under her cool, feather-soft fingers.

She had a dancer's respect for the body, and his was magnificent. He was lean but solidly built. His skin was smooth over the bulging muscles. Even still as he now was, hardly breathing under the sensuous play of her fingers, she could sense the vitality that was implicit in everything he did. It informed all his movements, giving them a graceful elegance that was beautiful to see.

"What are you thinking?" he asked softly.

"That you would have made a wonderful dancer."

Hank threw his head back and laughed. "I think your only interest in me is professional."

Sylvia didn't dare respond with the joke that came to her lips, that *his* only interest in *her* was professional. That was dangerous territory.

He took her hand then and said simply, "Come."

Hand in hand, as they had left the Adamses' garden the night that seemed so long ago, they went to her bed. Outside, the moonlight laid a bright path across the lake. It changed the mosquito netting into a gossamer cave where anything could happen, and it clothed Sylvia's rosy skin in a silver sheen.

Hank stood looking down at her. Her hair against her moon-paled shoulders was a fiery cascade. Her eyes, moon-washed, too, so that they were a paler green, smiled up at him.

"You look like Diana, the moon goddess," Hank said huskily.

"Diana was a huntress," Sylvia said teasingly.

Hank's voice dropped lower as he stretched his length beside hers. "Did she catch what she hunted?"

"Always," Sylvia replied softly. "She used silver arrows . . . like this."

Sylvia touched him with her cool, soft fingertips, exulting in the feel of his hard male nipples, his tough navel, and iron-hard stomach. *This is Hank,* an interior voice said. *This is the way he feels. I know his body now.*

She ran one finger across his strong white teeth, wanting to feel all of him, to know every part of him. He took her finger and dragged it over the inside of his lower lip. Then he drew it along her lips, painting them with the slight moisture. When his mouth sought hers again, it was in a long, sealing kiss.

Her breathing quickened. He could hear the soft rasping, the heightened taking in and letting out of breath, the sensual, enticing signal of desire. Looking down into her face, Hank thought he had never seen her eyes so large, so green now, the pupils dark and slightly dilated. Her breasts rose and fell visibly.

Hank lifted each one to his mouth in turn, holding it in the moonlight like a crystal goblet. He kissed the white mound into rosiness, then lingered over the soft pink peak, moistening it with his tongue, taking it between gentle teeth and tugging at it till it blossomed into a hard, throbbing nugget of delight.

Sylvia groaned under the exquisite pleasure he was giving her. She arched her back and writhed with her rapture.

The invitation was almost more than Hank could withstand. Again he was torn between the urgency of his desire and the delight of savoring her just a little while longer.

He continued to caress her breasts with his ardent, half-opened mouth, his tongue, and his hands. Then he dropped his mouth to her belly and left a path of kisses across its soft surface. He traced the soft angle of her hip and continued down her thigh, losing himself in the enticing hollows and curves of her body, oblivious in his joy of her passionate kneading of his shoulders, of the half-moons she was making in his firm flesh with her nails.

He started the erotic journey upward then, planting a kiss inside the high arch of her strong foot and in the tender area behind her knee. The kisses he trailed up her inner thigh were like a string of dynamite with a long fuse. The explosion that came when he reached the very heart of her desire shook Sylvia into an ecstasy of sweet agony and an electrifying glimpse of the rapture to come.

Her fingers clutched his hair, her hands clenching and unclenching as tremors of delight tore through her. She whispered his name, entreated him, said "please."

His heart swelled within him at these signs of her desire for him, but their fires had been banked so long that he had to be sure she wanted him now as voraciously as he wanted her.

He darted his tongue into the dimple in the center of her soft, tight stomach and rested it there while her stroking, imploring hands kneaded his shoulders, then smoothed along his back to curve around his small, hard buttocks.

Murmuring, "Silver arrows," she touched him all over till his desire for her coursed through him like hot, molten lava. But still he wouldn't take her. He couldn't let go of her, couldn't get over the mystery of her, this moon-silvered goddess he held in his arms. He had never known a woman like her. She was quicksilver, her moods changing from tenderness to raw passion in seconds.

Her breasts gleaming in the moonlight beckoned to him like snow to a thirsty traveler. He wanted to melt them with the heat of his mouth. Under the golden waterfall she had made of her hair, he kissed them reverently with his warm, moist lips; then he took each rouge-crested peak in his mouth and pulled gently on it.

Sylvia gasped with the ardor of her pleasure. Her nails dug into his strong shoulders. She writhed in a sweet, painful need for him. She felt volatile, frivolous, giddy with joy.

"Goddesses can be cruel when they don't get their way," she said lightly.

"What do you want, moon goddess?" Hank gently pushed aside her fiery curtain of hair and took her face between his hands. "Tell me."

Her movements under him, her hoarse breathing, the ardor of her response were all the invitation he needed, but he wanted to hear it from her lips too.

"I want *you,* Hank," she said, a joyous, teasing laugh bubbling up from the clear, sweet spring of her happiness.

"Oh, Sylvia," he whispered. He repeated her name, and a long shudder went through her. No one had ever said her name like that before, with so much awe, so much strength and tenderness. No one had ever made love to her like that, so gently yet so masterfully.

Then, suddenly, there was no more waiting possible. He had reached his limits. With one last kiss he lowered himself onto her soft, inviting body. She reached up, urging him to her, opening like a morning flower to receive him.

He entered her with gentle, velvety thrusts. She twined her strong dancer's legs around his hips and her arms around his neck. Exulting in her embrace, Hank called her name hoarsely, and she called back.

Their bodies, intimately entwined, rocked in the rhythm of a gloriously mad, pulsing dance. Hank's lithe, masterful body led her in a pas de deux that whirled onto ever new levels of rapture. Sylvia felt herself becoming more and more fully one with him, the barbaric, frenzied, thrusting rhythm bringing the longed-for ultimate nearness.

Soft little moans of joy escaped from Sylvia as the spiraling tension carried her to higher and higher planes of ecstasy until she reached the final, explosive instant of heart-bursting rapture.

Feeling the spasmodic shivering deep inside her body, knowing she was climaxing under him sent Hank over the edge. In the throes of his own fierce release he shouted triumphantly, the ancient cry of a man who has taken the woman he loves.

Still locked together, they stayed in a hush of wonder, trembling with the aftermath. At last they released each other and lay in a close embrace, glistening flesh against glistening flesh.

There was a lot to be said, but neither wanted to talk. Words might have spoiled the glorious sensations that flowed through them. Finally, in sated, exhausted contentment, they slept.

CHAPTER EIGHT

The morning light was soft and milky. Glancing out the bedroom window, Sylvia saw that the sky hadn't taken on color yet. The sun still wasn't hot enough to burn the mist from the lake.

She had awakened feeling completely refreshed; the coolness of the early dawn was a benediction after their fevered lovemaking.

It had been a night such as she had never known before. Their love had spanned a rainbow of pleasure, from the most subtle nuances of sensation to a wild abandonment of their individual selves in the rapture of shared ecstasy.

She glanced at Hank, still asleep beside her, his long limbs sprawled out on the bed, one muscular arm flung toward her. She studied the sharp planes of his face, his long, aristocratic nose, his firm chin, the sweep of his dark eyelashes against his cheek.

In spite of his gentleness—last night and on Caldera Street—he had the lean, pared-down look even in sleep of a man who could be dangerous. The smooth skin that she had stroked all over with her fingertips covered hard, powerful muscles. Nor was this a man who impulsively yielded to a moment of sensual pleasure. It was a man who could wait, a man who was always in control of himself.

She had learned his body last night—learned the feel of his strong, fine-boned hands, open and relaxed now against the sheet, as they fondled her into aching, reaching arousal time and again. She had felt the sinews of his long, muscular thighs against hers. She had taken his weight onto her, had held him inside her in a thundering stampede of breathtaking sensations.

She had tangled her fingers in his thick dark chest hair and traced the tapering line of its twin down his flat, hard abdomen. She had explored the leanness of his bare hips, the firmness of his rib cage, the taut muscles of his burly shoulders. In the throes of ecstasy her hands had curved around his small, hard buttocks and grasped his powerful thighs.

Last night she had known his superb body, and she had come to know him a little more. She had learned that he could be tender and even poetic, as he whispered love words while he caressed her. She saw the experience with other women that was implicit in his sexual self-confidence become concrete in the many ways he knew to give her pleasure. And she felt that energy of his, the powerful vitality that informed all his movements, transmuted into awesome, overwhelming maleness.

Sylvia had heard his breathing quicken, understood his gasps when words couldn't express ineffable joy, listened to him call her name in hoarse cries of exultation.

But, Sylvia mused looking down at him, she still didn't know him very well. And that could be risky. Because she thought she was a little bit in love with him. But what kind of fool would fall completely in love with an enigma, with a man of secrets, a man who was in love with danger?

Suddenly he opened his eyes. They were instantly alert

and an ocean-dark, cold blue. Then, seeing her, he relaxed. His expression became humorous and tender, and he smiled.

"What are you thinking of as you feast your eyes on my magnificent bod?"

"That you're a dangerous man."

He grew very still then. "Dangerous in what way?" he asked quietly.

Her heart was beating fast. She couldn't tell him the truth, that she was half in love with him. "Dangerous to your enemies," she said, hedging.

He leaned over her and drew one finger meditatively along her cheek. "And dangerous to you, Sylvia?"

Sylvia looked up at him, her eyes wide and serious. "I don't know yet." She paused. "Are you?"

But he didn't answer. He seemed lost in a reverie as he cupped the palm of his hand along her jaw, then slowly passed it down her lissome neck.

"You're so lovely," he murmured. "I want to look at you all the time, touch you all over, make love to you."

He had made love to her. Hank couldn't get over the marvel of it. What he had wanted since Caldera Street, what he had known had to happen had taken place. And it had been as he knew it would be. What he and the little dancer had was special, out of the ordinary. There was between them a magic that rarely occurred.

It could be called into play again and again. He could make her very happy, as he had last night. But could he make her happy in other ways? He didn't know. He didn't even know if he wanted to. He had never even had thoughts like this the morning after. She was his first love —if that's what she was.

He was stroking her now from her shoulders to the tops of her thighs, watching her skin go pink with love's glow under his hand, her lips moisten and part, her delicately carved lids become heavy and languorous over her green eyes.

As he adjusted his weight over her and bent to kiss her, Sylvia arched her body and put her arms around him. At this moment she loved him, as, she guessed, he loved her —for the moment. It was enough for now.

More than enough. More than enough could ever be, as with gentle thrusts he entered her, filled her with himself, carried her off with him in a barrier-breaking, heaven-scaling ascent to glory.

"Do you still think I'm dangerous?" He raised his head from the soft breast he had collapsed upon and grinned wickedly at her.

"Umm. Doubly so."

"I was known as a triple-threat man when I played football in college."

"You did something as normal and ordinary as play football?" Sylvia asked teasingly. "I would have thought you wore a trench coat over your diaper and played with coded blocks."

His funny, crooked smile flashed again. "Actually I was up to microdots in kindergarten." He rolled over onto his side and drew Sylvia into his arms.

"And writing with invisible ink in first grade," she responded with a laugh. "When did you start sleeping with beautiful spies?"

"Umm." He nuzzled her neck, and the musky male scent of him started a delicious stirring of arousal in her. "That's the part of my life that's really secret."

The contact between their bodies, the soft crushing of his moist lips on her neck were fanning her excitement to fever pitch. She pressed herself closer to him. "Were they prettier than I am?"

"Don't be silly," Hank answered, his voice going husky and deep. "You're the loveliest woman I've ever held in my arms."

He loved her then with his mouth and lips and teeth, and his clever hands, and his magnificent body, and when they lay entwined together again, sweat-slicked, exhausted, and deeply content, he murmured, "I told you I was a triple-threat man."

"Umm, such threats!" Sylvia said, and fell back to sleep, her golden hair mingling with the dark mat on his broad chest.

They stayed at Lake Bogado until early the next morning, and as they swam and picnicked and made love, the two days they spent together were, to Sylvia, days set aside in a tantalizing way from the tenor of her life in San Lorenzo.

As they drove back to the city, she said wistfully, "It was like being on vacation." Then, with a grimace: "Or more like getting time off from prison for good behavior."

Hank looked at her with surprise. "Do you dislike San Lorenzo that much?"

"I see it as a sort of hell, a steamy, blistering hell of danger and secrets and worry, of shadows and disguises, a place where quite possibly nobody is what he seems."

Hank was silent.

"I suppose you're thinking that it's Elena and Carlos who aren't what they seem," Sylvia went on.

"I *was* thinking something like that," Hank said dryly.

He could be right, Sylvia told herself. It was possible. How well did she really know Elena? The empathy that had so quickly grown up between them was not the same as knowing someone over a period of years. As for Carlos, wasn't he different here in his own country?

These were fugitive thoughts. The final push to belief didn't occur. But with these reflections came the old doubts about the man she had made such wonderful love with. Was he using her even to the point of lovemaking to get at Elena and Carlos?

Could you use a person you loved? Or did the two

situations cancel each other out? Ah, Sylvia reminded herself, but he never said he loved you. There's the rub.

The telephone rang thirty minutes to the dot after they had walked into the house.

Hank raised his dark eyebrows. "Someone knows we're home."

He strode to the phone and picked it up. His "hello" was dry and sardonic.

"It's for you," he said, and he handed the phone to Sylvia.

"Sylvia, this is Judit Mendieta. I hope I am not disturbing you."

"Not at all," Sylvia answered, aroused into alertness by the edginess in the young woman's voice.

"I have been trying to get hold of you to invite you to a luncheon at Las Palmas tomorrow."

"Sounds lovely. What's the occasion?"

"No occasion. It's just that several of us women in your classes would like to treat you for all you've done for us. Can you come? It's to be at one o'clock tomorrow."

"Yes, I'd love to. Thank you."

Sylvia put the phone down slowly. Judit had sounded more as if she were giving an order than an invitation. But perhaps it was just her student's quick, nervous temperament that had made her sound that way.

"Going somewhere?" Hank asked.

"Some of my women students are giving a luncheon for me tomorrow."

"Pretty ritzy bunch of students you have."

"Just middle-class."

And not wealthy middle-class, an interior voice reminded her. Not wealthy enough for Las Palmas. But Elena was. She had referred to her parents' membership in the exclusive club several times.

Sylvia felt her stomach knot up with excitement. This was another message from Elena; she was sure of it.

There had been that anxious note in Judit's voice, inappropriate to a simple luncheon invitation, and Judit, Sylvia remembered, was a friend of Elena's.

"So you're going then?"

The last person she wanted to know that she was going to meet Elena was Hank. Sylvia managed to smile calmly in spite of her agitation. "A day out with the girls," she said.

As her taxi slowed at the entrance to El Club de Las Palmas, Sylvia's heart fluttered with apprehension. The white-uniformed guard was an unexpected obstacle. Whose name should she use to be admitted? Judit had neglected to tell her.

The driver stopped at the guard's signal. Trusting to luck, Sylvia rolled down her window and gave the heavy-set man her most charming smile.

He smiled back, showing two yellow canines in his lower jaw and a long pink space between. "Senorita Vanegas?" he asked.

"Yes!" Sylvia called out, her voice singing with relief. With a polite bow the guard waved them forward.

As she paid the driver, Sylvia wondered about the openness with which Elena had let her name be used. When she entered the clubhouse, she glanced around the cool, dim lobby, hoping to see Elena there. But except for a group of three designer-dressed young matrons, obviously waiting for a fourth, the room was empty.

Sylvia wished fervently that Judit had told her what to expect. After the furtiveness of Elena's previous attempts to contact her this appointment in a semipublic place was puzzling.

She decided to play it safe and ask the receptionist for Senora, not Senorita, Vanegas since it was Elena's parents who held the club membership.

But the clerk flashed her dark eyes at Sylvia and shook

her head. "It is Senorita Vanegas who is here." She corrected Sylvia. "The senorita is on the patio."

Sylvia walked out the French doors onto the cement patio and its flower garden of yellow and white table umbrellas. She shielded her eyes from the sun and scanned the tables.

A languid hand and a long, graceful arm raised in greeting were Elena's. She was sitting at the farthest table, facing the door. Her face was shaded not only by the large canvas umbrella overhead but by a broad-brimmed panama hat as well.

Sylvia caught her breath. She had worried so much about Elena that it seemed a miracle her student should be here, sitting casually at a table in this pretty outdoor setting. Then her happiness and relief gave way to a spasm of annoyance. Twice she had gone to a great deal of trouble, perhaps even risk, to meet Elena at her request. Even this trip to Las Palmas had been costly in terms of taxi fare. Yet here was Elena, as nonchalant and cool-looking as if she had just driven from her parents' luxurious home for lunch and an afternoon of bridge at the country club.

"What fun that you could come," Elena trilled as Sylvia sat down at her table.

What should she say? Sylvia wondered. There were people all around them. Some were in swim attire; others, in tennis whites or short golfing skirts or chic little dresses for a summer lunch.

Elena was wearing a simple white linen sundress of expensive cut. Her thick blue-black hair was wound into a becoming chignon. She looked very smart and sophisticated, totally different from the hardworking, sweating dance student in a leotard or the frightened girl whose full print skirt had been the last Sylvia had seen of her on a sealed-off Caldera Street.

"I've been looking forward to it," Sylvia answered noncommittally. "By the way, how did the guard know I had come to see you?"

Elena's dark eyes sparkled mischievously. "I told him I was expecting a beautiful *norteamericana.*" Elena flicked a pink-tipped finger against her glass, tall and frosty and half full of an amber liquid. "Would you like a glass of maté before lunch?" Elena suddenly grimaced. "Or are you getting tired of our national drink?"

Sylvia laughed. "I think I've become an addict. I'll have to take some maté plants home with me and make my own Paraguayan tea."

As the waiter came and went several times to carry out her polite but imperious orders, Elena chitchatted gaily. She hadn't been in dance class lately because she and Mamá had gone on a shopping trip to Buenos Aires. Elena described the latest Paris fashions, which wouldn't reach poky old Paraguay for at least a year. She gossiped about dancers she and Sylvia knew. She even talked about the weather, how hot the summer was and did Sylvia mind it as much as most North Americans seemed to.

"Judit couldn't come?" Sylvia ventured when the salad was brought.

"No, unfortunately. But it's nicer this way. Just the two of us."

Sylvia didn't answer. She was thinking of the long taxi ride back to town, the cost; the time lost in coming out here for what, considering Elena's behavior, was probably just a whim on the girl's part; her disappointment, which gnawed viciously inside her. Her passionately honest, deeply serious friend was, in her own environment, just a superficial, conventional little debutante after all.

Sylvia began to let her irritation show. Deciding that caution was unnecessary, that Elena had just been playing silly games all along, Sylvia started to ask outright why Elena had wanted to see her.

But as if guessing Sylvia's intention, Elena startled her

into silence with an odd, unexpected little smile. "A friend of yours is here in the club," she said.

Hank! Sylvia thought. But the idea was absurd. How could Hank have gotten into this private club?

"He's in the pool," Elena said softly, her eyes intent on Sylvia.

On the far side of the sunny blue pool were clumps of wand-thin palm trees, their long, fringelike fronds all bending, in the breeze that had come up, in one direction like a corps de ballet. The cement deck was lined with buff-colored chaise longues covered with the club's green pads and yellow towels. The smell of suntan oil hung greasy and sweet on the warm air. Children playing in a small pool with nursemaids nearby babbled gravely in their own language. Young matrons, tanning in their St.-Tropez bikinis, showed the first signs of the fat to come, when their husbands would take mistresses with small waists and slim sides.

Sylvia registered all this subliminally before scanning the swimmers for a familiar face.

"He's on the diving board now," Elena said.

It took a moment for Sylvia to recognize Carlos in the stocky man who stood with small, fleshy feet planted on the diving board, chest out, stomach sucked in as though on parade.

A spasm of distaste shot through her at the self-consciousness, the sexual flaunting in Carlos's sustained posture on the diving board.

The image of Hank's nude body flashed into her mind. It had a purity and a sinewy grace that not only excited her but pleased her aesthetically. More than that, Hank had the self-confidence of a sexually successful man. It was the kind of aura that a sophisticated woman was immediately aware of and able to recognize for what it was.

Carlos lifted himself off the board then and pierced the air in a competent, perfectly executed dive.

Carlos *was* different in his native country, Sylvia reflected as she watched him cleave the blue water neatly. He seemed to preen himself on his sexual prowess, wanted it recognized, needed to prove it. He postured more and had acquired an oily charm that grated on her nerves.

Still, he was a friend, and one was loyal to friends. You saw them through their disagreeable phases, trusting that someday they would change. You were patient, Sylvia thought wryly, as she was now being patient with Elena, whose only care in the world seemed to be getting the waiter to bring the exact kind of salad dressing she wanted.

Carlos and Elena. Both members of the exclusive Las Palmas club, both part of the country's privileged class. Was Hank right then? Were they allies in some scheme she didn't know about?

A shadow fell across the table.

Carlos, loosely belted into a white terry-cloth robe, stood beside her.

"Sylvia! What an unexpected pleasure. I didn't know you came to Las Palmas."

"I'm a guest of Senorita Vanegas," Sylvia explained.

She introduced Elena and Carlos and watched them carefully for a sign of recognition.

But there was none.

Instead, after inviting Carlos to sit down, Elena launched into a nonstop spate of questions. Had Senor Ronderos been at the last club dance? Did he have children who participated in the club's activities? Did he think, as some people did, that the food in the club was not as good as it once was?

Sylvia raised her eyebrows in sustained surprise. This was a totally new Elena—a brittle, insensitive, snobbish woman who openly ignored her guest while discussing club affairs, as if to emphasize that Sylvia wasn't one of them.

Carlos fidgeted like a man forced by politeness to show an interest he didn't feel. Even so, his eyes kept straying to Sylvia.

As soon as Elena had run out of questions and gossip, he turned directly to Sylvia.

"How's the dance teaching coming?" A pained smile spread across his features. "It's been a long time since I've seen you to ask."

Sylvia laughed. "I'm afraid I've been busy." Immediately she wished she hadn't been so apologetic. She didn't have to apologize to Carlos for not seeing him.

"Not entirely with dance lessons, I believe."

There was something new in Carlos's expression. The reproach was still there, but an intense anger now burned in his dark eyes.

Sylvia drew away, shocked by Carlos's bitterness. Then, recovering herself, she retorted, "With living my own life in *your* country, Carlos, as I always do in *mine.*"

Carlos bowed his head slightly. "Of course. Unfortunately people often make mistakes in foreign countries that they wouldn't make in their own. Out of lonesomeness for their own countrymen, perhaps, they permit themselves to be taken up by people they wouldn't associate with at home."

Sylvia's anger grew. Carlos was making Hank sound like riffraff and her like a fool.

"Is that what happened to you in New York?" she asked acidly.

Carlos smiled patiently. "In New York I had a good friend—*you.*" The smile faded. The muscle around his jaw tightened with the point he was going to make. "As here you have me."

What could she say? Sylvia wondered, caught up for a

moment in a feeling of helplessness. Carlos wasn't talking about friendship. If there were any doubt in her mind, the yearning look in his eyes as he watched her would dispel it.

It was complusive, single-track passion Carlos felt. And she was the object of this obsessive love. Sylvia Goddard was the possession Carlos had told himself he had to have.

Sylvia didn't reply to Carlos's statement. She glanced toward Elena. Her friend wore a bland social smile, and her brown eyes, usually so vivacious and full of laughter, were as still as forest pools.

It was the first time, Sylvia thought, she hadn't been able to read Elena's feelings on her mobile features.

"Would you like to swim, Sylvia?" Carlos asked. "Perhaps Senorita Vanegas could lend you a suit. If not, there's a little shop in the club. Of course, I would take care of the cost." He laughed a little. "For the pleasure of swimming with you."

"I wasn't planning to swim," Sylvia said firmly. "I came to the club just to have lunch with my friend."

No use making a point of his offer to buy her an item of clothing, Sylvia decided, insulting though it was.

"Ah, yes, Senorita Vanegas," Carlos said. He fixed Elena with a policeman's eye—sharp, curious, and knowing. "You come to the club often, senorita? Like me, perhaps, to take a noontime dip before returning to your professional duties?"

Elena's laugh tinkled musically in the air. "You flatter me, Senor Ronderos. I come to the club to swim and have lunch with my friends and play tennis—all day long if I like."

Carlos nodded, as if satisfied that his placement of Elena Vanegas in the structure of San Lorenzo society had been correct. Then he bracketed the two women together in an inquiring gaze.

"Except," Elena went on, "when I am at Sylvia's dance studio. I'm one of her less talented students." She shrugged. "But I enjoy dance, and it's very slimming."

Dancing as a means of figure control? This from a woman who voluntarily worked herself to the point of exhaustion to improve her technique, who literally lived and breathed dance?

Whom was Elena trying to fool by this spoiled debutante act—Sylvia or Carlos?

As if satisfied about Elena, Carlos turned his attention full on Sylvia. He sighed heavily, comically. "If you won't swim with me, Sylvia, I'll have to swim alone. One more dip, then it's back to the old salt mine. But it's been a pleasure seeing you." His expression darkened. "Remember what I said about bad company. A wise woman knows her real friends."

A tremor of fear seized her. There was menace in Carlos's tone, and that old obsessive, brooding look was back in his eyes.

But she answered him stoutly. "I hope to keep your friendship, Carlos, and definitely plan to keep my other friends."

She hesitated just long enough before *friends* to let him read *lover* into the word, so there would be no doubt in his mind where he stood.

A dark, bitter look seared his plump face, as it had on the dance floor at his party. Again Sylvia saw the other side of Carlos's obsessive love for her—his equally obsessive jealousy and hatred of Hank. Fear raced along her nerves like a brush fire out of control. Had she innocently set Hank up for Carlos's vengeance by her unequivocal statement about her feelings?

But with Carlos's courtly bow to both women and his polite words of farewell her panic waned. No person continued for long to hate like that. Carlos's spasms of jealousy would pass. Even his love for her, if you could call it that, would fade once he had accepted the fact that it could never be returned.

"What were you thinking of just a little while ago?" Elena asked quietly. "You looked terribly distressed." Elena's large dark eyes were liquid with compassion and friendship as she looked at Sylvia.

This was the Elena she knew—this grave, gentle woman. Sylvia felt a surge of relief as if she had just heard that a friend who had been ill was out of danger.

"I was thinking of Carlos, but I'm afraid my thoughts were too lurid to tell you."

"Where Carlos is concerned, nothing is too lurid," Elena said flatly.

Sylvia looked at her friend's serious face for a long time. "I think you'd better start telling me what you brought me here to tell me," she finally said.

"Don't be surprised," Elena began, "if I laugh and smile while I talk about this man, whom I shall call Gustavo. I shall keep my voice low, like this, and I suggest that you smile a lot too. We are two ladies having lunch at a country club together, and that is all." Elena smiled charmingly. "Agreed?"

Sylvia smiled back at Elena and nodded, amazed at this exquisite young woman's experienced handling of the situation.

"May I assume that Hank Weston told you about his friend?" Elena asked.

"I know that he's an American journalist who has disappeared and that Hank is looking for him." Clearly, Elena wasn't going to mention Peter Burns's name either.

"But you don't know why he 'was disappeared,' as we sometimes say here." Elena looked off into the distance for a moment. "The expression is accurate, by the way. People don't just vanish; they are made to disappear."

"No, I don't know why. Nor does Hank, although I think he suspects."

Elena concentrated on dropping a cube of sugar into her espresso. She pulled the brim of her hat down farther, even though the afternoon sun still hadn't struck their table. Her face was completely shadowed now. With a chill Sylvia realized that this would make it very difficult for anyone to read her lips, even with binoculars.

"This person came here to get information he could use to expose Gustavo, particularly in the United States," Elena said. "He had inside intelligence that the man who was fostering a public image of himself as an American-educated businessman dedicated to democratic ideals was actually using very unsavory ways to prepare a power base for himself."

"For a political coup?"

"But of course."

Elena delicately but precisely cut through the layers of her napoleon with her fork. "He had evidence that Gustavo used murder, kidnapping, and torture against his political enemies, the last not only for information but for vengeance too. Gustavo is a very vindictive man."

She stopped a moment to chew a morsel of pastry, then resumed. "He also has an army of spies all over the country but particularly in San Lorenzo."

Sylvia grimaced, remembering the man in the tan suit and the intruder at the university.

"Smile," Elena reminded her softly. "Isn't this pastry good?" She raised a piece on her fork and looked at it. "Do you like it? I think the dough's remarkably light."

"Yes, it's delicious," Sylvia answered, smiling obediently.

"One of this person's informants turned him in to Gustavo, or so we believe. Gustavo had him kidnapped and held him in one of the private little jails he has here and there. The jail is always the house on the street where the neighbors know no family lives; where some of the people whom they see go in, never come out; where they can't hear any screams but know there's a cellar and a few soundproof rooms. Not wanting to find themselves in one of these houses, they say nothing."

Sylvia shuddered at the picture Elena was drawing for her. Then, remembering, she twisted her lips upward into a smile.

"You and he were lovers," she said, not asking a question but stating a fact to show her compassion for the anguish Elena must have suffered.

"Yes. I would have told you, but my friend said not to. He thought the fewer people who knew about us, the better, for my safety."

"Hank thinks you set this person up," Sylvia said flatly.

She watched Elena closely for her reaction to this accusation. To her surprise Elena nodded complacently.

"We had planned ahead of time that if my friend were disappeared, I was to make it look as though I were through with him. I was to talk against him and even have it appear as though I had set him up. These tactics were partly for my protection and partly to enable me to put our plan into effect."

"What plan?" Sylvia asked impatiently.

Elena poised another bite of pastry at the end of her fork and looked at it judiciously. "To find out where he had been taken and to rescue him." She popped the morsel into her mouth and closed her lips over it.

Sylvia stared at Elena, who nodded confidently in answer to her unspoken question, *how?* "Oh, I had the means. I'm part of a small but very efficient human rights group that has its own network of spies and operatives. Unfortunately we haven't been one hundred percent successful. But in my friend's case we were. We got him out and to a safe house, which is where he is now."

"That's wonderful," Sylvia said breathlessly.

"It's like a miracle. There isn't any doubt that Gustavo was planning to have this person killed after he had 'punished' him a little," Elena said grimly. "He couldn't let him go free with the kind of information *he* had."

"How long will your friend be safe where he is?"

"Long enough." Elena glanced at her watch. "Because in exactly four hours we'll be out of the country. I won't tell you how."

Sylvia nodded thoughtfully, still absorbing all this surprising information. "But why—?"

"Why did I expose myself in order to meet you here?"

"Yes."

A shadow fell across the table. Sylvia saw the look of fear that skimmed the joy from Elena's face. But it was only the waiter asking if they wanted more espresso.

She lives on the edge of her nerves, Sylvia thought, watching Elena's quick smile at the waiter.

While the coffee was being poured, Elena said in her fluty debutante's voice, "But you must talk more, Sylvia. I'm hogging the conversation with my silly gossip. Are you choreographing anything at the moment?"

For the next few minutes, Sylvia described the dance "Affirmation" to a smiling, nodding Elena.

"That's fascinating," Elena said. "I'm dying to see it when it's finished."

Sylvia didn't say that she had hoped Elena would dance the woman's role for her. Some small part of the distress Elena was suffering had to be the fear that something would happen to her and she would never dance again.

When the waiter finished fussing over the table and left, Elena picked another sugar cube out of the bowl with the dainty tongs and dropped it into her tiny cup of espresso. "I arranged to meet you here today because I wanted you to know that Gustavo is dangerous. He is not the friendly, innocuous man you knew in New York. He is a cruel, unpredictable, vindictive person who wields a great deal of power."

"Even if I accepted the truth of what you say, and frankly I'm inclined, for the first time, to do so, I still don't think Gustavo would hurt me. I really don't," Sylvia protested.

"You never know with people like him," Elena argued earnestly. "They can change very fast. That's why I tried to meet you on Caldera Street—because I thought you should know what he was really like, that he might turn nasty if you continued to reject him. But of course, the raid stopped that attempt. I tried again in your dance studio, but I left when I saw one of his spies watching the studio."

"Someone in my classes has been leaving your messages," Sylvia said.

"Yes, but I won't tell you who, aside from Judit, who you know made the phone call to you."

"I thought the 'bells' message left on the calculator was very clever, but why did you use that method?"

Elena beamed. "It was clever of you to catch on. One of my messages had been removed by some unknown person." *The one I couldn't find to show Hank,* Sylvia thought. "Although it was so innocuously worded as to present no danger to us, we couldn't tell whether its removal was accidental or not. While we were checking, I devised the message of the bells."

"It was very good of you, Elena, to keep trying to contact me. Actually heroic, considering the risk you ran."

"Frankly, I wouldn't have continued except for Hank." Sylvia froze, her espresso cup half raised to her lips. Her heart seemed to shrink with fear, to congeal and turn cold inside her chest. "True, knowing how Gustavo feels about you and how vengeful he can become when thwarted, I thought that he was always a potential danger to you, but it wasn't until you became involved with Hank that Gustavo became very, very dangerous."

Sylvia set the little china cup down with a bang. She looked at it blankly for a moment, surprised that it was still intact. "Dangerous out of jealousy?" she stammered.

"That and more."

Sylvia's heart was thumping against her ribs now. She stared wide-eyed as Elena threw her head back and laughed gaily. For a moment Sylvia thought the girl had gone mad. Then she remembered the subterfuge Elena had adopted and steeled herself for what was to come.

"Gustavo knows who Hank is, Sylvia," Elena said quietly, her large eyes dark and still with the seriousness of what she was saying.

Unconsciously Sylvia's hand flew to her mouth, and she swallowed hard. "How?" she asked in a voice that sounded strained and hoarse even to herself.

"One of Gustavo's spies thought he recognized Hank from some previous operation in Latin America. He told Gustavo. Gustavo put his sizable information network on Hank's trail and came up with Hank's real reason for being here—to look for his friend."

"I see," Sylvia said dully. "Then Hank is in danger." Fear seemed to have whited out all lesser emotions, the whole varied spectrum of feeling once available to her. She had become one giant soundless scream of dread.

"Great danger," Elena said gravely. "Now that this person has escaped, Gustavo is very likely to want Hank for interrogation."

"How about you, Elena? Are you in danger too?"

Elena shook her sleek dark head. "No. So far, Gustavo doesn't know about my connection with this person or to the human rights group. That's why I decided to risk coming out into the open today. I had to get the message to Hank that his friend was safe but he wasn't. Will you tell him, Sylvia?"

Her composure completely gone now in her fear for Hank's safety, Sylvia rose abruptly. "I'll go to him right now." She looked down distractedly at Elena. "Hank was hired by his friend's family," she said, only because it was always on her mind.

"From what this person tells me, I doubt that Hank cared about that. The man was Hank's friend. That's all that mattered to Hank. Smile, Sylvia," Elena warned.

Sylvia forced a bright smile. "Thanks for the lunch, Elena," she sang out gaily. "It was fun—gossiping, hearing your news, telling you about my latest dance. And the food was delicious. I'll have to exercise and diet all week to get rid of those scrumptious calories."

She wanted to put her arms around Elena, to thank her and wish her Godspeed in her flight from the country. But she couldn't. So Sylvia smiled again—sad-eyed, like a clown, she thought—and said, "The next time's on me." Then she turned and left the table.

As she walked past the pool, Sylvia darted a nervous glance at the diving board, the turquoise water, and the towel-draped chaise longues. Carlos was no longer there.

Sylvia shuddered. What if she got to Hank too late to save him?

CHAPTER NINE

Sylvia sat on the edge of the seat, face thrust forward, willing the taxi to go faster. Every once in a while her eyes met those of the driver in the rearview mirror, and his troll-like features took on new worry lines at her desperate look.

She used the old schoolgirl trick of trying to defuse the future by expecting the worst. But if it had worked in the past with exams and grades, it certainly didn't now. The pictures she drew of what might be happening to Hank at the moment were so horrifying that she had to force them from her mind.

Swinging to the other extreme, she told herself that she was being silly, that Hank would be there, safe and sound, when she got home. She would give him Elena's message. Then, with Peter safe, there'd be no reason for Hank to stay in the country any longer. *Her* contract with the university would be up in two months. They could meet in New York.

And then?

Sylvia stopped short in her thinking. This was the hurdle she had to jump, the self-knowledge she had to come to. Did she love Hank?

There, in the ancient cab with the cracked plastic seats, hurtling itself at Sylvia's order through the streets of San Lorenzo, Sylvia answered herself. *Yes, I love him, and my heart will die its own death if anything has happened to him.*

She paid the driver and got out her key. She was trembling so, her fingers fumbled at the lock. When she finally got the door open, she stepped inside, breathing in the silence, the deadness of the house.

"Hank!" she called, making her voice sing out, demanding by her own normality that everything be as it should.

When he didn't answer, she called again and heard the fear in her voice.

The third time was a whispered "Hank?" and a silent *Please, God, let him be all right.*

"He's just stepped out," she said, unconsciously speaking aloud as she forced herself away from the door.

Reaching the living room, she felt a sense of déjà vu superimposed on shock because in some recess of her mind she had expected this: chairs overturned; a lamp crashed to the floor, its bulb a pond of broken ice; books swept off a table.

A heavy glass paperweight in the center of the rug was probably the weapon Hank had grabbed to defend himself.

Carlos's men must have gotten into the house by a ruse, and Carlos would have given them the order right after he had left Las Palmas. Because she had rejected him? Sylvia wondered with anguish. Or wouldn't he, regardless of his feelings toward her, have wanted Hank anyway because of Peter's escape?

Sylvia was suddenly seized with terror at the thought of Carlos's tremendous power. She felt chilled as if all her surface warmth were fleeing an indefensible outer position to make a last stand somewhere inside her.

"There's nothing I can do," she said, speaking aloud again. "Nothing. Nothing."

Believing neither in the sufficiency of Hank's strength or her stamina nor in the power of good over evil, Sylvia willed herself to stop the insidious ebbing away of her courage. Carlos and men like him *wanted* people to feel terrorized. That made it easy for them to get their way.

Then Elena's slim, indomitable form came into Sylvia's mind. Elena had rescued Peter, so there was a chance after all.

But Elena had help. *You're alone in a foreign country,* an interior voice pointed out. *And by the time you got the wheels of bureaucracy moving, it might be too late.*

Sylvia stuck her chin out and said defiantly to the overturned furniture and broken glass, "All right, alone then."

She changed into a dress of pink cotton lawn that she seldom wore because the sailor top was cut very low. She undid her coronet and brushed her hair till it flowed in copper ripples over her shoulders. She retouched her makeup and applied a heavy evening perfume.

She looked at herself briefly, her lip curled with distaste. Then her eyes hardened. She was going to rescue Hank, no matter what it took. For one moment, she wavered again and turned cold with dread. What if Carlos had already done away with Hank? She resolutely brushed the idea away. She couldn't allow herself to think like that.

Hank's car seemed still to hold his smell, a sense of his being there. Sylvia looked around for something of his and found his wraparound sunglasses in the glove compartment. On impulse she put them in her bag as a talisman.

The location of Ronderos Enterprises was well known. It occupied the entire area of a small industrial park built by Carlos Ronderos about twenty miles outside town.

Sylvia gave the guard at the gate her name and told him she had an appointment with Senor Ronderos. She waited while he stepped into his sentry box and called through to the office.

She could see into the area framed by a high stone wall. Ronderos Enterprises consisted of a unit of three adjoining cinder-block buildings, two broad stories high, flanked on each side by a building still in the framing stage.

The industrial park had been carved out of wooded land, and some trees had been left standing. The place had been further beautified by scarlet bougainvillaeas and tangerine-colored hibiscus bushes. All this planting must have been done to impress visitors, Sylvia thought, since the buildings were windowless boxes.

The guard, who was built like an oil drum draped in horizon blue, finally told Sylvia she might enter. He pointed out the building that housed Senor Ronderos's office and pushed a button. The red-and-white-striped steel barrier slid upward, and Sylvia drove through.

A car was leaving on the other side. It waited a moment for the barricade on that side to lift. Then it went on.

Sylvia parked the car but didn't lock it. It was empty anyway. She clutched her bag with Hank's sunglasses inside and crossed the sunny courtyard to the central one of the three concrete buildings.

She stepped into a softly lit air-conditioned reception area that was Contemporary American Corporation. There was a pretty receptionist at a desk, a carpet of deep green pile, walnut-paneled walls, and more green plants than in a vegetarian restaurant.

A guard stepped out from behind the shrubbery and with a polite smile asked to examine her handbag. He was younger and slimmer and looked better in horizon blue than his counterpart at the gate. But his tanned neck was creased by a long white scar, and his jacket bulged over his right hip.

Sylvia advanced to the glossy brunette at the desk and gave her name. "Senor Ronderos is expecting me," she added unnecessarily.

The receptionist pushed a button and spoke softly into an intercom.

After a short wait a glossy brunette clone appeared. "Senorita Goddard?" she asked in a milk-and-honey voice.

Sylvia nodded.

"I will take you to Senor Ronderos now."

As Sylvia followed the receptionist, she felt herself relaxing, unwinding, her nerves going limp in the subdued, pleasant atmosphere, like a patient in an expensive private hospital no longer fearing surgery.

They entered a richly paneled, carpeted elevator, which moved silently upward. When it stopped, the receptionist, who had stood poised with ruby-tipped fingers pressed together, said smoothly, "This way," and proceeded down a carpeted corridor to a massive door of quebracho, the ax-breaking hardwood of Paraguay.

The receptionist knocked, then opened the door. "Senorita Goddard is here," she announced. She stood aside to let Sylvia enter.

Carlos came forward from a desk that was a solid block of leather-topped black mahogany. It seemed to take him forever to cross the expanse of carpet between them. Sylvia waited, noticing things about him she never had before. His step was mincing and precise. The smile on his lips didn't reach his anthracite black eyes. It seldom did, she recollected.

"I was surprised—and delighted—when I was told you were here, Sylvia," he said, taking both her hands in his.

"But your hands are cold. Is something wrong?" He motioned her to one of a pair of deep couches covered with black-and-yellow-spotted jaguar skins. "Would you like something to drink? A brandy, or coffee?"

"Coffee, please." She needed time to think. This tastefully decorated building with its soft-voiced personnel had thrown her off. She had expected a grimmer ambience, more in line with Elena's description of Carlos's activities.

As Carlos took the long walk back to his desk to call his secretary, Sylvia debated whether to ask immediately to see Hank or to flatter Carlos by requesting his help in finding Hank. She absentmindedly watched Carlos jab at the intercom with his right index finger and bark out an order for coffee. At the same time his tubby body rocked almost imperceptibly back and forth.

It would be best, she decided, not to accuse Carlos or put him on the defensive.

So when he sat down by her side on one of the sofas and a tray of coffee things had been put on the low table in front of them, Sylvia smiled pleasantly at him. She poured a stream of the dark, rich South American coffee from a silver carafe into the thin white porcelain cup he held out to her and said with earnest frankness, "Hank Weston was taken from my home by force this afternoon. I thought perhaps you might be able to help me find him."

"What makes you think I could help in a matter like that?" Carlos asked indulgently, and for a moment Sylvia wondered if everything Elena had told her had been false.

But the moment passed. There wasn't a false bone in Elena's small body. Sylvia was sure of it.

"You have the reputation of being a man of great influence. I didn't think such a simple request would be beyond your power." Sylvia waited a moment, then drove the barb in. "Is it?"

Carlos lost his cool. He rose excitedly from the sofa. He took several short steps in one direction on the thick carpet, then wheeled and faced her. His face was flushed, and a blue vein in his forehead stood out from the thick milky skin.

"Why do you care so much for this man, Sylvia? He's not worthy of you. He's a mercenary. He would work for anyone for money. He comes looking for a trashy journalist, this Peter Burns. Why? Out of friendship? No! For money. He's riffraff, trash. Have you lost your sense of self so badly here that you can fall in love with a man like that?"

"Then you have him," Sylvia said quietly. She slid one hand between the cushions so Carlos couldn't see her clenched fist, the nails digging into her palm. Her heart raced painfully. She was sick with fear for Hank. So much rode on how she handled Carlos, but she didn't know if she could outthink him in the dangerous game that lay ahead.

Carlos moved his shoulders in a massive shrug. Sylvia had a flash of recall—their thick pale skin and tufts of black hair as Carlos preened on the diving board—and controlled the grimace of disgust that came to her lips.

He sat down beside her and took her hands in his again. He uncurled her clenched fingers and kissed her palm.

"Forget about him, Sylvia. His kind has a woman every place he goes. I could make you happier than he could, believe me. I would give you as big a dance company as you wanted, hire the greatest dancers in the world. We were such good friends once. Remember?" He began kissing her fingers one by one. Sylvia willed herself to relax, to permit it without the tensing up that would show resistance. "It isn't far from friendship to love. Or, at least, affection."

His eyes swept her hair, her smooth white throat, and the delicate cleavage that showed under the sailor blouse.

Sliding his hands around her waist, he put his lips to her silky hair. "And I would settle for affection. I've wanted you since the first time I saw you dance. I've never forgotten how you looked. I thought I had never seen a woman so delicately made yet so sensual. All your exquisite womanliness was evident in your shape and your movements. It needed only the right man to make it flower, and I knew I was that man. I've waited a long time for you to come to me, Sylvia."

Sylvia used her dancer's training, her professional control over her muscles, to stay limp and relaxed. But she felt her insides writhing and twisting at the touch of Carlos's hands and the feel of his lips against her hair.

Keep it light, play for time, she told herself, hoping against hope that she wouldn't have to make the ultimate trade for Hank's life.

She moved Carlos's hands, now drifting upward to her breasts, and sprang to her feet.

Forcing a gay little laugh, she said, "What makes you think I've *come to you,* as you put it?"

Carlos looked her over with a cool, measuring eye. "Your dress, your perfume. I'm not exactly a babe in the woods when it comes to women, you know."

"I'm sure you're very successful," Sylvia murmured.

"Which is why I can make you happy." Carlos smiled indulgently at her. "You'll see. We will have a wonderful time together. We could even travel all over the world—wherever there's a dance company that interests you." He lowered his voice seductively. "And sometimes you would dance for me alone, wouldn't you, Sylvia?" He leaned forward and captured her hand.

A feeling of horror grew within her at the picture Carlos was painting. She would become a rich man's mistress, no longer an independent artist but a plaything to be pampered with furs and clothes, to be shown off as she walked into the famous restaurants of Europe on Carlos's arm, to be enjoyed at night, as a lover, a dancer. She looked down at the hand clasping hers, at the black hairs sprouting from its back, the stubby fingers and soft slug-white palm. And this with a man who was physically repulsive to her, a man who would violate her pure dancer's body with lust, not love.

She dropped his hand and moved quickly away. Lengthening her stride, she reached his desk and leaned against it. "What do you plan to do with Hank?" she asked bluntly, chin lifted and her green eyes full on his.

Carlos got up and stood facing her. "What do you care? Why do you bother so much about this man?"

Sylvia shrugged. "It's only natural, isn't it?"

"Because you were lovers, you mean." An angry flush spread over Carlos's face. His eyes got a burning, hateful look again. "What does one do with trash?" he screamed at Sylvia. "One gets rid of it so it doesn't pollute decent society."

Sylvia felt faint. There was no doubt at all about what Carlos meant to do to Hank. She put her hands behind her and dug her nails into the fine leather of the desk. The time for the ultimate trade-off had come.

But would Carlos be willing to make it? To trade one obsession for another? Hank's life for her love?

Sylvia trembled with fear at the gamble she was about to take. From being repulsed by Carlos's touch she now thought she would do anything he asked just to see Hank set free.

She pitched her voice low, made it coolly logical yet with an overlay of warmth. "There are many ways of getting rid of what one doesn't want. Send Weston out of your country. Tell him not to come back."

"That wouldn't serve my purpose," Carlos answered brusquely.

It must be Peter Burns, Sylvia thought. *He plans to extract information from Hank about how Peter escaped. Then he'll kill Hank.*

"One can always set up a different order of priorities." Sylvia smiled at him in an arch way that made her feel sick.

"Meaning?" he said quickly, the avid gleam in his eyes showing that he had an inkling of what she intended.

To pretend love would be absurd. Even affection wouldn't work. For a man like Carlos only one approach was possible: domination and submission, the owner and the possessed.

"A trade. Set Hank free, and I'll be yours."

Her emerald eyes smoldered with an unmistakable invitation. She stuck her lower lip out in a sexy pout. Moving away from the desk slightly, she arched her back, lifting her perfectly shaped breasts seductively.

Sylvia could hear Carlos's sharp intake of breath. His eyes burned with desire as he took in her provocative pose.

She had him! Sylvia thought triumphantly. But Hank wasn't free yet. She would have to use all her skill in playing the game to the end.

Carlos's eyes narrowed; his expression became calculating. "For how long?"

"Till you tire of me."

"I would never tire of *you,* Sylvia," Carlos protested. But a satisfied smile spread over his tallowy face at Sylvia's recognition of his superior position in the proposed relationship.

He took a step toward her. "When will you come?"

"When Hank is free."

"But then you might change your mind."

Sylvia's eyes flashed. "You have my word of honor."

Carlos advanced across the wide expanse of carpet. "We are alone here." He gestured toward a dark rosewood cabinet and one of the couches. "We could sip a leisurely brandy. Then perhaps you would give me evidence of your good faith."

Slowly now, with the pride of a property owner, he surveyed the sharply outlined mounds of her soft breasts under the close-fitting dress and the graceful roundness of her hips.

The fastest racehorse, Sylvia thought. *The biggest Mercedes. And now me.* Soon Carlos would have everything he wanted.

She had to fight to keep a bitter twist from her lips and, as Carlos drew nearer, to hold her body relaxed, in the inviting posture she had assumed.

"Let me see Weston first," she said lightly. "I know that you would never mistreat a prisoner, but sometimes guards get carried away . . ."

She left the sentence unfinished, because she couldn't go on. The mere thought of what Ronderos's strong-arm men might have done to Hank made her feel sick.

Carlos stopped where he was. "You're very solicitous about this mercenary, aren't you?" he said dryly.

Sylvia grinned. "I promised his mother."

Carlos threw his head back and laughed at Sylvia's joke. "That's very good. You 'promised his mother.' Men of his kind don't even have mothers. Or at least don't know who they are." He laughed again. "But all right. If that's what you want, I'll have Weston brought in."

He looked at Sylvia shrewdly, then fished in his pants pocket. He pulled out a small key and handed it to her.

"I'm going to leave the office for a few minutes. While I'm gone, you can get the brandy out. One quick look at Weston should be all you'll need. Then we'll enjoy ourselves."

He strutted out of the office, leaving Sylvia staring after him. Carlos wasn't wooing her any longer. He owned her.

And women were more disposable than a custom Mercedes-Benz.

Even worse than her picture of what life as Carlos's mistress would be like was Sylvia's sudden fear that Carlos might double-cross her. He would let her see Hank, then have him taken away to be interrogated and shot. He would make up some story, and as Carlos's virtual prisoner she would never know what had happened to Hank.

She couldn't believe that or she would go mad, Sylvia told herself. She had to have faith. She and Carlos had been friends once. Surely he would remember that time of comradeship and loyalty and not go back on his word.

She considered escape but discounted the possibility almost immediately. Somewhere inside this windowless building there had to be an army of blue-uniformed guards. The soft lights and soft-voiced receptionists were only window dressing.

Remembering Carlos's order to get the brandy out, Sylvia got up and went to the rosewood liquor cabinet. From the rows of bottles she selected a well-aged French brandy and put it and two large snifters on the coffee table in front of the couch.

Invitation to an assignation, she thought wryly, looking at the props for the love scene Carlos planned. Then she sat down to wait, wondering how Hank would look when the guards marched him in, trying not to think the worst, forcing herself to keep her courage high.

It's the only way, she told herself. *If your morale's good, you'll be able to think . . . and possibly help him. If you go to pieces, what good will you be to him?*

When she heard the door open, she jumped up, but it was only Carlos.

"You *are* anxious, aren't you?" Carlos said sarcastically, searching her face with his black eyes. "Don't worry. You'll see your lover now. Your *old* lover." He chuckled so that his plump chin shook and disappeared into his stiff collar. Without a chin, Sylvia thought, Carlos's pale face resembled a balloon with features painted on it.

If only she could say, *But you're only a balloon!* and see him float away.

Businesslike now, Carlos crossed to the desk and stepped behind it. His right index finger punched at the intercom, and he barked an order into the speaker in a shotgun Guaraní that Sylvia couldn't understand. And again he seemed to rock back and forth like one of those wooden Russian dolls, weighted at the bottom. He listened a moment, spoke again, then turned the intercom off.

Hank would be there soon. Sylvia's mouth felt as though it had been stuffed with cotton for days. She tried to swallow but couldn't.

"Would you give us a few minutes alone together?" she asked, trying for a light, casual tone but hearing her voice crack from fear and strain.

"Why do you want that when you're starting a new life with me?" Carlos asked coldly.

Be careful, go slowly, Sylvia warned herself.

She shrugged. "I should say good-bye to him after all." She lowered her voice seductively and waved her hand first at the bottle and glasses on the table, then at the couch. "Then we'll have our brandy."

"You will have to say your good-byes in front of me—and a guard," Carlos said abruptly. "It's enough that I'm letting you see him." His glance drifted toward the couch. "And please don't make a scene. It would put me off and interfere with my pleasure."

Sylvia nodded obediently.

What she had closed her eyes to all along had just become blindingly clear to her. Egocentric, emotionally callous, and cruel, Carlos was more monster than human being.

She heard footsteps then, the thud of boots on concrete. Mystified, she glanced toward the paneled wall where the sounds came from. There was a door there she hadn't noticed before because it blended in with the paneling.

Fear seemed to sit on her chest like a bird of prey, squeezing her breath, as she watched the door open. Two men in horizon blue uniforms shoved a third into the room. That man was Hank Weston.

CHAPTER TEN

Sylvia's hand flew to her mouth. A hoarse gasp escaped her.

Hank's shirt was ripped, and there was an ugly bruise on his cheek. But his eyes were alert, so he hadn't been drugged, and he stood with his usual self-confident stance. She let her shoulders droop in relief. He had been roughed up in Carlos's jail or while fighting off his kidnappers. But, thank God, that was all.

She could see the guarded surprise in his sharp blue eyes as he took in the world he had been suddenly thrust into—the luxurious office and the two graven figures of Carlos and Sylvia, watching him. There was a flicker of love in their azure depths when they rested on her for a moment. Then the scene was broken up as Carlos jerked his head toward one of the guards and barked an order. The man did a military about-face and, with Carlos watching, returned the way he had come in.

Before the door shut completely behind the guard, Sylvia gazed curiously at the space beyond it. Whatever lay at the end of that corridor, hidden from the pretty receptionists and the visitors to Carlos's business office, was concealed for good reason.

Sylvia glanced quickly at Hank. He stood poised on the balls of his feet, his big, graceful body ready to move in an instant. His eyes ransacked the room, searching out entrances and exits. They flicked to the remaining guard, who had stationed himself at the quebracho door, and then to Carlos. And finally, with one eyebrow raised, back to Sylvia.

She got his message immediately. Why only one guard? Hank wasn't even handcuffed. And Carlos didn't seem armed, but then Carlos hired others to do his killing.

It wouldn't be impossible, Sylvia thought, for a man like Hank to overpower the guard and knock Carlos out. So there had to be a signal, some way of getting a number of armed men into the office in a moment.

But what signal? The office was as banally normal as any bank president could desire.

Sylvia closed her eyes for a moment. There *was* something unusual about the office. She was sure of it. In time it would come to her. But she didn't have time. She had to retrieve the fact *now.*

Her thoughts became desperate racers, each one arriving at the finish line only to be told by a critical interior voice that the result was wrong. Frustrated, she sought kinetic release, as always, for her tension.

She thrust her hands in the pockets of her dress and raised up on her toes. *The movement recalled another: the way Carlos had rocked back and forth, first when he buzzed his secretary for coffee and then when he called the guards to bring in Hank.*

Her wry joke—Invitation to an Assignation—flashed through Sylvia's mind. Carlos wouldn't want witnesses to *that.* But he *would* want someone watching while a practically unguarded prisoner was in his office.

The answer exploded in her mind. Carlos used a one-way viewing screen for his protection. Normally on, so that dozens of guards could be brought into the room immediately if necessary, it could be turned off in an instant when Carlos so wished.

Desperately hoping that her deduction was correct, Sylvia duplicated Carlos's rocking movement. As she had thought, this put her slightly off balance, causing her right foot to come in contact with the floor first—in contact with a hypothetical buzzer.

Sylvia's mind took a quantum leap to a plan so daring, only desperation made it thinkable. As dangerous as Carlos's reaction would be if he caught on, Hank's would be even riskier.

She looked at Hank lovingly, pleadingly, hoping he'd get her message for patience. Then, with slow deliberation, knowing the eyes of both men were on her, she moved closer to Carlos and put her hand on his shoulder.

Carlos smiled with insulting satisfaction. She could read in his eyes his conviction that all women were whores, ready anytime to ditch a loser and go with the winner. Then he glanced meaningfully at Sylvia. *Get on with it,* his look seemed to say. *Tell him good-bye now.*

Sylvia trailed her fingers down Carlos's arm. She could hear Hank's quick sucking in of breath, but she didn't dare look at him.

She glanced ostentatiously at the ornate clock on Carlos's desk.

"There's something I have to tell you, Carlos." She paused, her heart thundering against her ribs, her mouth dry with fear. Carlos arched an eyebrow. She could hear the rasp of Hank's breathing. "Peter Burns is across the border," she said quietly. "He's out of the country now."

Hank gasped audibly. Out of the corner of her eye Sylvia saw the guard lunge forward, his hand on the holster strapped to his shiny black belt.

She kept her eyes on Carlos. His lips paled to the color

of cement as he compressed them in an effort to hide any reaction. His shoe-button eyes licked the room like a lizard's tongue, and Sylvia guessed his mind was working at evaluating this information.

Sylvia put her hand on his arm again, trusting because it was the second time that her touch wouldn't startle him, if anything could reach him in his present state of shock. She stepped behind him, lightly transferring her hand to his other arm in a soothing, reassuring caress. *The perfect mistress,* she thought, *breaking a piece of bad news.*

Dear God, let this be right, she prayed silently. She passed her foot lightly over the carpet. All it encountered was the thick pile of the rug. Disappointment stabbed painfully sharp. She made another pass, bearing down harder this time.

Sylvia closed her eyes in relief. Under her right foot was a small metal disk.

She raised her foot and pressed down hard on it. No bells went off, no sirens; no guards came rushing in.

What happened? Did some electronic device shut down? A screen go blank? She had no way of knowing.

"Who told you this about Burns?" Carlos's voice was hoarse and strained.

Sylvia was jubilant. Carlos had believed her.

"That's not important," she answered. "I have a proposition to make to you."

"You *have?*" Carlos jeered. He had recovered all his arrogant confidence. His eyes went to the guard, and the man's hand moved again to his gun. Carlos turned back to Sylvia with a mocking look, as if to say, *I hold all the chips; what proposition could you possibly make?*

But Sylvia's chin only went higher. Her eyes bore into Carlos's with the hardness of emeralds. "With Peter gone there's no point in your holding Hank any longer. Let Hank and me leave, and we'll see to it that Peter won't print what he's found out about you."

"We already have a deal." Carlos curled his upper lip in a sneer. "You gave me your word of honor. Remember? I was to set Weston free in return for your . . . what's the old-fashioned English word, *favors?*"

"We've been friends for a long time, Carlos." Sylvia spoke slowly, seriously, her eyes locked on his. "Do this for me, as a friend. Let us both go. You won't lose anything by it. In fact, you'll gain. As I said before, I give you my word Peter won't use the information he has about you."

"You gave me your word before, Sylvia," Carlos said dryly. "I'm afraid you're not very reliable. Once you and Weston are out of the country, Peter Burns will be able to publish anything he wants about me." His pale lips spread in a sly smile. "But if one of you stayed, there'd be no danger of that, would there?" He looked from Sylvia to Hank, and back to Sylvia again. "Which one will it be? I'll leave it up to you to decide. But I don't mind telling you, I hope it's you, Sylvia." Carlos glanced at the bruise on Hank's face. His eyes narrowed in another kind of smile. "Still, there are all kinds of fun."

That sadistic smile did it. "*I'll* stay," Sylvia said, forcing firmness into her voice, speaking overly loud to cover the quaver she thought she heard. "Let Hank go."

What happened after that had the jumpy, chaotic speed of a video tape on fast forward.

Hank yelled, "Get down!" as he lunged at Carlos.

Sylvia threw herself on the floor and wrapped her arms around her head. She heard the soft thud of a bullet as it struck the desk, then the crackle of wood splintering. When she looked up cautiously, Hank had Carlos in front of him, his arms pinned back and in Hank's strong grasp.

Holding Carlos as a shield, Hank snarled, "Tell your trained ape to drop his gun, or I'll hurt you a lot worse than you're hurting now."

He bent Carlos's right arm high behind his back. Carlos grimaced with pain, and sweat broke out on his forehead.

"Something tells me you can't take much of this. You can just dish it out, right, friend?"

Hank bent the arm even farther back. Carlos screamed, and sweat glistened on his brow.

"Put your gun down," he shouted to the guard.

"Tell him to drop it on the floor and push it toward the center with his foot," Hank said.

Carlos gave the order.

Sylvia watched the large black revolver slither along the rug.

"Pick the gun up, Sylvia," Hank commanded.

She went to the service revolver, her first impulse to handle it gingerly. But that wouldn't do. She had to show confidence. So she closed her fingers around the heavy butt and, raising the gun, pointed it without wavering at the guard.

Sylvia thought she heard Hank murmur, "Good girl," behind her, but she wasn't sure. There was a dull roaring in her ears. Events seemed to be occurring in slow motion now. She had passed beyond fear into a state of detached disbelief, of wonder that any of this was really happening: that Hank was no longer a prisoner under guard but the man on top and that she, who had always loathed violence, was holding a gun on someone.

"We're going to take care of lover boy here first," Hank said.

"What are you going to do to me?" Carlos screamed.

"Not half what I'd like to after seeing some of the people your thugs have worked over. There are handcuffs in the guard's rear pocket, Sylvia. Keep the gun on him and take them out. They took them off me, I suppose because Carlos wanted to make a good impression on you."

Hank barked in a mixture of Spanish and Guaraní at

the guard, "Keep your hands up. All the time. If you let 'em drop just once, she'll drill you. Did you get that, Sylvia?"

"Yes, Hank." Shoulders back, heels coming down confidently on the thick rug, Sylvia strode over to the guard. The shiny steel handcuffs protruded from the single rear pocket in his horizon blue uniform. Sylvia reached around him and pulled them out. Then, backing away, her gun still on the guard, she passed the handcuffs behind her to Hank.

Hank locked one of the pair around Carlos's wrist and the other around the leg of a heavy oak library table holding short stacks of magazines, waiting room-style.

Hank waved a hand at the magazines. "You won't be bored, Ronderos. I'm leaving you lots of reading material."

Carlos sat down heavily on the rug. The same feeling of unreality that had gripped Sylvia a few minutes before now seemed to have taken hold in Carlos. His eyes had glazed over, and his face was slack-jawed with incomprehension.

He kept glancing at an area of wall directly opposite. Sylvia guessed he was wondering what had happened to the one-way screen, his fail-safe. He didn't seem to connect Sylvia with the fact that it was obviously nonoperative. He didn't look at Sylvia at all.

It was probably the first time, Sylvia figured, that Carlos had ever suffered a defeat. His father's money and his father-in-law's position had greased his road to success, and his own unsavory tactics had ensured his amassing of ever more wealth and power.

When Carlos snapped out of it, he'd be a very nasty customer indeed.

Hank must have thought the same thing. He looked down at Carlos, slouched against the table leg, and said, "Keep your eye on the guard, Sylvia."

She heard the crack of knuckle against bone. When she dared a glance, Carlos was prone on the carpet, unconscious.

"Give me the gun," Hank ordered.

Sylvia put it in the palm of his hand, and his long fingers closed over it.

Was Hank going to shoot the guard? It was possible, she thought. He came from that world, the sphere of violence, of guns, and brutality.

She wiped her hand on the side of her skirt, as though the gun had been dirty. Her hands were shaking and her breath was catching in her chest, coming hard as she waited for what Hank would do.

You're acting like a nut case, Sylvia. The man's a menace. If he has to be put away, so be it. . . .

But not by Hank. Not by the man I love. Because I'm not sure I could still love him if he did.

As Hank walked purposefully toward the guard, gun in hand, the man's dark eyes rolled with fear, showing a large expanse of yellowish white. He put both hands out as if to supplicate the big man advancing on him, but Hank grabbed him by the throat and backed him up against the wall.

Sylvia turned her head. There was a loud cracking sound, but it came from a blow, not a bullet.

"Help me strip this guy," Hank said. "I'm going to use his uniform to get us out of here. But we've got to be fast about it."

Sylvia knelt by the limp figure of the guard stretched out on the rug. She unbuttoned his tunic and worked it off his shoulders.

"They check people leaving, as well as going in, Hank."

"I've got a plan." He tugged a boot off one of the guard's feet. "Phew! This guy must wear his socks till they drop off."

"What's your plan?"

"First, tell me something. Did Carlos make you do anything you didn't want to?"

Sylvia laughed shortly. "That was to come later."

"Thank God!" Hank looked gravely into her eyes. "I don't know how I can thank you for offering yourself to save me."

Sylvia gazed back at him, drinking in the clear sapphire of his eyes and every feature of his dear face. She raised her finger and touched his bruise lightly. "Just in case we don't make it out of here, I want you to know, I love you, Hank."

Some words broke from him, but Sylvia didn't know what they were. It was as if language had failed him for the moment. He put both hands on her arms and gripped her hard. "I love you, Sylvia, more, so help me, than I ever thought it possible to love anyone." Then he turned away, averting his face, wrenched with emotion.

He slipped his broad shoulders into the guard's shirt and started buttoning it. "We're going to have to tie this joker up and gag both of them. What happened to the alarm? There has to be one here. How come we got lucky and it didn't go off?"

"Luck, nothing! It's a one-way screen, and I deactivated it."

"What a woman! The next time I'm in a jam I want you right alongside me."

Completely dressed in horizon blue now from forage cap to pants, Hank posed for a moment. "How do I look—like the bluebird of happiness?"

"More like the tenor in *The Merry Widow,* darling."

Hank grunted. "We're going to tie Frankenstein here with electric cord from one of those lamps. If you can't yank it out, get some scissors from the desk."

Hank worked calmly and quickly at tieing the guard up and gagging both men.

"What's your plan, Hank?" Sylvia asked when he had finished.

"I'm going to imitate Carlos's voice and phone through an order to his secretary to let us out."

"Do you think you can do that well enough to fool her?" Sylvia asked doubtfully.

Hank nodded. "That's how you learn a foreign language, through imitation. And I've developed the knack. Besides, the intercom will distort my voice."

He stood looking down at the array of buttons. "It must be line one," he mused aloud.

He pushed the button, and the secretary's voice came on the line. "Yes, Senor Ronderos," the woman said in a soft, musical voice that massaged the nerves.

"My guest has become ill," Hank snapped out. He had Carlos's intonation down pat, Sylvia thought, and her fingers relaxed so that her nails no longer bit into her palms. "I've summoned a guard to help her out to the parking lot. He'll drive her in her car to a doctor. Give the gate guard the go-ahead signal immediately."

Sylvia held her breath, waiting for the secretary's reply. It seemed aeons in coming. She glanced at Hank and saw a muscle twitch along his lower jaw. Then he winked at her, a huge "chins-up" wink, and Sylvia felt better.

"Yes, Senor Ronderos." The secretary's voice trilled back over the intercom. "I will phone down to the guard at the gate immediately."

"Good! I'll be busy for the rest of the afternoon, so don't put any calls through."

"And no dictation?" The secretary's voice was kittenish.

Hank raised an eyebrow and grinned. "Not this afternoon." He turned the intercom off. "Let's go, Sylvia."

He pulled the visor of the cap down and took her arm. "Lean on me and look sick."

"That won't be hard. It's the way I feel."

They closed the door behind them and walked out into the hall. Sylvia leaned heavily on Hank's arm and, head down, seemed to watch every painful step she took to the elevator. Hank solicitously kept his head bent toward her. All the way to the front door of the building, Sylvia felt a prickling along her spine as she waited for a shouted order to stop.

Then they were outside, in the shade of the trees. Sylvia stared at the bright flowers, at the people passing back and forth, the phalanx of cars in the parking lot. This world had been going on all the time, she thought with wonder, while she and Hank had been living so intensely, so dangerously. The very ordinariness of life suddenly seemed very dear to her.

She glanced up at Hank. His long jaw was rigid with tension. How could he choose to live like this—always on the edge of danger?

"This is the risky part," Hank muttered as he handed Sylvia into her car and slid behind the wheel.

"You mean, if the guard didn't get the message or didn't believe it or gets suspicious."

"Right," Hank drawled as he turned the key in the ignition. "Look sick and fasten your seat belt. If there's any trouble, I'm smashing through, and they can chase us."

"Smashing through a steel barrier?"

"Hell, no. I'm heading for the sentry box. That's only wood."

"Hank, wait!" Sylvia fumbled in her handbag. "Those blue eyes of yours are a dead giveaway. I put your sunglasses in my bag . . . just to have something of yours with me."

Hank looked at her with humorous tenderness and put the glasses on. "What a woman! You think of everything."

As the car moved slowly toward the gate, Sylvia muttered, "I feel sick."

"Good. If you could faint or vomit or go into a coughing spasm, it'd be even better."

"You swine!"

Hank grinned, then quickly wiped the smile off his face. They were at the sentry box. The guard glanced suspiciously inside the car. Hank stared straight ahead, ramrod-stiff and soldierlike, with both hands on the wheel. The bruise on his face was not on the guard's side, Sylvia noticed, and she thanked God for *that.*

Sylvia sat slumped in her seat as if in her sick condition any movement would be distressing. Her mouth was dry with fear and her heartbeat was out of control as she waited . . . and waited.

Finally the red and white barrier rose slowly in the air, so slowly that, still terrified, she imagined Carlos or the guard regaining consciousness, freeing himself, and calling down an order to stop them.

Then her breath eased out of her with relief. The car was moving forward. It passed under the barrier and kept going till Ronderos Enterprises disappeared behind it.

"Jesus!" Hank said. "I never want to go through anything like *that* again."

"I thought you liked danger," Sylvia said teasingly, giddy with joy for the moment.

Hank chuckled. "Maybe I'm getting old."

"How long do you figure Carlos and the guard will remain unconscious?" Sylvia asked, her heart giving an anxious little jump.

"Not long enough."

"So what are we going to do, chief?"

"Remember Emily Adams's promise to help us if we ever needed it?"

"A terrific idea!" She was on an emotional seesaw, Sylvia thought ruefully. There were no in-betweens. It was either elation and relief or a painful, heart-stopping fear.

"I hope so," Hank answered morosely.

Sylvia's spirits sank again. Their situation was almost hopeless. Even if Emily Adams helped them, what chance did they have of escaping with all of Carlos's power mobilized against them?

Hank looked in the rearview mirror constantly. Both he and Sylvia listened tensely for the sound of a distant siren. The trip to the Adamses' house was agonizingly long.

When they finally reached it, Hank said, "I'd park somewhere else, but that would only get *those* people in trouble, and Emily and Frank have some protection as foreigners."

Emily opened the door. She took a step backward and her features sharpened with alarm when she saw the uniform. Then she recognized Hank. Her glance zeroed in on the bruise on his cheek. She turned to Sylvia and examined her swiftly as though to ascertain the extent of the harm that had befallen them. Then, with a worried look, she opened the door wider and said tersely, "Come in."

The familiar environment, the comfortable surroundings brought a pang of nostalgia to Sylvia. How innocent she had been when she first started coming to this house. She had considered Carlos a good friend. She had been thankful to him for expediting her appointment as a dance teacher at the university and was determined to repay his faith in her by working hard to create the nucleus of a dance company in San Lorenzo.

Elena Vanegas had been just one of her more talented students, not a girl she would follow to Caldera Street.

Sylvia glanced at Hank as they followed Emily to a room in the rear of the house. Her eyes traced the clean line of his profile, the jutting strength of his chin. There was a faint white crescent of a scar near his lower lip that she hadn't noticed before. And she had thought she knew every bone and muscle, every mark on his face and body!

It was here in this house that she had first really known Hank. No matter what happened to them now, she wouldn't ever want to go back to that time when she didn't know him, when she hadn't felt the weight of his arms around her, his lips alternately cajoling and fiercely claiming her, when she hadn't held him inside her, lover and beloved fused into one.

"We can talk here," Emily said, motioning them to chairs. "The servants all are in the other part of the house." She sat down and surveyed them again with her keen blue eyes. "What happened?" she asked calmly.

Hank took off his uniform cap and laid it on his knees as if he had just remembered he was wearing it. "A little trouble with Carlos Ronderos. At the moment, he's sitting on the floor of his office, manacled to a table leg, gagged, and unconscious."

Emily accepted this piece of information with composure. "I never did like Ronderos anyway," she said with an ironic smile.

A grin flashed across Hank's face. "We had somewhat better reason than that for knocking him out."

"I wouldn't doubt it," Emily said dryly.

"Unfortunately, Carlos won't stay unconscious forever. For all I know, he's already looking for us."

Emily's anxiety showed on her face, but her voice remained controlled and low. "What are your plans?"

"To get out of the country as soon as possible."

"They'll probably set up roadblocks. You'd better take my car."

"How about the car we came in?" Hank asked.

"No problem. A French couple have moved out of a house two blocks from here and gone back to Paris for a vacation. She told me the combination of the lock on the garage so that I could take care of a delivery of some goods for her. I'll put your car in there."

"Sounds good," Hank said.

Emily looked them over, her sharp eyes narrowed appraisingly. "In the meantime, we've got to disguise you two so that you're not immediately recognizable. Fortunately you're close enough to Frank's size, Hank, so that you can wear his clothes." She frowned as she continued to study him. "I don't know what else to do," she mused aloud. Her face suddenly lit with joy. "I've got it!" she called out, clapping her hands together. "A mustache!"

"I don't think I'll have time to grow one," Hank pointed out.

"I mean a false one, of course. We used to have amateur theatricals here to keep ourselves from going mad with boredom. Frank always got to play the dapper older man, the friend of the family, the worldly doctor, the sophisticated villain. I know his makeup box with a lovely black pencil mustache in it is still in his bureau drawer."

She turned to Sylvia, and her eyes rested on the golden red hair that rippled over her shoulders.

Sylvia held out a lock of her hair. "You want to cut it, right?"

"There isn't time," Emily said tersely. She surveyed Sylvia with a frown. "What can we do?" she asked worriedly. Then she hesitated, blushed a little, and put her hand to her own sleek, stylishly cut brown hair. "I use a tint, just a color rinse really to hide the gray. . . ."

Sylvia pretended surprise. "Emily! I would never have known."

"So how would you like to be a brunette instead of a redhead?"

"If my hair looked as nice as yours, I'd love it."

"Good," Emily said, continuing to look Sylvia over. "And we'll use different makeup and clothes—mine, in fact. What we want is a different *immediate* effect. All of

Ronderos's men will have been told to look for a man and woman with a certain appearance, and you two will have a slightly dissimilar one, that's all. Agreed?"

Hank and Sylvia nodded.

Emily got up then. "We'll start with the mustache for Hank. Wait here, both of you, and I'll get it."

When she returned, her arms were draped with clothes. She gave one set along with a small box and another marked "Spirit Gum" to Hank. "There's a bathroom just outside this room," she said. "Turn right."

As Hank left the room, Emily handed a seersucker skirt and jacket in a narrow tan pencil stripe and a white cotton blouse to Sylvia. "You can put these on while I get the rinse and other materials."

Emily returned with a plastic bottle labeled "Sunset Brown," a pan of water, towels, and a blow dryer. She positioned Sylvia on a straight chair and draped a towel around her. "Obviously it's none of my business, but may I ask why you were wearing such a tarty-looking outfit? I've never seen you in anything like that."

Sylvia made a wry face. "I was going to seduce Carlos."

Emily looked startled. "Whatever for?" she asked as she started to dampen Sylvia's hair.

"So he'd let Hank go free."

"Why had Carlos taken Hank?"

"To get information about Peter Burns, a journalist who had material that would expose Carlos and who had escaped from one of Carlos's jails. Hank came to San Lorenzo, looking for Peter. Peter's family was paying Hank." This was still a sore point with her, one she couldn't get over. Now, hearing herself tell Emily, Sylvia realized she had done so with a subconscious purpose—to find out what Emily thought of Hank's behavior.

As for revealing that Hank wasn't a businessman, the head of Americo Import and Export, surely it was a little late to be worrying about *that,* an interior voice said.

From behind her, as she squeezed "Sunset Brown" over Sylvia's hair, Emily said, "Although I never told you because I didn't think it necessary or advisable, Frank made inquiries in certain channels about Hank. There's nothing against him. He's never worked for cruel or dishonest people or repressive governments. I see no harm in Peter's family paying him for his work. Do you?"

Sylvia thought for a while. "No, of course not," she finally said in a low voice. "I didn't really think Hank could have done anything wrong. But—"

"But you wondered." Emily ran her fingers through Sylvia's hair, spreading the tint evenly. "Naturally you wondered. Every woman does about the man she's fallen in love with. I think unconsciously we're looking for the perfect hero, and there ain't no such animal. Or if there is, I've never met him. And at my age I've met *everybody*, my dear."

Emily clicked on the blow dryer, and both women fell silent.

"There, it's done," Emily said finally, "and it looks pretty good if I do say so myself. There's a mirror on the inside of that closet door. Take a look—why don't you?—while I remove this stuff."

Sylvia glanced briefly at her reflection in the mirror. She wasn't greatly interested in hair color at the moment. Her mind was busy with Emily's remark about looking for the perfect hero.

Maybe in that safe, assured time when life was thought of in terms of years, not minutes, she had unconsciously expected that this man who had come to her with personality and character fully developed, stamped with his own unique individuality, should, in some unthought-out way, conform to her expectations. But she no longer did. She loved Hank as he was. She didn't want him to change for her sake.

Still, Sylvia mused, her thoughts progressing logically,

if this life of spying and dangerous secrets, of pursuit and probable death if captured, was Hank's life, how could she possibly share it with him? Even if they had a future, could it be a future together?

Hank entered then, and they looked at each other and laughed.

Fingering the neat little black mustache on his upper lip, Hank asked, "How do you like it?"

"I love it! It makes you look suave, debonair, and smooth."

"Right," Hank drawled. "And it's short so it doesn't get in the soup."

"How do you like me?" Sylvia put one hand to the back of her hair and the other on her hip, and gave Hank a sultry south-of-the-border look.

"Wow! Another gorgeous woman." Hank's eyes softened then. "I love you, Sylvia." He went to her and folded her gently in his arms.

"Oh, Hank!" Sylvia cried. She threw her arms around his neck and pressed her face to his chest.

Hank raised her chin so that her eyes met his. "Ssh, don't cry. All that mascara will run. We'll get out of this, little stranger, just as we got out of Caldera Street."

He kissed her then, pouring all his love and strength into her, promising her with the fierceness of his lips that someday she would know his passion again, holding out to her the delight of laughter-filled nights as he nibbled gently at her earlobe.

He was still holding her, Sylvia's face tucked into the crook of his shoulder like a sheltering bird, his arms protectively around her, when Emily came in.

"It's time to go," she said gently. She handed Hank a wallet full of guaraní notes and the car keys. "You're in luck too. The tank's full. I've put a large Thermos of good hot strong American coffee and some sandwiches on the front seat. As soon as you've gone, I'll put your car in the

Legrandes' garage." She held up one finger as though something had just occurred to her. "Do you have a gun, Hank?"

Hank nodded. "The one I took off the guard."

"Don't you think you'd better leave it here? If you're stopped and searched in a street sweep, you won't stand a chance with a gun on you."

Hank handed the older woman the black service revolver. "Good thinking, Emily."

"How can we ever thank you for all you've done for us?" Sylvia said, her eyes misting over.

Emily smiled. "Send me an invitation to the wedding. But you must go now," she added urgently.

Sylvia bent forward and, placing her hands on Emily's thin shoulders, kissed her cheek.

Emily put her hand out to Hank, who took it in both of his.

"Good-bye, Emily. Play it cool. You and Frank may be questioned, but Carlos won't dare touch you."

Emily's eyes flashed blue as a jay's wing. "Just let him try!"

Sylvia walked out the front door beside Hank. It had been an illusion that she was safe inside the Adamses' house. There was no place in this country that she and Hank were safe. But here out in the open, under the hard blue sky and amid the acid green foliage, she felt hunted, and she was seized by an overwhelming, atavistic impulse to run, to hide anywhere.

Hank gripped her hand. The firmness of his grasp, the confidence in it restored her courage. She pressed his hand and smiled to herself, not realizing he was watching her.

"What are you thinking?" he asked.

"That if anyone could get us out of this mess, you could."

"You'd better believe it!" Hank said heartily.

But as her eyes turned away from him, he grimaced. It would take an army, not one free-lance soldier of fortune, to save them now.

CHAPTER ELEVEN

"Where are we going?" Sylvia asked.

"We're going to try for the airport and hope Carlos doesn't come to and have it covered before we get there."

"And if we don't make it?"

Hank flashed her an insouciant grin. "Then we'll have to play it by ear."

"Sounds like fun," Sylvia said in a deadpan. She stared out at the green fields on both sides of the road. "I don't suppose we'll have time for a picnic."

"Something tells me we won't. I'm hungry, though. Friend Carlos doesn't believe in wasting food on his prisoners. How about handing over one of Emily's sandwiches?"

Sylvia took a Saran-wrapped sandwich out of the bag Emily had given her. "Roast beef on rye okay?"

"With mayo or without?"

"Emily's into nouvelle cuisine. I think it's without." Sylvia unwrapped the sandwich and placed it in his outstretched hand. Their fingers touched, and the electricity that was always there between them came alive. A tingle of love, of desire, of longing for him ran through Sylvia.

She breathed deeply to take in his scent, the warmth from his body, the knowledge that he was actually there beside her when she hadn't thought she would ever again know that solid, comforting joy.

Sylvia watched while he took gargantuan bites, and her heart turned over at the thought that he had actually been hungry, that he had probably passed the night in fear of being hurt, that he had, in fact, actually been manhandled by Carlos's thugs. "Do you think you could manage some of that good hot strong American coffee while you're driving?" she asked tenderly.

"You bet!"

Sylvia poured a cupful out of the Thermos and tasted it. "It's not scalding anyway."

"Aren't you going to eat too?" Hank asked, taking the cup and glancing at her.

"When you're finished. We'll take turns."

"I think maybe you'd better eat now," Hank drawled.

"You mean, like the condemned man ate a hearty supper?"

"I wouldn't go so far as to say *that*, but there seems to be a lot of blue on the horizon."

Sylvia looked out her window. Cars packed with men in horizon blue uniforms were driving slowly in both directions on the highway. Some had pulled over to the side of the road, where the men watched the passing cars through field glasses. "I see what you mean," Sylvia murmured. Her heart had started its painful thumping again. "I take it Sleeping Beauty has awakened."

Hank nodded grimly. "And everyone in his castle."

Sylvia took the half-drained cup of coffee he held out to her. "What was it like, Hank, beyond that door you and the guards came through?"

"It was bad. I don't really want to talk about it."

Sylvia glanced quickly at him. Suddenly he looked grim and shut in upon himself. "I understand, sweetheart, but how did Carlos manage to keep his business and his secret activities separate from each other?"

Hank shrugged. "That part was easy. The walls in the interrogation rooms and cells were completely soundproof, and prisoners were brought into the underground garage in the middle of the night and whisked upstairs in the service elevator. I learned all that while asking questions about Peter; prisoners always have ways of communicating with each other. But forget Carlos. I almost fell over when you said Peter had made it out of the country. It was terrific news. Who told you? Elena?"

Sylvia murmured, "Yes," and gulped nervously. "Is that a roadblock up there ahead of us?" Her voice was faint with the terror she felt. She suddenly realized how flimsy their disguises were. Hank's mustache and her tinted hair wouldn't fool a discerning child, much less men who, with Carlos's customary efficiency, must have been given detailed descriptions of the fugitives.

Hank peered through the windshield at the cars stretched across the road and the armed blue-uniformed men standing by them.

"It's either that or a conclave of campfire girls, and I tend to think it's the former."

"How can Carlos get away with it—blocking an entire road?"

"After a day and a night in one of Carlos's jails I'm beginning to think there isn't much Carlos *can't* get away with," Hank muttered.

"Well, what do we do now?" she demanded nervously.

Hank looked in the rearview mirror. "No one's following us. That means they haven't tumbled to the fact that we're using Emily's car. There's a dirt road up ahead that leads off from the highway, probably to a farm. I'm going to turn off there. I'll slow down, though, and wait till traffic bunches together a little. That'll give this flock of bluebirds more to watch."

Hank eased up on the accelerator and kept pace with the cars around him. Then he steered Emily's little car off the highway and onto a red dirt road.

The car was immediately dwarfed on both sides by ten-foot-high stalks of sugarcane topped by feathery, rosy silver tassels that waved in the warm breeze.

"Wow!" Hank exclaimed. "You couldn't ask for a better hiding place."

"But all good things come to an end. What do we do after we run out of sugarcane?"

"The river's that way." Hank jerked his chin forward. "Remember the rental boats we saw tied up along it when we took the steamer upriver?"

"Rowboats and river canoes, some with outboards."

"Well, we're going to get ourselves one. I think Carlos will concentrate on the highway instead of the river."

"I agree. And then?"

Hank glanced at her and smiled. "You ask a lot of embarrassing questions for a beautiful woman, don't you?"

"I'm trying to figure out when I'll get to eat my sandwich."

"You can eat it now or save it for the boat trip. I think we're in clover, or at least sugarcane. *If* we can get our hands on a boat and *if* Carlos isn't having the river watched, we should be able to sail all the way to Brazil."

"Umm. I hear there's lots of coffee in Brazil. Maybe I'll eat my sandwich then." Sylvia looked at the green forest of sugarcane. "Whoever owns this little plantation certainly isn't bothering with it."

"They're late in harvesting it. The cane should be cut before the flowers appear."

"How much you know!" Sylvia feigned wide-eyed admiration.

"Keep it up," Hank answered with a grin. "My ego doesn't make fine distinctions. Ah, here are the willing workers. They're starting down there, at the far end of the field."

As the car bumped along on the rutted road, Sylvia looked where Hank was pointing. Almost lost in a bright red dirt furrow between two rows of tall green plants was a line of *campesinos* in wide-brimmed straw hats and thin, long-sleeved cotton shirts that clung to their stooped backs in the damp heat like a second whiter skin.

"I hope they like us," Sylvia said as the car drew closer to the row of sugarcane the men were cutting. "Look at the size of those knives."

Each cutter had a large steel knife with a blade about five inches wide and eighteen inches long with a hook on the back. As Hank slowed down, Sylvia watched the men move mechanically down the row, cutting the cane close to the ground. They stripped off the leaves with the hook, cut off the top of the stalk at the last joint, and threw the cut stalks onto heaps to be gathered up later.

"Uh-oh," Sylvia murmured suddenly. "Here comes Mr. McGregor, and we're in his lettuce patch."

A swarthy, barrel-shaped man dressed in tight khaki pants and a white shirt that ballooned out over his belly strode belligerently out of one of the furrows toward the car. A rifle nestled in the crook of his arm. As the car slowed and stopped, he took the gun and pointed it at the windshield.

"This is private property, senor," he said grimly.

"Put on the silly American act," Hank whispered to Sylvia. He leaned out the window and yelled, "Sorry, but we're lost. We're looking for the river."

"You understand Guaraní, senor?" The small eyes narrowed to slits in the fat cheeks.

Hank pointed to the rifle and answered in Spanish. "I understand guns, senor."

Sylvia joined the conversation from her window. "I'm afraid it's all my fault, senor. I've never seen sugarcane growing before. When we saw your road, we thought we'd enter just a little ways. Then we couldn't turn around without damaging your valuable plants, and of course, we didn't want to do that. We're from Iowa back home. Have you ever been there? We don't have sugarcane, but we grow a lot of corn. I think as a farmer you'd find some of our hybrid experiments very interesting." She rattled on in Spanish with an ear-piercing American accent, hardly paying attention to what she said, unleashing a torrent of pseudoscientific details on the plantation owner.

It worked. With a muttered oath of exasperation the man lifted his rifle and waved them on. "The river is straight ahead. Half a mile."

As he shifted gears and the car lurched forward again, Hank shot Sylvia an admiring look. "You were terrific. Mr. McGregor couldn't have stood another minute of that."

Sylvia smiled back at him. "Aren't you glad you brought me along?"

"Just wait till I get you on that slow boat to Brazil."

"Not too slow, I hope."

"No complaining, please. So far everything's gone just great."

But it was whistling in the dark, Hank thought. All this joking to keep their courage up. It would take every bit of his skill and wits to get them to a safe place. And even that wouldn't be enough. What they needed mostly was luck.

And luck was still with them, Hank decided, when they got out of the car and looked down on the river from the low bluff above it. For a time at least.

"There's our ship," Sylvia said, pointing to the rusty funnel with the Maltese cross and the name *Cruz de Malta* painted on the side. The steamer had docked at a boat landing, where the usual tableau of vendors and passengers was being enacted. "Could we sail upriver on the steamer?"

"Too risky and too slow. What I have in mind is our own boat. Look there!" He pointed to a small school of rowboats tied up and bobbing on the pale coffee brown water.

"We're *rowing* to Brazil?" Sylvia's voice was dramatic with disbelief.

"We're going fishing. That's what the boats are being rented for. According to the sign on that shack, the guy sells tackle and bait. And there's an outboard motor in the bottom of one of them. I can see it from here. We need an occupation, an excuse for being on the river, and fishing will give it to us."

"What will happen when we don't return the boat?"

"Killjoy! We'll be in Brazil by then. Don't worry, I'll get the boat back to its owner when we're finished with it. Right now I'm going to drive the car as far as it'll go in this wooded area and leave it."

He opened the car door and took out Emily's Thermos and the lunch bag. "Keep these. They'll give us a bona fide look, as well as feed us."

When he rejoined Sylvia after parking and locking the car, she said, "Don't you think the boat owner will be suspicious of us, a pair of gringos going fishing this far from civilization?"

"That's exactly *why* we're going fishing here—for adventure." Hank waggled an eyebrow at her, and Sylvia laughed.

"Yeah, right," she answered, and took his hand as they scrambled down the hill.

The whole transaction—for the boat, bait, and fishing tackle—was completed quickly. "How about selling us an extra can of gasoline?" Hank asked the boat owner, a brown-skinned mestizo with high, flat cheekbones. "In case we feel adventurous and want to fish way upriver. Or is there a village farther along where we can buy supplies?"

The man shrugged. "There is no village farther up the river. The next one is the last one." He looked at Hank and Sylvia shrewdly. "Gasoline is very expensive here. But if you *have* to go farther, of course, you will not mind paying for it."

He watched greedily while Hank built a tower of guaranis in his palm.

Before the boat owner's fist closed over the wad, Hank pulled out more bills and added them to the others. "There'll be the same number of these when we come back this way," Hank said.

The man waved the hand holding the bills in the air. "It is clear that you'll come back, senor."

As the boatman left to get the extra gasoline, Sylvia said, "Something tells me he didn't buy that two gringos fishing for adventure bit you fed him."

Hank grunted. "I'm hoping our gringo gold will persuade him not to tell Carlos's river village spies about us."

With a jerri can of gasoline in the boat their provisioning was complete. As they shot away from shore, the noisy rumble of the engine brought passengers on the *Cruz de Malta* to the railings.

"I wonder if the man in the tan suit is there," Sylvia mused aloud. "Maybe the *Maltese Cross* is his regular beat."

"A floating boondocks for foul-ups," Hank said absentmindedly. If one of Carlos's spies *was* on the steamer, a radioed message could bring a cutter full of armed men surging through the water at them in no time.

All they could do now was put as much distance as possible between them and Carlos and hope for the best.

They steered a straight course upriver, passing strips of dense green jungle that suddenly opened up to vast green savannas with rolling hills in the background. Villages of thatch-roofed huts appeared here and there, and the putt-putt of their motor brought people crowding to the riverbanks to look and wave.

The air even on the river was warm, thick, heavy, sluggish. And the sun in the open boat burned their skins like a branding iron.

When he considered it safe, Hank said, "Let's get out of this for a while," and steered the boat into the shade of some overhanging trees. They passed Emily's Thermos of coffee back and forth between them and ate what was left of her sandwiches.

"Any ideas about what you want for dinner?" Hank asked. "We're stopping at the next hamlet for a Thermos refill and some food to take along."

"How about lobster salad and a chilled white wine?"

"Will you settle for a beef sandwich on manioc bread and yerba maté tea?"

Sylvia nodded and wiped the sweat from her face with her arm. "If there's candlelight and music to go with them." She cupped her hands and leaned over the edge of the boat to splash her face with river water.

Water still dripping through her fingers, she froze. With a whir that sounded like the wings of a gigantic mechanical insect, a helicopter beat the air directly above them.

The noise seemed to penetrate to the very center of her skull. She had to fight the impulse to throw herself flat in the bottom of the boat and fold her arms over her head.

"Don't panic," Hank said calmly. "He can't see us. It's lucky we pulled in when we did. And if he does get a glimpse of us, we'll just be two people fishing."

Quickly but deliberately Hank baited the two fishing lines and handed one to Sylvia. They cast over the side of the boat and waited.

"If we catch one, you're going to have to take it off the hook," Sylvia said.

"If we catch one, I'm throwing it back."

"To propitiate the river god or because you don't like fish?" *Keep it light, keep it cool,* Sylvia thought, *no matter how hard your heart is beating.*

Hank didn't answer. All his energies were focused on listening to the helicopter.

Finally, when the roar had subsided to a distant pulsing, Hank said, "He's turning back." He pulled in his line and Sylvia's and started the engine. "Let's get going. We'll stop for supplies soon, then spend the night where we can."

The sun was low in the sky when the village came in sight, and the air was perceptibly, if barely, cooler.

"Ah, the usual welcoming crowd," Hank said, tying up at a tree stump sticking out of the water. A line of villagers stood watching silently from the riverbank.

"These people aren't waving, Hank."

"They're probably thinking, *There goes the neighborhood.*"

"Well, tell them it's not my kind of town anyway," Sylvia muttered, looking at the one-room windowless houses with thatch roofs.

They got out of the boat, and the crowd parted to let them pass. The children smiled shyly at Hank's greetings, called out in Guaraní. The women, in simple long-sleeved cotton dresses and cloth turbans wound around their heads, stared with sullen expressions on their broad, passive faces.

What was odd about the scene, Hank thought, was the presence of so many men in the usual *campesino* garb of wide-brimmed straw hats and cotton shirts and pants. Why weren't they still in their fields at this time?

He didn't like the looks of it. They were pretty far upriver, isolated from any larger town, and these people seemed more hostile than curious.

For a moment Hank considered going back to the boat with Sylvia, but it was always a bad idea to turn your back to a crowd like this. So he held the large Thermos up confidently and asked where he could get some yerba maté tea and some bread and beef.

One man answered first, the others furnishing a chorus, and Hank marked him as the leader. He looked to be almost pure Guaraní Indian and was tall and broadly built with a powerful chest.

He pointed to a dirt road behind him. Hank motioned to the Guaraní and the others to precede Sylvia and him. With the Guaraní in the lead, the crowd turned and moved forward up the red dirt road, flowing across it and engulfing it amoebalike.

"You're very polite," Sylvia said lightly, folding her fingers inside Hank's big hand. It was comforting just to touch him. It gave her an immediate sensation of being safe, of assurance that somehow he would pull them through.

"I didn't want them behind us, making off with the outboard motor."

"All joking aside, I'm not crazy about this situation, Hank. Since they're in front of us, why don't *we* make off, *using* the outboard?"

He squeezed her hand reassuringly. "Because even though they're in front, they're watching us." He didn't want to say it, but he sensed that they were the crowd's prisoners, that if they turned and ran back to the river, the crowd would turn into a mob, led by the Guaraní, and that mob would be in howling pursuit of them.

So they trudged along in the wake of the crowd, in a fine cloud of red dust, to a small stucco building—a palace compared to the thatch-roofed mud-and-wattle dwellings—where the villagers stationed themselves on both sides of an open door.

"It's like a military wedding," Sylvia said brightly.

"They're probably waiting to carry our packages for us," Hank answered.

Still holding hands, they passed between the lines of murmuring dark-eyed watchers and entered the building. The floor was dirt; the only light came from the setting sun outside. Rows of roughhewn shelves had been nailed to the wall. They held flyspecked cans of food, their labels yellow and peeling; bolts of cloth in the prints the women's dresses were made of; and a jumbled assortment of pots and cheap dishes, umbrellas, and articles of clothing. A crate of pineapples rested on the floor. A refrigerator, its white enamel chipped and rusted, stood against the wall behind the wooden counter. A curtain of print cloth hung in a doorway where a heavy quebracho door with a modern lock stood open.

An elderly man sat on a high stool, his elbows resting on the counter, his pale blue eyes behind steel-rimmed spectacles fixed on Hank and Sylvia. His thinning hair, neatly combed over a pink, almost bald head, was a graying blond. His fair, thin skin was freckled and ruddy. A long-healed thin scar crossed the right cheekbone.

He spoke first.

"Good afternoon. Madame, sir? Monsieur, madame? Mein Herr, gnädige Fray? Which is it?"

Only the German was pronounced without an accent, Hank noticed.

"We're Americans," Hank explained. "We're doing a little fishing on the river and need some supplies. The friendly villagers led us to your store."

The storekeeper laughed, a thin, brittle sound that crackled against the rumble of whispers from outside the door. A gold tooth on the upper right side of his mouth flashed in the sun.

"The *friendly* villagers. That's very good. The *brutish* villagers are *trained* to bring everyone to my store. Not that we get many visitors, we're too far upriver for that, and certainly not tourists or"—he hesitated meaningfully—"fishermen."

"Then how do you survive, if I may ask?" Hank said politely. "Economically, I mean."

The man waved his arm around the dim interior. "This is a company store. I grow pineapples. My plantation is a little inland from here. The men of the village work for me."

"And the families buy all their goods from you," Hank said.

The storekeeper bowed his pink head to indicate yes. That explained the villagers' poverty-stricken, mean looks, Hank thought. They worked this guy's pineapple plantation for low wages and paid high prices in the only store for miles around.

"Well," Hank said briskly, "I guess we'd better do our shopping before the sun goes down. May we just go around and help ourselves?"

"There's no need to hurry. We have electricity here. I have my own generator naturally." He turned to Sylvia. "I have a fan too. Would you like me to turn it on? I've gotten accustomed to the heat. It doesn't bother me." He touched his finger to his scar. "But I have to stay out of the sun. It makes cancers on my skin," he explained. He glanced at Sylvia's green eyes and fair complexion and smiled. "We members of the northern races don't belong in the tropics."

Sylvia ignored the remark. There was something repulsive about the man that had nothing to do with the scar on his cheek. She would have said there was an emanation of evil from him, except that it would have sounded overblown and melodramatic.

A fan would be a relief in the hot, stale atmosphere, but she sensed that nothing extraneous, nothing that would delay their departure should be introduced into the situation. So she said decisively, "I would like to be on the river before the sun goes completely down. I hear the sunsets are beautiful here. So if we may get our supplies now . . ." She held the large Thermos out. "Could you fill this with hot yerba maté, please? And we'll need some fruit, manioc bread, cheese, and dried beef jerky if you have them."

"My wife will get those things for you," the elderly storekeeper said. "And while she's doing it, please have a glass of iced maté with me. The water has been boiled, by the way. It's so seldom that I get the chance to talk with people of my own kind."

Of what "kind" was his wife then? Sylvia wondered.

The man clapped his thin, wrinkled hands, mottled with the dark liver spots of age.

Immediately a slender young girl, her face a light copper color, her hair a dark river falling straight to her shoulders, pushed the print curtain aside and entered the store. A belt around her simple cotton dress held a bunch of keys that jingled lightly as she walked. And Sylvia wondered if they didn't also serve to let her husband know at all times where she was.

The girl stood, barefoot and graceful in front of the storekeeper, her dark, deep-set eyes expressionless, her face passively stoic. At the oldest she was sixteen. And she was exotically beautiful.

Sylvia's stomach churned with disgust. She heard Hank draw his breath in sharply and knew his reaction was the same as hers.

The man issued some orders to the young girl in a clipped Guaraní that gutturalized the liquid vowels. Then he got down from the high stool and came out from behind the counter.

Holding himself at attention, *almost* clicking his heels, the storekeeper said, "Allow me to introduce myself. I am Otto Lang, third-generation Paraguayan. My family immigrated in 1900," he added proudly.

Hank bowed to Lang's wife, who had not been introduced, and gave Lang a casual nod of acknowledgment. "We appreciate your offer of tea, Mr. Lang, but we won't have time for it. We'll leave as soon as our supplies are ready." He pulled out his wallet. "Can you start totaling it up now?"

Lang smiled apologetically. "Lisa—the name I gave her—is slow. I really must insist that you be my guests while you wait." He waved his hand toward the curtain and smiled at Sylvia. "Please."

Was it her imagination, Sylvia wondered, or did the rustle of voices outside increase in volume, creating an audible pressure to remind them that the villagers were still there?

Lisa wasn't going from shelf to shelf, picking up supplies either. She was standing watching Lang. What orders had he really given his young wife? Sylvia wondered. The storekeeper's rapid, accented Guaraní had been incomprehensible to her. Sylvia glanced at Hank. Had *he* understood more?

With a slight movement of one burly shoulder Hank indicated acceptance. There was no way out. They'd have to go along with the storekeeper's invitation. And Sylvia walked past the print curtain Lang held open.

The change was startling. She stepped into a room that was carpeted and crowded with heavy pieces of overstuffed furniture, marble-topped tables, floor lamps with tasseled shades. It was like stepping back into a prior time. When? Sylvia asked herself. Remembering old movies, she guessed the 1930s and probably Europe.

"Do you like it?" Lang asked. "As one gets older, one becomes nostalgic for the ambience of one's youth." He waved his hand at the contents of the room. "It took a little searching, but I finally found the objects I wanted and had them shipped here."

"This is third-generation Paraguayan?" Hank asked dryly.

Lang was quick with his answer. "I have never hidden my German ancestry. My home is in the style of the European middle class." He shrugged contemptuously. "The store is for the natives."

"Speaking of natives, how come so many men are just idling around, not working?" Hank asked.

"Workers get cocky when there's full employment. Surely you've noticed that in your own country. There's no shortage of labor here, so for my workers' own good I 'manage' employment, so to speak, on my pineapple plantation. That way everyone has enough for survival but not enough to cause trouble for me . . . and therefore for themselves."

"*Manipulate* would be a better word than *manage,* I think," Hank said. "You use forced periodic unemployment to keep your workers submissive, so what you have, in effect, is a pool of slave labor."

His shot in the dark had hit, Hank noticed. Lang's sandy lashes blinked nervously over his pale blue eyes. He turned abruptly away from Hank and to Sylvia. Indicating a green velour-covered chair, he said, "Please."

With a glance at Hank, Sylvia sat down. Hank sat opposite her. His mind was busy putting two and two together. Lang's age, just right for the Nazi era and World War II. His German origins. The fact that he had holed himself up in a remote river village in South America. The scar on his cheek; the SS, the Nazis' infamous elite corps, had its own code in which dueling was allowed.

For a moment Hank let his imagination clothe a younger, stronger Lang from head to foot in black—a black cap bearing a silver death's-head, a black tunic over a brown shirt with black leather buttons, and black tie, black breeches, and black jackboots.

It all added up, Hank thought. And if he was right, it

was quite possible that the nostalgic Otto Lang had kept a souvenir from his days of glory, a souvenir it might be worthwhile to find.

"Lisa will bring our tea now." Lang walked to the doorway and clapped his hands.

"And our supplies," Hank called after him.

"Of course," Lang replied.

While the storekeeper's back was turned, Sylvia looked inquiringly at Hank.

He frowned and shook his head to show his worry. "Be careful," he mouthed.

That was silly, he thought. To be careful, you had to have a choice of action. There was none here. Although they could no longer hear the murmurs of the crowd outside, the people—or at least the men—were still there, he was sure.

For whatever reason, they were prisoners of Otto Lang. Was the man possibly demented, perhaps senile, and so eager for company that he would force travelers to stay?

Or had he guessed that Hank and Sylvia were fugitives, and was he holding them for a reward? Perhaps from Carlos, Hank thought. It was logical to assume, considering the man in the tan suit on the *Cruz de Malta,* that Carlos's network of spies extended this far.

Lisa passed through the room, eyes shyly down, on her way to what was evidently the kitchen. The house was built like a railroad flat, one room opening off into the next. From its size Hank figured it contained, in all, three rooms and a bath.

Without any preamble Hank stood up abruptly and announced, "I'm going to use your bathroom, Mr. Lang."

Lang half rose from his seat. "I'll show you where it is."

"Not necessary," Hank said in a bluff, hearty tone. "You stay there with my wife. I'm sure she has a lot of questions to ask you about the furnishings."

Hank grinned as he turned his back on the pair. He could hear Sylvia behind him. "Is any of your furniture a modern adaptation of Biedermeier? I've heard of Biedermeier furniture," she prattled on, "but I'm afraid I don't know much about it. Could you . . ."

Her voice faded. He was in the bedroom now. He flicked his eye over the massive double bed, the fancy veneered bureau, the landscapes of pine forests and cloud-topped mountains on the walls.

What he was looking for would be hidden, but it would be there. Lang was a transparent example of his type. He would have kept at least one sentimental souvenir, one reminder of his true identity, one denial of the fact that he was just an old village storekeeper in a third-rate country.

But what?

The silver death's-head signet ring worn by SS commanders? Or the even more elitist SS dagger, granted only to men of higher rank?

Lang's air of authority and his obvious intelligence led Hank to decide upon the dagger.

But he had no time to search for it. Lang was in the room behind him; Lisa in the kitchen in front.

Lisa! Lang wouldn't bother to hide his Nazi past from a Guaraní Indian girl. She shared his bed, poor thing. Lisa would know.

Hank passed quickly into the kitchen. The slender, nubile young woman was pouring maté from a pitcher into three glasses on a tray.

Hank smiled. "Your husband wants me to see his knife, the one in the bedroom," he said in Guaraní. "Can you tell me where it is?"

She looked at him blankly. *She knows I'm lying,* Hank thought. *When has Lang ever wanted to show his precious dagger to anyone?*

Hank ran his eyes over her gracefully curved body. *But she hates Lang. She must. How could it be otherwise? Her family must have sold her, and instead of being loved by a strong young man of her choice, she has to submit to God knows what acts the old Nazi imposes on her.*

"I need to see it," Hank said softly, his eyes holding hers in a compassionate look. "No harm will come to you, I promise."

The stubborn, impassive expression vanished. The girl's eyes suddenly flashed with fire. A moment's rebellion could be hers. Instantly, decisively she put the pitcher down and glided silently into the bedroom.

Hank followed and watched her every move, at the same time keeping the doorway in his line of peripheral vision. He had promised that she would come to no harm, and he meant to keep that promise.

Lisa opened the central one of three drawers in the shiny bureau. She beckoned to Hank. When he was beside her, she pressed the wooden back of the drawer. A panel slid open.

The niche had been lined with black velvet. A slim black object rested on the cloth. Hank took it out. It was a cheap leather scabbard. The treasure was inside.

Hank slowly slid out a gleaming steel dagger. Its cross guard bore the dread death's-head of the SS.

He turned it over in his hands, wondering at any man's deliberately choosing the dedication to evil it symbolized. Then he felt Lisa's soft fingers on his. She took the dagger from him and quickly replaced it in its scabbard and its hiding place.

She caught up with him a minute later as he was about to reenter the living room. She was carrying the tray of glasses.

"I offered to help her," Hank boomed out heartily. "But she wouldn't let me."

"One doesn't help servants," Lang said dryly.

Lang was dangerous to them. Hank knew that now. A high-ranking SS officer, he was undoubtedly a Nazi war criminal who had fled retribution by going to South America. Protected by Carlos, he ran his pineapple plantation as he wished, using his workers almost as forced labor.

It was obvious he was going to keep them there. No one had gotten the supplies Hank ordered. The tea and conversation were just to lull his prisoners' suspicions, to make it easier to hold them.

But if force had to be resorted to, it was there, in the crowd outside, Lang's workers, totally dependent upon him for the manioc bread they ate every day.

Sylvia and he would have to get away somehow before Carlos and his men arrived because Hank didn't doubt that Carlos would want to be in on this "kill," the capture of the man and woman who had outwitted him.

Taking off from the tea she was drinking, Sylvia was now quizzing Lang about the growing habits of the yerba tree and other plant life of the country. Hank shot her a look of approval. She picked it up and answered with a slight lowering of her eyelids and a faint smile.

And as the conversation droned on, with Sylvia asking question after question and the flattered storekeeper answering, Hank planned their escape from SS Oberführer Otto Lang—or whatever his name and rank had been—and his mob outside.

He looked around at the nearly empty glasses of iced tea. An old man's kidneys were weak. Whom would Lang call in to guard his prisoners while he went to the bathroom to relieve himself? Not one of the men outside, Hank thought. That would be too blatant and might alarm the prisoners.

Lang would probably summon Lisa. And Lisa was already Hank's friend.

Hank raised his glass. "May I have another glass of iced tea, please? Sylvia, how about you? You must join us, Mr. Lang. A good host never lets his guests drink alone."

With a smug smile—who could ask for stupider, more amenable prisoners than these?—Lang clapped his hands for Lisa.

And the tea party went on.

CHAPTER TWELVE

Hank smiled to himself as the old Nazi fidgeted in his seat and glanced toward the kitchen where Lisa was. His third glass of iced Paraguayan tea rested on the table beside him.

Finally the storekeeper made a decision. He got to his feet, clapped his hands for Lisa, and waited, shifting his weight nervously from one foot to the other.

When Lisa entered with her usual graceful, unhurried walk, Lang barked an order at her in Guaraní and bolted out of the room.

Hank rose immediately. He took Sylvia's hands in his and pulled her to her feet.

"Let's go, sweetheart. We're leaving our host without saying good-bye."

Sylvia glanced toward the Guaraní girl, her dark eyes inscrutably fixed on them.

"I think Lisa's on our side," Hank said softly. He spoke in a rapid, almost fluent Guaraní to the Indian girl. A smile brightened her features, and she nodded a yes.

Sylvia's hand flew to her mouth in horror as Hank suddenly swerved and hit Lisa on the jaw. He caught the girl's limp body in his arms as it fell and laid her gently on the floor.

"She agreed to let us escape, but we don't have time to tie her up," Hank explained. "It was the only way I could think of to protect her from Lang when he comes back and . . ."

He didn't finish the sentence. He saw the question in her eyes and knew their thoughts had led them both to the same conclusion, the logical one in their situation—to grab Lang and hold him hostage for their safe passage through the crowd. But then what would they do with Lang?

Would Hank commit the ultimate act and kill the old man? Sylvia's eyes seemed to ask. Did even he, the man she loved, do such things, so common in his profession?

"And finds us gone," Hank added.

He bent down and unsnapped the ring of keys from Lisa's belt. When they left the room, he locked the heavy door behind them. Then, holding the key ring with one hand, he grasped Sylvia's hand firmly with the other.

They stood for a moment in the store, listening to the voices outside. The unending drone filled the dark interior like the muttered threats of malevolent old crones.

Sylvia felt her heart lurch with unreasonable, superstitious dread. She tightened her grip on Hank's hand.

"Spooky, isn't it?" he said, and she could hear the grin in his voice.

Her apprehension grew as they stepped to the doorway and she looked out on the mob massed outside. There were no longer any children and very few women in the crowd—a bad sign.

Sylvia wondered what Hank planned to do. There hadn't been time for him to tell her. What *could* he do?

The whispering stopped as the brown, woodenlike faces turned to them. There was no hostility, no curiosity, not even surprise. The eyes were dark voids; the features, blank.

The mob was simply there, as the river was always there, or the jungle. If she and Hank took one step forward away from the doorway into that mass of people, they would be swallowed up as the river and the jungle indifferently took in its victims and, according to Lang's orders, either spit out to be returned to him or stomped to death by the anonymous herd.

Hank raised the key ring high in the air so that everyone could see it. He waited till the whispering, which had started again, stopped, till the only sound was the dry crackling of the palm fronds as they rubbed against each other in the breeze from the river.

Then he said, speaking slowly and emphatically in Guaraní, "Senor Lang is locked in. The store is yours."

Sylvia watched comprehension move ponderously across the rigid faces. An avaricious gleam lit the dark eyes of a few, then spread like wildfire from one stoic face to the next. The crowd moved forward with the inexorable sweep of the tide. Hank put his arm around Sylvia's waist and pulled her away seconds before the first looters squeezed through the narrow doorway.

"Let's go before that mob changes its mind or Lang gets to them and they start chasing us."

They stayed off the dirt road now and filtered their way through the jungle to the river. They came to a thicket of bamboo that the villagers had evidently been thinning, for numerous shoots lay on the ground. They stopped in its densest part and stared glumly ahead of them. The boat was there, but the outboard motor was gone.

Hank glanced up the river. It was the quickest way out of the country and therefore the first place Lang's Indians or Carlos's men would search for them. He looked across at the jungle on the opposite side. It would take their enemies awhile to figure that he and Sylvia would actually tackle the Gran Chaco and its thousands of miles of "Green Hell" in order to get to Bolivia. So, tough as the terrain was, it was the way they would have to take.

"As soon as it's dark enough," he said, "we're going to try to get the boat and cross the river to the other side. We'll be going into the Chaco then. There should be enough water in the streams to keep us going a fair distance by boat. Then we'll just have to hoof it. We're going to hide now and hope that the looters find enough in the store to keep themselves busy for the next hour or so."

"It didn't look like Bergdorf's to me," Sylvia said.

Hank grinned. He touched her lightly on the arm and said, "C'mon."

From the silence in the village behind them it was evident that everyone had gone to the looting party. Hank led Sylvia back into the jungle. They walked, staying parallel with the river, looking for a hiding place, till Hank suddenly brought her to an abrupt stop in the tangled undergrowth. His grip on her arm bit like iron, but Sylvia hardly felt the pain. Like Hank, she was listening with an acuteness of concentration that was almost painful.

There was someone behind them, someone who was practiced in stealth, in tracking in silence, in avoiding all the sounds a man made in the jungle.

Nonetheless, the whispery sound of dirt and leaves yielding to the pressure of feet, the displacement of air as a body or bodies moved through it were transmitted to them as they stood holding their breaths.

With all her senses on edge, her nerves quivering to ensure her survival, Sylvia followed Hank as he started moving through the jungle again. She ordered her muscles into their dance mode, making her body featherlight, her balance sure. But still the sounds behind them continued, stopping when they did, then resuming.

Where the jungle dipped right down to the river, forming an undulating green border for a series of little coves and inlets in the grayish brown stream, Hank motioned to Sylvia to follow him. He plucked several broad reeds from the riverbank and, handing some to her, demonstrated what he was about to do.

Then, holding one of the reeds upright, he slipped into the water and immersed himself completely. Seconds later Sylvia saw a pool of bubbles break the surface of the water.

She followed him into the river, letting herself sink until her feet touched the mud bottom. Adjusting the hollow reed so that one end was in her mouth and the other just cleared the water, she commenced to use it as a breathing tube.

Time seemed endless in that uncomfortable position. She was saturated with the river's chill. Her very bones felt cold and wet.

Then Hank put a warning hand on her arm. She saw him surface. A few minutes later he reached down and pulled her up out of the water.

"We fooled 'em that time," he said. "Whoever was following us is gone. It's dark now. Let's see if we can get that boat."

"And if we can't?" Sylvia said, shivering.

"We'll have to swim across the river underwater."

"You've got to be kidding!"

As they followed the river back to the boat, the voices of the villagers were loud in the still air.

"Ah, the happy looters have returned," Hank said.

"Do you think they freed Lang?"

"I have an idea they'll wait until morning. There was beer in the store. They'll probably party all night, then let the old bastard out. What more can he do to them than he's already done?"

"Who was he, Hank, really?"

"Undoubtedly a Nazi war criminal who escaped to South America, as many of them did. I found his cute little SS dagger in his bedroom, or rather his poor slave, Lisa, found it for me. He had the SS dueling scar. He flinched when I mentioned slave labor—"

"What's his connection to Carlos, if any?" Sylvia asked.

"He's almost surely under Carlos's protection."

"And reports to Carlos."

"Right," Hank drawled. "That's why we've got to hope we can get across the Chaco."

"Hope?"

"Part of it's forested, but a lot of it's open ground."

And Carlos has a helicopter, Sylvia thought. *But first things first,* she told herself. Like getting away from Otto Lang.

They reached the boat, still tied to its tree stump.

"If they kept the boat, they must have kept the oars," Hank muttered as he felt around in the bottom of the boat. "Where the hell are they?"

"Maybe they hid them just in case we *did* get back to the boat."

"It doesn't matter." Hank straightened up. "Poling would be better, anyway, both in the swamps of the Chaco and for crossing the river, which is full of sandbars at this point. The river's low enough so that you can just about see them. Wait here. I'll be right back."

Standing there in the dark with the stars so close that they seemed to be pressing down on her, Sylvia listened to the bursts of laughter and drunken shouts from the village. The noise would drown out any sounds she and Hank might make, but it was also frightening. A drunken mob would be completely out of control.

A dark shape suddenly loomed up in the darkness beside her. Sylvia jumped and without thinking started to scream. A warm hand clamped itself across her mouth.

"It's me, Sylvia," Hank whispered, taking his hand away. "I had to stop you from screaming."

Sylvia took a deep breath. "You did right, Hank. I was all set to hit high C."

"I got two poles from some of that fallen bamboo. We can shove off now."

Sylvia took one of the bamboo poles and climbed into the boat, while Hank groped around in the dark until he got the anchoring rope untied. Then he jumped in and, using a pole, pushed the boat away from the riverbank.

The trip across the river seemed to take an eternity. In the black night they kept striking the numerous sandbars. They went aground once, and it took all of Hank's strength to get them off again. Worse, tree stumps sharpened by the current and floating quebracho logs threatened to tear a hole in the boat or stave in the side.

When they finally reached the opposite bank, they were exhausted and Sylvia was shivering dangerously.

"We're going to have to get out of these clothes and sleep," Hank said, "or we won't be able to go on."

They looked across the river at the fires burning on the opposite bank.

"You don't think they've set fire to the store with Lang and Lisa in it, do you?" Sylvia asked in a horrified voice.

"No. They wouldn't dare do anything to Lang. For one thing, they'd be afraid of the authorities. For another, he's their bread and butter, meager as it is. They're probably celebrating, that's all. But one thing we can be sure of: No one is going to bother us till morning."

Sylvia looked around at the strip of sandy riverbank backed by the dark, looming jungle beyond.

"I've seen better hotels," she said.

"But not quieter ones. No elevators, no drunken conventioneers. Why don't we pull the boat up off the beach so it won't be seen, just in case?"

As they dragged the boat into the jungle, Sylvia listened to Hank's ragged, hoarse breathing. He had started shivering too.

"Let's undress, Hank, or we'll end up with a tropical

fever. The air's warm enough. It's just being wet that's bad." She started unbuttoning his shirt.

Hank chuckled. "That's what I like, a sexy woman. Nothing stops her—not drunken natives, not Nazi war criminals, an open-air hotel. *Nothing!*"

"Ssh, this is medicinal."

Sylvia spread all their wet clothes out on the ground to dry and stood for a moment listening. The jungle was silent, but she could feel its teeming life all around her. "I'll tell you one thing about this hotel. It gets four stars for loneliness."

There was no answer.

"Hank?" Her voice trembled between a whisper and a scream.

A loud, rattling snore came out of the darkness, and Sylvia laughed with relief. Then the snoring stopped as Hank was seized by a spasm of shivering. Only body warmth could save them now. Sylvia lay down on the leafy ground and pressed herself close to him till his strong body was still and she fell into a deep, dreamless sleep.

She woke up to a finger of light, the pale gold of earliest morning, reaching down from between the trees. Luxuriating in the sensation of being warm and well rested, she stretched out in Hank's arms.

The lapping of Hank's wiry hair against her breast as his chest rose and fell set up a tide of physical longing for him. She ran her hand down his side lingeringly, feeling the silkiness of his skin with her fingertips, letting its allure thrill all her senses, then palming the bold contours of the muscles underneath.

She reached around him and cupped his small, firm buttocks. Then she trailed her hand down the back of his sinewy thigh.

Hank groaned and opened his eyes. "Can't a guy sleep in his own jungle bedroom?"

Sylvia wound her arms around Hank's bare torso. "Not

when there are Indians on the other side of the river, and you're the only cowboy around."

"Thanks for the compliment," Hank said laconically. "I suppose the boat's our covered wagon."

Sylvia nuzzled his strong, corded neck. "Umm. Better hurry before the arrows start flying."

"Loving you is one thing I never want to hurry." Hank raised her lips to his and drank all their morning sweetness from them. His hands molded her bare shoulders, then swept down her back, curving around the firm globes of her derriere. "I have to know that you're here, still here," he said huskily, "that nothing happened to you during the night, that nothing ever will happen to you."

"I know how you feel, Hank," she said wistfully. "I feel the same way."

It was true. Their lives were so precarious now that mere survival had become the unexpected, the miraculous event. Just seeing Hank, feeling the solidity of his flesh, knowing he was there were a phenomenon full of joy, but one that held no assurance of being repeated.

The knowledge that they might not see tomorrow gave their lovemaking a poignant desperation that heightened their wild abandonment to their desire for each other. If these moments were to be their last, they would be islands of pleasure, of joy and laughter in the dangerous sea they were drifting in.

Hank hugged her to him, holding her fiercely to his long, lean body, his hands pressing her close to his pulsing need. The touch of his flesh against her smooth skin jolted the knot of coiled desire within Sylvia into a glorious ball of fire hurtling itself across the vaulted sky of her longing.

She whimpered, and he kissed her softly, asking her without words to wait just a little. Taking her cue from him, she relaxed, and inserting her hands between his back and the ground, she explored his firm muscles and strong, straight spine. Then she stopped.

"Do you have an extra vertebra?" she asked, laughing.

Hank reached behind him. "I think it's a stone," he answered with a chuckle, flinging it from him.

He reached up then and caught her breasts in the palms of his hands like ripe fruit. Pulling at each erotic bud with his lips, he hardened it into a life-giving seed.

His palms worked their way down to her midriff and rounded her hips. Then his sensitive fingertips took over to stroke the tender flesh of her inner thigh, barely touching the surface, making each nerve sing like a violin string, till Sylvia could hardly stand the ache of frustrated need burning within her.

"I want you, Hank, darling," she moaned, but he silenced her cry with his lips in a long, passionate kiss that anticipated the deeper possession to come. Her fingers touched him in poignant yearning, but he held off, bent on heightening her desire with sweet torture of his hands, fingers, lips, and tongue.

Sylvia knew his arousal was as powerful as hers, but she now shared his desire to prolong their ecstasy, to make the joy they had in each other last as long as possible. Her hands were drawn inexorably to his broad, finely muscled chest. Then she let them drift downward to plane across his hard, flat stomach. Her palms cupped his lean bare hips and paid soft tribute to his maleness.

At last there could be no more waiting for either of them. As he entered her smoothly, Sylvia felt time contract to that moment, her world shrink to their joining. Nothing in her life had ever been so right or so beautiful. With deliberate slowness Hank rocked against her till she joined his rhythm. Hearts racing in unison, breast to chest, they crested height after height of ecstasy as their lovemaking sped ever deeper and faster to the final gasping, glorious climax.

Then, as Hank slid from her body and held her close, Sylvia whispered, "I love you." And he answered with the same tender words.

He covered her face with kisses, his warm breath drying the tears. "Don't cry, darling," he said. "We'll get out of this. Remember Caldera Street."

"I know. It's just a release of tension, I guess."

"What have you got to be tense about?" Hank asked jokingly. "Just because we're being chased by a bunch of drunken Guaraní Indians—correction, Guaranís with terrific hangovers—a storekeeper with an inventory problem, and a sadistic South American and are about to enter the most inhospitable terrain known to man. Where's your sense of adventure, woman?"

Sylvia laughed. "Considerably dampened . . . like my clothes." She fingered Emily's blouse and skirt. "Shouldn't we be getting dressed and calling room service?"

"Right. I'll have three eggs any way they want to cook them and about a pound of bacon."

When they had put on their still-damp clothes, they stood for a moment staring at each other.

"You look different," Hank said, puzzled.

"So do you. Your mustache's gone."

"And your hair's red again."

Sylvia put her hand to her hair. "The tint washed off in the river, like your mustache. There go our disguises!"

"At least we're ourselves again," Hank said cheerfully.

They stood with their arms around each other, staring at the opposite riverbank. Some of the beach fires were still smoldering, sending bedraggled columns of smoke into the now flamboyantly blue sky. There was no sign of activity, no going to and fro of the villagers.

"They're probably sleeping it off," Hank said with a grunt. "We'd better make tracks while we can. It'll take Carlos and Lang awhile to zero in on us." By that time, he thought morosely, they'd be out in the open, easy prey for Carlos's helicopter, but that was a bridge he'd cross when they got to it.

The heavy summer rains had filled the riverbeds with muddy streams that meandered through the thick, swampy jungle of the eastern Chaco. In a few months, when no rain would fall, the bogs and swamps would again become the cracked, parched skin of that desolate land, and the dry ribs of the riverbeds would lie open to the cobalt blue sky.

Hank stood in the prow of the boat, holding the long bamboo pole in both hands, working it slowly forward through a dense growth of reeds and water plants, while Sylvia worked another bamboo pole behind him.

"It's like a tropical greenhouse," Sylvia said, surveying the dense, sharply green jungle growth around them.

"The Green Hell of Paraguay," Hank answered grimly.

"Alligators?" Sylvia asked warily.

"Wait. The trip's just begun."

"I'd hate to miss anything in this 'me Tarzan, you Jane' flick."

"Just don't throw your popcorn in the bottom of the boat. That's all I ask."

"That reminds me—not that I really needed a reminder—what are we going to eat in this jungle paradise?"

"Feel around in my hip pocket."

"Really, Lord Greystoke! I don't think I should take that liberty."

"It's all right. Just don't tell Jane. And don't rock the boat!" Hank yelled as Sylvia started toward him.

She steadied her movements, put her hand in Hank's pocket, and pulled out a soft slab in a flyspecked yellowed wrapper with faded printing on it. "What is it?" she asked doubtfully.

"Chocolate. I swiped it from Lang's store. Go ahead and eat it."

"What about you?"

"I had some last night when you were asleep."

Sylvia laughed. "Yeah, sure. If you hadn't snored, I would have thought you were dead, not just asleep."

"I don't snore," Hank said defensively.

Sylvia just looked away and smiled.

The chocolate was stale and tasted of the river. It had gotten wet and dried out and was starting to melt again. But it was ambrosia to Sylvia. She scrupulously ate only her share, but she savored every morsel of the old candy bar and licked her fingers before she rewrapped the half she left for Hank.

"You don't have a glass of water to go with that chocolate, do you, Hank?" Sylvia asked.

He glanced up at the gray-bellied clouds hanging like dark fleece from the tall blue sky. "I will soon. We'll catch some rainwater."

Sylvia turned her empty hands upward. "Using what?"

"How about your blouse?"

"How about *your* shirt?"

Hank grinned. "I asked first. Just take it off and lay it on the bottom of the boat. Shape it into a sort of container."

Sylvia unbuttoned her blouse and removed it. Emily's jacket had been discarded long ago. She spread the blouse out and knotted several ends to stiffen them. Then she raised her head to the sky.

Hank looked at her, at the clean line of her small, determined jaw, her slender neck, her exquisitely shaped breasts, and his throat constricted. He loved her so much. The thought that she would have given herself to Carlos in exchange for his life stirred him as nothing else ever had.

Running his eyes over her sweaty face and the fingers she had hungrily started licking again, Hank made a vow.

If they ever got out of the mess they were in, he was going to make her happy for the rest of her life.

She looked at him through her fingers and smiled. "What are you thinking of?" she asked.

"That when all this is over, I want to marry you." His voice broke a little. "Take care of you."

She teased him a little, the green of her eyes glinting between narrowed eyelids. "What are you going to put on your business cards? Mr. and Mrs. Soldier of Fortune?"

Hank shook his head slowly. "I'm giving it up. I've had my fill of this kind of life. It'll be the nine to five for me, the house in the suburbs, and cutting the grass on weekends."

"Hank! I love you, darling, and I'd love to be married to you, but you'll never give it up. You couldn't. Danger's in your blood."

"You're wrong, Syl. It's not worth it to me, not when it puts you in danger. I would have killed Carlos with my bare hands if he had laid a finger on you."

She stared at him, a kernel of hope slowly germinating inside her. Was it possible? Could they have a life together? It seemed too much to expect in spite of what Hank had just said.

Then, suddenly, the heavens opened up. Rain poured out of the sky in arrow-straight, pelting torrents. They raised their faces to it and opened their mouths, catching the precious water, wetting their lips with it, drinking it in. They stuck their tongues out, too, as though there were no surface they didn't want to bless with water.

In thanksgiving Sylvia raised her face and arms to the sky.

"You look like a rain goddess!" Hank yelled, laughing.

"I feel like one. Ooh, it's so lovely, Hank. Just to be cool and fresh and not sticky."

The sight of her, water running from her hair and

cascading over her smooth, uptilted breasts, made Hank want her again. She glanced lovingly at him, and he felt his body tighten and harden at the promise of her.

He started to pole the boat toward shore, looking at her all the time, letting his love for her and his desire come together like two great rivers inside him.

Sylvia watched him. His shirt was plastered to his skin so that his nipples made little points in the fine cotton. The chest hair that showed under the half-opened shirt glistened with drops of water. His brilliant blue eyes were hot and searching, and Sylvia reveled in the desire she had aroused in him and anticipation of the joy she would give him.

Hank pulled the boat in under a large tree with thick overhanging branches.

"Let's get out," he said. "It's fairly dry under the tree. Or at least no wetter than we are," he added with a laugh.

"What about my shirt?" Sylvia wailed, pointing to the blouse in which a pool of rainwater had collected. "I can't go around bare-breasted forever."

"I don't see why not," Hank said huskily. "*I* like it."

After helping Sylvia out of the boat, he pulled her to him and folded her in his arms.

"I wonder what it would be like to make love in a bed and with dry clothes on," Sylvia murmured as her breasts pressed against the wet cotton of his shirt.

"What clothes?" Hank murmured, bending to take her lips with his.

Suddenly they jumped. With pounding heart Sylvia buried her face in Hank's chest. The harsh clatter of a helicopter tore up the air in the near distance. Then it was right over them, raking the treetops as it passed to and fro. Sylvia began to shiver violently, the suddenness of the attack unnerving her.

"It's all right, Sylvia," Hank whispered. "We're completely hidden. He can't possibly see us or the boat. We'll just stay here till he goes back."

His eyes searched the jungle around them. "I'm looking for something to hold the rainwater so you can put your blouse back on."

"Do you think we're going to be captured?" Sylvia whispered fearfully.

Hank grinned. "Heck, no. I just can't keep my mind on my work with you like that."

He let his eye travel upward along a tall, graceful trunk that ended in a cap of featherlike leaves sheltering clusters of coconuts. The tree was too high and smooth for him to climb, but several coconuts lay on the ground at its base.

"I'm going to get one of those coconuts and use it for our water," Hank said.

He picked up a coconut and smashed it against the tree. When he had worked the husk loose from the fruit inside, he held it up. *"Voilà!* Our dinner tonight."

"Good. I much prefer coconut to steak and lobster."

Together they managed to pour most of the rainwater into the coconut shell.

"We'll drink this before we push off again," Hank said. "You don't have to put that wet shirt on now," he added tenderly. "The rain's stopped. If you spread it out, it should dry in an hour or two."

Sylvia looked up through the canopy of green leaves at the blue sky above. "The helicopter's gone."

All Hank said was "Umm."

"But he'll be back."

"Maybe yes, maybe no. Not having found anything, he might just give up."

He didn't believe this, but it was important to keep her courage and hope up.

"Lang must have gotten free and told Carlos," Sylvia said. Her voice was flat and unemotional. It was a logical conclusion, and logic called for coolness and a clear-sighted view of things.

Hank moved his burly shoulders in a casual shrug. "It looks that way. Let's drink our water and shove off. I don't think the chopper's going to make another pass, and even if it does, the trees will give us cover."

They continued down the ever-narrowing river through an immense matted jungle. Trees, massive, enormous, towered above them, shutting out the sun. The greenness all around them was overwhelming. The little boat seemed submerged in it like a submarine underwater.

Sometimes they passed snouted, toothy caimans sunning themselves on the sandy banks, and each blanched visibly at the sight. Long snakes of a kind they didn't know slithered into the water now and then.

They watched, horrified, as the riverbanks gradually closed in on them and the river became a reed-choked stream in a sea of mud. At times Sylvia poled while Hank got out and pushed the boat through what water there was. Other times they dragged it over the mud flats till the river surfaced again.

The day seemed endless. They were mud-stained and muscle-sore. Where their clothes had been torn on bushes and overhanging branches, long red scratches marked their arms and legs. Sylvia's blouse was ripped across the shoulder, and she had slashed Emily's too-long skirt into a ragged mini that allowed her greater freedom of movement.

The sun now shone fiercely down on them through the diminishing number of trees. Their nerves were frazzled with fear—fear of alligators and snakes, of the helicopter that might spot them on its next pass, of Carlos and his henchman, the SS criminal Lang.

"We're going to sleep in the boat tonight, Sylvia," Hank said. "It's probably the last day we'll be able to use it. The river's disappearing faster than an ice cube in July."

"Don't mention ice," Sylvia said, groaning. "I'd like to be packed in it from head to toe."

"I'd like to see 'em stacked in a tall glass of Scotch," Hank mused. "I'd take a sip, hold an ice cube in my mouth, let it melt. . . ."

Sylvia shook her head. "Not me. I'm not getting out of my ice pack even to drink Scotch."

"You won't have to," Hank said soothingly. "I'll bring you a glass with a bent straw."

They curled up together then in the boat and tried to sleep.

"I don't suppose an alligator could make it into the boat?" Sylvia said with a false little chuckle.

"Not a chance. That's why we're sleeping in it instead of onshore."

"But I suppose one of those huge snakes could drop in."

"Why would he? What have we got that he'd want?" Hank pointed out logically.

Still, as Sylvia slept, Hank forced himself to stay awake, a coconut at his side, a feeble weapon but the only one he had. While he listened to the night sounds of the jungle—the roar of a jaguar as it captured its prey, the chatter of a pack of monkeys, the myriad cries of birds—he thought of the events of the last few days.

Sylvia had told him of her meeting with Elena Vanegas at the country club. He had been wrong about Vanegas, but he wasn't keeping score on himself. The important thing was Peter was safe.

Hank raised his eyebrows. Peter was his last assignment. He'd never take another. He was going to be the spy who knew when to fold.

Surprise at his own decision turned to relief. Until now he hadn't realized how tired of the game he'd become.

For the first time his life seemed infinitely precious because it belonged not only to him but to the woman he loved, the woman who needed him.

Somehow, if they made it to the border, out of Paraguay, he would have to convince her that he wasn't a danger junkie, that he was capable of commitment, and that she, Sylvia Goddard, was the woman he was committed to.

The border! Hank snorted in self-derision. Thousands of miles of open country—cattle lands and scrub forests—lay between them and the border. Where would they hide from Carlos's helicopter in the Gran Chaco?

Hank began to sleep fitfully, dozing off against his will, then forcing himself awake and always clutching his "cannonball," the hard coconut. Then as the night sky began to pale and the jungle became safe, he permitted himself to fall into a deep, restful sleep.

Suddenly Hank woke up, instantly alert, to a sound close by.

Sylvia was swinging her arms in the air and clapping her hands softly over her head.

"Morning, darling. I'm trying to unkink my shoulders. I feel as though I spent the night in a rowboat."

Hank laughed and looked up into the sky. "It's light enough to get going again. Let's have some coconut and move out."

As Sylvia chewed on the crunchy, semi-tough coconut, she said, "Ugh, I'll never order coconut cream pie in a restaurant again."

"It's keeping us alive," Hank pointed out. What would they live on once they left the swampy jungle? he wondered. There were some cattle ranches and isolated settlements owned by foreigners in the Chaco, but he didn't know how to reach them. They'd have to trust to luck and hope to meet up with some friendly ranchers.

They were able to pole the boat along only a few miles farther. Hank climbed a tree to see if the river widened again, but it didn't.

"It's the end of the river," he said, climbing down. "There's nothing but swamp ahead. Let's hide the boat where it can't be seen from the air and continue on foot."

They dragged the rowboat into a dense thicket and covered it with branches. Then they drank some coconut milk, passing the shell back and forth, and started out on foot.

They had to work their way slowly through the viscous mass of bog and shifting sands. The slimy, gooey mud sometimes reached as high as Sylvia's thighs, and every step was a giant effort. They held on to trees and sturdy bushes as they went and resolutely kept their minds from thoughts of alligators and snakes.

Hank kept ahead of Sylvia. "Keep calling to me," he said, "so I know you're there."

"Where do you think I'd be—dancing in Lincoln Center?"

"I'll take you dancing when we get back."

"Do spies dance?" Sylvia asked teasingly. "I've never heard of it. They don't in films."

"Those aren't real spies."

"Oh!" Sylvia answered.

She stumbled then on a buried tree root. To regain her balance, she reached out for a tree. But it was too far, and her nails scraped maddeningly down the bark. The thick, sticky mud sucked at her, pulling her down. Breathless from shock and the near fall, when she opened her mouth to call Hank, no sound came.

She was surprised that this could be happening to her, this nightmare in which she was unable to run or scream for help. Then the mud was up to her armpits, and she began to panic.

"Sylvia!" Hank called out. "How come you're not talking to me?"

He turned around then.

"My God!" he exclaimed. He was at her side in an instant. Reaching one hand up to a branch, he extended the other to her. "Hold on!" he yelled.

It took all his powerful muscular strength to pull Sylvia out of the bog. When she was safe, he folded her in his arms and stroked her leaf-strewn hair and comforted her.

"I don't like this damn place," she said, sobbing. "I know I wouldn't have drowned with you there, but it was horrible to feel myself sinking, sinking."

"Ssh, love," he crooned. "We'll be out of it soon. I can practically see open land from here."

Soon the trees grew sparse. The swamp dried up. The jungle disappeared.

They were on a vast plain of cracked earth and dry grayish green shrubs. The sun was a pale, angry-looking disk in a metallic blue, cloudless sky.

But there was nothing up in the sky as yet. Either Carlos's helicopter was late or Carlos had called off the search for them. For now Hank was satisfied. They trudged on, keeping the sun behind them and heading due west.

They walked for two hours, then stopped to wet their lips with coconut milk and to rest. The mud had dried quickly on their clothes, and they brushed it off. Sylvia wore her shirt partially buttoned and the sleeves rolled up.

After they had rested the fifteen minutes they allowed themselves, they started out again.

An hour or so later Hank shouted, "Hey! Am I dreaming, or is that a house out there, in that clump of trees?"

"It's probably a mirage," Sylvia grumbled, her eyes on the ground. She raised her head and yelled, "It's a house! A real house!"

"More like a ranch probably. Hey, some people are coming out. Two men and a woman. They see us." Hank waved both arms in the air, and the people waved back. One of the men left the others and entered a building adjacent to the house. A few minutes later a pickup truck drove out.

With tears in her eyes Sylvia watched the truck approach. Now that the ordeal was over, she could let herself cry. Hank had a smile of deep joy on his face. Their rescue had come sooner than he expected.

When the battered old pickup drew abreast of them, the driver yelled, "*Buenos días, amigos.* How ya doin'?"

Hank and Sylvia stared dumbfounded. The accented Spanish and the greeting both were unmistakably American.

CHAPTER THIRTEEN

"Name's Chuck Fowler." A grin slashed across his sharp-featured face. "But my friends call me Brute."

"What do your enemies call you?" Hank asked, irritated by Fowler's grandiose airs.

The grin turned into a nasty sneer. "They don't call me . . . period."

For safety's sake Sylvia introduced Hank and herself as Matt and Betty.

Fowler leaned out of the cab of the truck and shook hands with Sylvia, then patronizingly shook Hank's outstretched hand. "I own a ranch down the road a piece."

Hank's eyes narrowed. Fowler's hand was soft for a working rancher.

Fowler surveyed them both appraisingly. "Looks to me like you two are on the lam," he drawled, and his long, bony face lit with a pleased smile. "What are you into? Drugs? The black market?"

"Nothing illegal," Hank answered. "We got separated from our tour group. That's all."

Fowler's slate-colored eyes went mean and hard at that. Sylvia watched fascinated as his Adam's apple moved up and down in his turkey-thin throat in an obvious effort at self-control. He had a day's growth of dark beard and a pallor that was unusual in that sunny climate.

"Get in," Fowler said. "I'll take you back to the ranch. Give you some grub and water."

Hank helped Sylvia up into the cab and squeezed in beside her. Fowler's bold, searching look reminded Sylvia that she was braless, that her skirt was terribly short, her blouse torn and incompletely buttoned. Although the cab was like a metallic oven, she quickly buttoned her blouse as far as it would go.

Fowler's eyes narrowed gleefully. Sylvia bit her lower lip. She had played his game by responding to his lecherous glances. But what else could she have done?

As if to test her further, Fowler slid his hand quickly up her leg before placing it on the gearshift. Sylvia pulled away sharply and leaned into Hank.

She glanced up at Hank. If he had seen what Fowler just tried, he would have torn the rancher limb from limb. But Hank was staring straight ahead, looking at the house in the distance. He was frowning, and his face had a taut, alert look as if he were puzzling something out ahead of time, to be ready for trouble if it came.

When the truck shuddered to a stop in front of the house, Hank jumped out and held his arms up for Sylvia, while Fowler watched with hooded eyes.

"What do you raise here?" Hank asked, looking around at the dilapidated house and bare land.

"Nothing much now. We had a nice cash crop of marijuana going, but the fuzz made us cut it all down." He gave Hank a look charged with significance. "I don't know what you heard, but the cops *do* make it out this far." Suddenly his whole demeanor changed. The sharply cut planes of his face stretched in a wide grin. He moved his hands in an expansive gesture. "But we've got prospects for something big," he said boastfully. "A whole new field is opening up. Because it's so big, a man would need protection for his operation." Fowler eyed them speculatively. "But that might not be too hard to arrange."

"I told you before we're not on the lam," Hank answered coldly. "Can we go inside now? My wife's about ready to drop."

"You two are married?" Fowler gave Sylvia another blatantly appraising glance. "That's nice," he said in a dead monotone as if he didn't believe it.

He led the way into the house then, calling out, "Hey, Darlene, Jake! Here's that couple I went to get. Come out here and say hello like nice polite folks."

A man—like Fowler—somewhere in his thirties came out of another room. His gray, grease-stained tank top had ridden up over his belly, which hung meat pink over his jeans, almost hiding the frayed rope holding them up. He was barefoot, and the spaces between his toes were encrusted with old dirt.

"Where's Darlene?" Fowler snapped.

"She's coming," the other man whined. His eyes skidded toward Sylvia. "She's making herself purty for the company."

The woman who shuffled in shortly afterward had once been pretty. You could tell that, Sylvia thought, from her fine features and very blue eyes. She was thin now almost to the point of emaciation. Her skin was sallow, and her dark hair lacked luster. Worst of all, her eyes were vacant; her expression was remote, as though she had escaped from the world and were camping out, waiting till a better one was built.

Fowler did the honors. "Darlene, Jake, this here's Matt and Betty. Mister and missus," he added with a huge wink.

Jake didn't even bother looking at Hank. His eyes came to rest on Sylvia and stuck there.

Darlene looked both of them over with faint curiosity as if they were animals in a zoo or specimens under a microscope. Her eyes were as void of compassion as they were of every other emotion.

"We'll pay you for any water and food you can give us," Hank said. "Then we'll take off."

"Going where?" Fowler asked, amused.

Hank didn't answer. He pointed to his lips and throat and mouthed, "Thirsty."

With a heavy shrug Darlene clattered off in a pair of dirty satin mules trimmed with pink feathers. She returned with a plastic container of water and two jam jar glasses.

All three watched curiously as Hank and Sylvia gulped the water down.

"We'll have more later," Hank said. "It's not good to drink too much at first."

Darlene nodded and slip-slopped back into the kitchen. This time back she carried a plate of bread and cheese. She put it on a wooden crate that served as a table and motioned Hank and Sylvia to a mortally wounded couch spilling gray cottony entrails.

Hank cut a large hunk of bread and handed it to Sylvia. Then he cut a piece of the yellow cheese for her.

"See?" Fowler said to Jake. "Hubby helps wife first. That way he earns brownie points." His bold eyes drifted to the outline of Sylvia's breasts under the thin white shirt. "Get enough points, you get a reward."

Darlene didn't seem interested. She turned her back on the group and left.

"You go, too, Jake," Fowler commanded. "I'm the only one with enough manners to take care of company."

"Where do you get your food, Fowler?" Hank asked curtly. He had picked up on the man's glances at Sylvia, and his face had turned an angry dark red.

"There are a couple of cattle ranches around here. We

buy from them." He turned to Sylvia. "I guess you could go for a real nice steak, couldn't you?" He rubbed his long-fingered hands together. "Maybe if things work out, we'll have it later with a bottle of vino."

"The cheese and bread were enough for me." Sylvia glanced at Hank. Fowler made her nervous. He stripped her with his eyes every time he looked at her, and he seemed mean enough to try anything.

Hank got to his feet and with almost sleight-of-hand dexterity slipped the cheese knife into his pocket and pulled his wallet out. "How much do I owe you, Fowler?"

Fowler waved his hand disparagingly at the wallet. "Hey, man, that's hospitality. You don't have to pay me. But it's not nice to steal from your host. Darlene needs that knife to cut our grapefruit." He thrust his left hand out palm up for the knife. At the same time he drew a gun out of his pocket with the other and pointed it at Hank. He inclined his head slightly toward Sylvia. *He looks like a rattlesnake,* she thought, *with that triangular-shaped face and long, skinny, swiveling neck.* "You like grapefruit in the morning, don't you, honey?" he said insinuatingly.

Sylvia could see Hank measuring his chances of taking Fowler. But they were nil. The man was deadly, and the gun gave him all the power.

Hank laid the knife in the outstretched palm and smiled. "Thought we'd need it when we pushed on. The Chaco's a pretty wild place."

Fowler nodded grimly. He pressed his thin lips together as if to dam up what he wanted to say.

A crescendo of dread mounted in Sylvia. *He's not going to let us go,* she thought. *He was about to say,* "If *you push on,*" *or something like that, but he thought better of it because he didn't want to arouse our suspicions.*

"Darlene would like for you to stay to supper," he finally said.

"We want to get going," Hank answered. "So thank Darlene for us and tell her 'next time.' "

"That's not polite, mister." With sudden, sickening violence Fowler drew his hand back and hurled the knife at the table. It stuck in the wood, point down, and quivered there. Sylvia stared at it, mesmerized like a rabbit caught in a pair of headlights. A knife was primitive, brutal, direct, a nastier kind of threat than a gun.

She forced her eyes away from the knife and looked at Fowler. His face was flushed and contorted with anger; his pale eyes flicked back and forth, from Hank to Sylvia.

Something about the way he held his head, the unsteady wavering of his eyes, and his twisted mouth struck Sylvia with the lightning-bolt swiftness of insight. Fowler was, at best, emotionally unstable; at the worst, crazy.

Hank had come to the same conclusion. She could see it in the warning look he gave her.

With his gun still on Hank and Sylvia, Fowler yanked the knife out of the table and wiped it on the seat of his jeans. The violence seemed to have relaxed him. His face was calm and had its usual pallor back.

"I don't like wise guys, mister," he explained. "Also, it's not polite to say no to a lady who's been slaving over a hot stove all day. Is it, honey?"

His flat, expressionless eyes stroked Sylvia's figure again, lingering on the silhouette of her breasts and her small, rounded hips.

A muscle on Hank's jaw began to jump dangerously. He looked ready to lunge at Fowler in spite of the gun. Almost imperceptibly Sylvia shook her head at him, sending a signal of no.

Fowler waved the gun in the direction of the kitchen. "Suppose you go in the kitchen and do woman's work with Darlene, while me and your hubby chat awhile."

He's sending me into the kitchen so he can kill him, an interior voice screamed. *He's going to take Hank outside and shoot him.*

"No," she said, flushing with determination, her eyes steady on his. "Not unless Hank comes too. You're not separating us."

Fowler let out a hoot of laughter. "Hey, you've got spunk. I like that in a woman." He ran his eyes down Sylvia once more. Then he grinned, a slow, dirty grin. "Maybe I'll earn some brownie points myself. We'll *all* go to the kitchen." He waved the gun at Hank. "Get going."

When they entered the kitchen, Darlene looked up for a moment, then went back to filing her nails.

The sink was piled high with dishes and pots and pans. The linoleum on the floor was cracked and dirty. A fan on the table churned the air slowly, lifting a strand of Darlene's lank hair, then letting it fall again, as though the effort had been too much.

"Where's Jake?" Fowler asked.

Darlene moved her head to indicate a room behind her.

"Watch 'em." Fowler handed the gun to Darlene. She took it with a yawn but straightened in her chair and held the gun steadily on Hank and Sylvia.

Fowler left the room.

"Would you like us to do the dishes for you?" Sylvia asked.

"Sure, why not?"

"Is there a place we can wash first?"

"That's it, right there where you're going to be washing the dishes. We got a one-holer out back, and the fellers rigged up a shower. But for now you gotta use the sink. There's a bucket of well water heating on the stove."

Turning their backs on Darlene, Hank and Sylvia started to wash the dishes. Sylvia winced at the limp dirty dishrag, but at least there was soap and hot water.

"I'm going to jump that Brute bastard when I can, Sylvia," Hank said out the side of his mouth.

"It would be three against one, and they're armed."

"I don't care. I've seen the way he looks at you, and he's not laying a finger on you. I'll kill him first."

Sylvia sighed. This was a new fear, that Fowler's leering interest in her would lead Hank to do something rash.

When Fowler returned to the kitchen, he took the gun from Darlene and said tersely, "Make supper."

Darlene slowly pulled herself to her feet. "There's a bowl of chili in the fridge, you two. One of you can heat it up. The other can slice some bread."

She leaned against the wall and watched them, giving directions now and then.

Sylvia set the table with the broken pieces of crockery she found in a cupboard. When she put five chipped plates down, Fowler said, "Take one off. Jake ain't eating with us. He don't feel too good."

A few minutes later, as they sat down at the table in front of the plates of chili, the rattle and roar of the old pickup's engine reached the kitchen.

"Jake going out for some Alka-Seltzer?" Hank asked.

"Could be."

With the same snakelike quickness with which he had thrown the knife into the table, Fowler picked up a plate and brought it edge down with terrific force on Hank's hand.

"I told you I didn't like wise guys," he snarled.

Hank went pale with the pain of the blow, but he didn't wince or flinch. Using his other hand, he righted the plate and said, "You oughta watch that, Fowler, dropping things. Could be the sign of a nerve disorder. The kind that results in paralysis. Know what I mean?"

Fowler growled something unintelligible. He handed Darlene the gun and started to shovel the gooey brown chili into his mouth. When he had finished, he grabbed the gun out of Darlene's hand and watched Hank and Sylvia while Darlene ate.

Jake did not return. But his absence hovered ghostlike over the table.

When they had reached the end of the meal and the coffee, which managed to be both dishwasher weak and bitter at the same time, Fowler began flicking his eyes from the greasy alarm clock by the stove to the door. Hank watched, tense and alert. *He's sent Jake somewhere, probably to the closest cattle ranch, with a message to Carlos that we're here. There must be a reward for us. It won't take long for Jake to get to the ranch, and it shouldn't take long for Carlos to fly here with a couple of men.*

He glanced at Fowler. The man was a pro. He had the kind of pallor that prison gave a man, the kind no amount of sun ever rubbed out.

And his woman was no proud little Guaraní like Otto Lang's Lisa, who could be appealed to for help. Darlene's face and body looked raddled from drugs, poor nutrition, and abuse. She had been reduced to an apathetic husk who went through the motions of living, and that was all.

Fowler was showing signs of worry. His eyes bounced from the clock to the door and back again with the rhythm of a tennis ball. Where was Jake? By this time, Hank figured, he should have been back with the good news—message given; mission accomplished.

Suddenly Fowler seemed to make a decision. He got to his feet and, holding the gun on Hank and Sylvia, said, "Come on, you two. Get up and start moving."

"Are we going somewhere?" Hank asked innocently.

"Shut up, wise guy." Over his shoulder he called out to Darlene, "Stay here."

The air outside hit them like a blast from an open furnace. Sylvia raised her hand against the eye-singeing glare of the late-afternoon sun, but Fowler snarled, "Put your hand down."

He marched them into a shed with a corrugated tin roof. Hank recognized it as the place he had seen the pickup truck leave. Oil stains on the cement floor and a couple of oily rags corroborated his guess that the building was used as a garage.

The sun beating down on the tin roof made the airless shed a sweatbox. The heat seemed to come out of the cinder-block walls and press down on them from the roof. It set up a violent throbbing in Sylvia's temples and made her feel nauseated and giddy.

"So long, you two. Don't do anything I wouldn't do." With a chuckle at his own witticism Fowler backed out of the shed, keeping the gun on them as he went. Moments later they heard the rasp of a chain and the snap of the padlock.

They stood looking around at their cement prison. There was no place to sit but the floor. No food or water. No air but the slight amount that entered under the wooden door.

"Well-built little place," Hank said.

"You can say *that* again. What's going on, do you think?"

"I think Jake was sent to the nearest ranch to get word to Carlos that Fowler has us. Only I guess something must have happened to Jake. Maybe that old pickup broke down. Or maybe he forgot what he was going for. Jake doesn't look too sharp to me. Anyway, I think Brute's gone to do something about it, but he had to secure us first. He couldn't leave us with Darlene for too long because she might just lay the gun down and start filing her nails again. So he had to lock us up."

"That makes sense." Sylvia looked around at the four bare walls and the floor. "How long do you think he'll leave us here?"

"Not too long, I should think." Hank didn't add what was in his mind: Carlos's reward for them must have stipulated "alive," and that alone would put a time limit on their stay in the shed.

Sylvia ripped at the buttons of her shirt. "It's like an oven."

Hank put his hand out to her. "C'mon, we're going to walk."

"In this heat? You must be crazy. We'll have a heart attack."

"No, we won't. We have to stay active and think about something else. We'll walk slowly and talk."

He took her hand, and they started to walk around the perimeter of the shed. "First of all, where are we going to live after we leave this charming country and get married?"

"Do secret agents have wives?" Sylvia asked doubtfully.

"They do, but they always leave them home. That's why I'm quitting the game. I don't want to be away from you for long stretches of time. I don't want you to have to worry about me. And because of you, I don't want anything to happen to me. I didn't care that much before, but now I do."

Sylvia stopped in her tracks. "Oh, Hank, I don't know what to say. I'm so touched." Tears poured from her eyes as though from an overflow mechanism. Their love suddenly seemed pathetic, doomed. She was exhausted from their trek through the swamps. She felt as though her body would explode with the heat in the shed. The chili had made her nauseated and thirsty. All her defenses were down; her emotional bank account was overdrawn. She cried too easily, startled too quickly. And a refrain in her head kept repeating, "Brute's crazy. He's crazy, crazy, crazy."

Hank took her in his arms and kissed her tears away. "You taste salty, like the sea," he said.

She tried to laugh and ended up sounding wistful. "I'm trying to remember what it feels like. The salty tang of the air at the Cape."

"Sailing. Running before the wind. The jib bellying out before the wind's thrust."

"Coarse grass waving on sand dunes."

"We'll see it all again, Sylvia. We will, I promise you." But even as he said it and as he kissed her again and again, Hank didn't think that they would. The net had really closed around them this time.

He was still holding her when they heard the steady purr of an engine overhead. Sylvia stiffened in his arms. "The helicopter!" she cried with unreasoning, almost superstitious fear.

"No, it's a single-engine plane. Probably belongs to one of the cattle ranchers in the area." *Or, more likely,* he thought grimly, *it's Carlos arriving with a couple of his men.*

The sound of the plane faded, and they started walking again. Anything was better than just passively waiting. Hank slipped his hand up under the bottom of her shirt and held her around the waist. Hot as it was in the hut, he knew she would want the warmth of his hand against her bare skin, would want the closeness of him.

As if his gesture and the heat and the fear and the waiting had reminded her of Caldera Street, Sylvia said, "I never told you, because to talk about my work before I've gotten it to a certain point vitiates its force, but I've been choreographing a dance that's an outgrowth of our experience on Caldera Street.

"I'm still developing it, but basically it's about a man and a woman who are imprisoned within themselves and who free themselves by coming together and loving each other. I call it 'Affirmation.' "

What Sylvia said detonated inside Hank with all the force of suddenly revealed truth. The freedom he had enjoyed all these years by remaining uncommitted had turned out to be illusory. *Freedom for what?* an anonymous interior voice asked scornfully. *To go from country to country, adventure to adventure, as though life were only a series of cour-*

age-proving episodes? To seek release from the tension of physical danger in sex?

He thought back to Caldera Street. Had he started to love her then? Had he fallen in love with her voice and the shape of her face and the exquisite femininity of her body, with that special quality she had of courage combined with vulnerability?

He thought that he had and that his love for her had become the house he lived in, that if he lost her, he would be dispossessed for the rest of his life. There would always be sex, but there would never be another woman he would love as he loved her.

"What will the dance be like?" Hank asked tenderly.

"Originally I conceived of it as a pas de deux and without props, but now I think I'll use many pairs of dancers to make sure the universality of the theme is clear. And I'll use boxes—not real boxes, of course, but right-angle frames—to show the prisons people make for themselves. How does that sound to you?"

"Like something I'd want very much to see." Hank's voice was husky with emotion. A thought shrilled through his head: *Christ, what agony this must be for her, to be cooped up in this small space, not knowing whether she'll ever dance again.*

The chain rattled outside. Hank felt a sharp twist of fear. Brute had come back with Carlos.

But there was only one man, a black silhouette in the yellow wedge of sunlight that erupted through the opened door. Fowler stood there, legs spread wide, gun in hand, like a movie gunslinger. While he kicked the door shut, his eyes went to Sylvia's unbuttoned blouse and Hank's hand under it.

Sylvia quickly drew the edges together over her breasts and kept her hand there, clutching the material. As she did so, she watched Fowler's Adam's apple move slowly up and down in a huge gulp. The pupils of his pale eyes dilated, and his mouth went slack.

"Did Jake make it back yet?" Hank asked, taking his hand from Sylvia but standing close to her as she buttoned her blouse.

"None of your business."

Fowler held the gun on Hank, but his eyes kept straying to Sylvia. He had looped a length of rope around his waist, cowboy style, and she guessed what he planned. He would tie Hank up, then rape her.

She felt sick. She couldn't expect Hank to save her, not against a man with a gun. It was the certainty of it, the feeling that there was no escaping this fate that disheartened her. Would she fight? Probably not. Weren't you supposed to give in to save your life?

Fowler's left hand went to the rope while he motioned Hank to the wall with his gun. Hank backed away from him slowly, his eyes never leaving the gun.

Thinking to distract Fowler, Sylvia followed. Her hand went to her blouse buttons teasingly, and she smiled seductively at him.

"Get away," he snarled, his eyes and gun steady on Hank.

That had been stupid of her, Sylvia thought. It had accomplished nothing and might have made him think she would be a willing partner.

But Fowler's attention was diverted for the moment he took to answer Sylvia.

In that instant Hank took a long step back. He kicked upward at the gun and sent it flying out of Fowler's hand. It landed with a clatter some feet away on the cement floor. Fowler ran for it, but in one long, lunging slide of his body Hank reached the gun first.

He stood up and pointed it at Fowler. "Get the rope off him, Sylvia."

Sylvia felt a surge of revulsion at the thought of touching the man. She had to will herself just to draw close to him and worked quickly, keeping her eyes constantly on the rope to shut out the leer on his pale, skull-like face.

Hank tied Fowler's hands and feet behind him and stuck an oily rag in his mouth.

"Chew on that for a while, you slimy bastard," Hank snarled.

He took Sylvia's hand, and they left the shed. While Hank padlocked the door, they could hear Fowler thudding his heels against the cement floor, but only faintly.

"He'll tire of that after a while." Hank chuckled. "I'm not sure Darlene would even work up the interest or energy to rescue him. And for all we know, good old Jake's on his way to La Paz right now in the pickup."

Staying close to the side of the shed and keeping on the blind side of the house, they gradually worked their way onto a dirt road that ran through a semiarid plain.

There was nothing in the sky but a vulture circling over the grayish green scrub. And no sign of the pickup on the dusty road that stretched for miles ahead.

"Where are we going, Hank?" Sylvia asked.

"Remember Brute's boast that he expected to be in on something big soon?"

"Drugs?"

Hank nodded. "Probably cocaine. Bolivia produces a lot of coca—cocaine's made from the leaves—but the U.S. is pushing a campaign there against production and export, so processing facilities are being moved into Paraguay and Brazil. A lot of these cattle ranchers own their own planes and have their own airstrips. Aircraft movements across the borders here are practically uncontrolled by civil aviation authorities. So the stuff can be flown from Bolivia to a cocaine laboratory in Paraguay without any hassle."

"Where did we fit into this picture?"

"It was obvious Brute knew we were running from somebody. Considering the power Carlos has in this country and the fact that we don't look like crooks who would be running from the law, Brute could well have figured that we were fleeing from Carlos. So he sends Jake out to the nearest rancher to get the message to Carlos that he's holding us. Only Brute isn't interested in a monetary reward for catching us. Remember his boast about getting into something big and needing protection? I think maybe he was going to trade us to Carlos in exchange for being cut in on the drug trade, maybe to set up a processing lab in that stinking shed of his."

"You think Carlos is running drugs then?"

"Yes, I do. It all hangs together. The drug traffic is big in South America. It means money and power, the sort of thing Carlos would go for."

"Carlos already has money and power."

"You know the saying 'You never can be too thin or too rich'? Well, if you're into money and power, you never can have enough of either. Also, part of Carlos's interest might be preemptive. As that guy Mark said at the Adamses' picnic, Carlos wouldn't want any behind-the-scenes drug king getting *more* money and power than he has."

Remembering her defense of Carlos at that time, Sylvia made a wry face. How wrong, how dangerously wrong she had been!

"What *we* need," Hank continued, "is some rancher who's not in the drug trade to fly us out of here."

"Otherwise?"

Hank looked up into the blue bowl of sky. "Otherwise, we cross the Chaco on foot." *Except that we'll never make it,* he added silently. *Because, aside from the fact that it's thousands of miles of semidesert, we'll be sitting ducks for Carlos's spotter helicopter.*

"Hank," Sylvia said in a low, hushed voice, "there's the pickup."

There it was, indeed, sitting right in the middle of the

dirt road. It looked abandoned. And for one crazy moment Hank thought it might have been boobytrapped. Otherwise, why would it be there? So inviting. The answer to his dream for transportation.

CHAPTER FOURTEEN

"Seems funny that good ol' Jake would stop right in the middle of the road," Hank said.

"Ran out of gas maybe?"

"There's a can in the back of the pickup," Hank said. "I saw it."

"Do you think he's in the truck?"

"If he is, he's dead. It must be a hundred twenty degrees inside that cab."

They fell silent then and walked faster in spite of the heat. The scene had an eerie, surrealist quality to it: a desert, a dirt road, sky, and a pickup truck right in the middle of all that emptiness.

As they got closer, the scene became even stranger. Whatever could be pried loose, knocked off, or extracted from the pickup had been. Floorboards, fenders, muffler, hub caps, reflectors lay strewn in the dirt.

"It's been vandalized!" Sylvia said. This was such an urban crime, she was amazed to see it in this streetless void.

"Not exactly," Hank answered thoughtfully. "The tires haven't been slashed, for one thing."

"Theft?"

"Nothing seems to be missing."

"What then?" Sylvia asked persistently.

"I think whoever took the truck apart was looking for something. Fowler might have boasted about the big cocaine deal he had working, maybe not distinguishing between present and future, and someone thought he had stashed the coke in the pickup."

"How about Jake?" They were close to the truck now, and she was wary of what she might see. It didn't seem likely that the truck would have been picked apart like this and they'd find Jake sitting in the cab reading *War and Peace.*

"Wait here," Hank said. "I'll go see."

There was nobody nastier than a thwarted drug dealer, and he didn't want Sylvia looking at a mutilated body before he could cover it up.

But the pickup was empty. Whoever had done the job on the truck had taken Jake away with them.

The hood was up, but the engine hadn't been removed. The truck's four wheels were in place. Suddenly Hank's haggard look disappeared. He laughed with glee.

"What's so funny?" Sylvia called out.

"Nothing." He slapped the hood. "But I think we've got wheels."

Sylvia came up and looked into the cab. The dashboard had been pried loose, the seats ripped open, the door handles smashed.

"How are you going to start it?"

Hank grinned. "Easy. I'll hot-wire her."

"You know how to do that?"

"Spies are really just handymen in trench coats." Hank climbed into the cab of the pickup.

"I guess you didn't find Jake," Sylvia said, looking around.

"Nope. Whoever was looking for the coke and didn't

find it in the pickup undoubtedly took good ol' Jake away for a little questioning."

Hank's long fingers began playing with wires exposed by the loosened dashboard. He rooted around on the floor of the cab till he found a screwdriver. Then he jumped out and, after going to the open hood, touched the starter with the screwdriver.

The motor sputtered, coughed, choked, coughed again, and finally settled down into a sustained, breathy rasp. Hank slammed the hood down and helped Sylvia up into the cab. With one long step he climbed in on the other side. He rubbed his hands together exuberantly. "Man, this beat-up little job looks better than a Rolls-Royce to me."

They drove due west across the vast arid plain till their gas ran out. Then they locked the doors, wrapped the stuffing from the ripped seats around themselves for warmth against the desert chill, and fell asleep in each other's arms.

Sylvia woke up to the sound of a deep, throaty roar and Hank's arms tightening around her.

"What is it?" she asked groggily.

"Look straight ahead through the windshield."

The moon lit the scene with a bright, artificial-looking light. Loping toward the truck, covering the ground quickly on its short legs, was a buff-colored big cat with black spots.

The animal looked beautiful and cruel. Sylvia was mesmerized by it as it came closer and closer. She felt no fear, high up in the cab of the truck, but Hank's hand slid against her leg as he drew Fowler's gun out of his pocket.

"It's a jaguar," she said with a little gasp.

"Yes, they're fairly common in the Chaco. The people call it *el tigre,* 'the tiger.' "

"What would it live on here?"

"The usual small animals and, if it gets a chance, cattle.

We may be near a cattle ranch. If we are, what do you say we hit the friendly rancher up for a plane ride to Bolivia?"

"What if he isn't friendly?"

They both watched for a moment as the big cat stared full at the truck, his eyes a glittering, translucent green in the moonlight.

"Don't borrow trouble," Hank said, laughing. "That's like saying, 'What if that *tigre* reaches one of its paws up and opens the door?' "

"I'm not worried about *that.* He couldn't; it's locked."

Hank groaned. "Here I am stuck in the Chaco with a stand-up comic." He took her in his arms and cuddled her against him. "On the other hand, who needs a bed and a down comforter? I've got you and Styrofoam stuffing."

"And a pussycat."

The jaguar roared again, very close this time.

"By the way, I wouldn't go outside tonight if I were you," Hank said. He started to kiss her, letting his lips drift across her cheekbones and face.

"What makes you think I would want to?" Sylvia murmured contentedly.

They slept in each other's arms the rest of the night. Sylvia woke up with the gauzy recollection of having dreamed that she was in Otto Lang's house. Hovering in the world between waking and dreaming, she listened to an indistinct sound of human voices. She opened her eyes slowly. The truck was surrounded by men holding rifles.

That's why you dreamed you were back at Otto Lang's, Sylvia told herself. *It's another jolly crowd scene.*

Some of the men stared through the windshield at her; others were looking at the ground and talking excitedly to each other, evidently about the tracks made by the jaguar. The men wore leather chaps cut in long strips for coolness in the torrid Chaco, neckerchiefs, broad-brimmed felt hats, and boots—the costume of the vaquero, the cowboy.

Hank rolled down his window and started talking to the man who, to judge from the silver on his belt and rifle, was the leader. Some of the others joined in. Sylvia heard *el tigre* and the Guaraní word *yaguaro* and let all her breath out in a sigh of relief.

Hank confirmed her guess. "The jaguar got a steer that wandered away from the herd last night. There's a woods and a small river in the area. Jaguars are different from the other big cats. They like water, and the men figure that's where he headed."

"Then there *is* a cattle ranch here," Sylvia said.

"You'd better believe it—three hundred thousand acres, the Estancia Juan de Cuyas. That's the head honcho himself." Hank indicated with a minimal movement of his head the fortyish man with the silver-embossed rifle who had joined the others in admiring the size of the jaguar's paw prints. "He never misses a jaguar hunt, he told me."

"Can he help us, do you think?"

"I'm going to ask him now."

When De Cuyas raised his head, Hank said, "I suppose with a spread that big you have a plane."

The handsome aquiline-featured rancher laughed at the possibility that he might not own an airplane.

"Could you fly us into Bolivia?" Hank asked earnestly. "You can name your own sum."

De Cuyas peered inside the cab, looking past Hank at Sylvia. She returned his gaze with a hauteur that was all smoke screen for the way she felt, which was sticky and dirty and embarrassed. She hadn't washed or changed her clothes in what seemed like years. Her grooming had consisted of finger-combing her hair, washing her face with spit, and brushing the mud off the blouse and skirt that now barely covered her. The only person she could stand having look at her was Hank, and that was only because he loved her and because he was as filthy as she.

From Sylvia, De Cuyas's sharp-eyed inspection went to the ripped interior of the cab. His eyes returned to Hank, and he shook his head slowly and definitely.

"I'm not running drugs," Hank said, "although I think the guys who tore the truck apart were. We have to get to Bolivia. Someone is chasing us."

"The law?" the rancher asked.

Hank decided to take a chance. De Cuyas looked like his own man, one who wouldn't either fear Carlos or need to curry favor with him. The size of his spread reinforced this guess.

"Somebody outside the law," Hank answered. He looked at the rancher meaningfully. "Somebody who makes his own laws . . . and enforces them."

De Cuyas studied Hank for a long time. He looked the truck over again, and Sylvia.

"This truck isn't yours?"

"No, it belongs to some renegade Americans. They held us captive while one of them went off to send word of where we were to the man following us. We escaped and found the truck ripped up as you see it and abandoned in the middle of the road."

"Where is the man who was driving it?" the rancher asked.

"Disappeared. I don't know for sure, but I imagine the guys who tore the truck apart looking for drugs took him away with them."

De Cuyas smiled faintly, and the dapper pencil mustache, a twin to the one Emily Adams had pasted on Hank which the river had washed away, moved with his smile. "And *la cucaracha grande,* the big cockroach, which is what the villagers around here call the helicopter, hasn't spotted you?"

"I don't think so."

The rancher suddenly turned and spit forcefully. The saliva left a dark, moist circle in the dirt and raised a miniature dust storm.

"We don't like cockroaches around here," he explained. He went on briskly, laying out his plan of action. "I will send a man back to the ranch with you, while we hunt *el tigre.* He will have instructions to my wife to welcome you. She will give you a meal and some clothes. You may bathe in my house, and when I return with a beautiful yellow and black pelt, we will discuss your flight to Bolivia."

De Cuyas rapped on the cab door. "In the meanwhile, since it is a long walk to the ranch, I suggest you get out of your truck now and drink some water and eat."

Hank unlocked the door and jumped out of the truck. At a hand signal from De Cuyas he was immediately surrounded by a ring of rifles.

Sylvia cried, "Stop! What are you doing to him?" and opened the truck door to get out.

One of the men swung his rifle around and pointed it at her.

De Cuyas muttered something, and the man lowered his rifle. But he kept his eyes on her, and Sylvia sensed that the unspoken command was to stay in the truck.

Leaving the door open, she watched the rancher move his hands rapidly down Hank's sides and back and his legs. A surge of relief swept through her. They were only frisking Hank after all. De Cuyas pulled Fowler's gun out of Hank's pocket and, hefting it in his palm, looked questioningly at him.

"That belonged to the guy we escaped from," Hank said. He snorted ironically. "A man named Brute."

De Cuyas stuck the gun in his belt. "For our own protection, you understand."

Hank shrugged. He wasn't about to argue with twenty armed men.

He helped Sylvia out of the truck. Flasks of water were thrust into their hands. The water was warm, but it tasted better than anything Sylvia had ever drunk.

The same man who had handed them the water flasks, an Indian whose mahogany skin glistened in the hot morning sun, now gave Hank a hunk of manioc bread. Hank tore it in two and handed half to Sylvia.

The Indian motioned to Hank and Sylvia to follow him, and still clutching the water flasks and the bread, they set off for the Estancia Juan de Cuyas. The Indian was not a Guaraní, they discovered, but belonged to the Toba-Maskoi tribe, which had lived in the Chaco for centuries. Although communication was difficult, they understood that they could drink all the water in the flasks because the ranch wasn't more than a few hours' walk away.

"I don't know whether to drink it or wash with it," Sylvia said ruefully. "Now that I'm not hungry or miserable with thirst, all I can think of is a bath and getting out of these clothes. Poor Emily, the only place she could ever wear this outfit again would be a come-as-a-swamp-rat party."

Hank chuckled. "Which isn't exactly Emily's style."

"Do you think Carlos will give her a hard time for helping us escape?" Up till now Sylvia hadn't even had the courage to put this fear into words. But the thought had tortured her often, mostly in the silent reaches of the night when she woke up and couldn't go back to sleep.

Hank shook his head emphatically. "Not a chance. It would cause too much of a stink in the international community, to say nothing of trouble with our State Department. Whatever he might do to us could be covered up, but the Adamses are too prominent in San Lorenzo."

"How about her car?"

"We'll get word to Emily when we reach New York, although it's probably been found by now and returned to her."

As the buildings of the De Cuyas ranch came into view, Hank looked around with keen interest. There was a cattle stockade and pens, several low sheds, a building that was obviously a bunkhouse, and a windowless brick structure the wooden door of which, unlike the others, was padlocked. A storeroom of some kind, Hank figured.

The few gauchos they met touched their fingers to their wide-brimmed felt hats in greeting, then continued with their work.

"Where is everybody?" Sylvia said, looking around at the near-empty grounds.

"Out hunting *el tigre* probably."

A maid came to the door. Pointing to Hank and Sylvia, the guide said a few words to her; then, with a shy smile of farewell, he silently padded off.

The maid led them into the *sala,* where Senora de Cuyas, a raven-haired matron of forty, greeted them as though weary swamp rats appeared on her doorstep every day.

"You are hungry? Thirsty?" Her eyes dropped to Sylvia's muddy blouse and skirt. "Or do you want a bath first, and some clean clothes?"

Sylvia closed her eyes in what felt like the first stage of delirious ecstasy. "Oh, a bath, please."

Another maid, small and sturdily built, led them down a long corridor to adjoining rooms—high-ceilinged, cool, dim rooms with long white curtains and blinds closed against the sun and dark furniture against white plastered walls. When the little maid left Sylvia's room to draw a bath, they fell into a wordless embrace.

She couldn't believe they both were here, alive, holding each other. It seemed a miracle like the water and the manioc bread the Indian had given her.

But would he ever be as daily to her as bread? When he had gotten them both to safety, would he leave her? Sylvia looked up into Hank's gaunt, bearded face.

"You want to know if you can take a bath with me, right?" Hank said.

"Right." Sylvia giggled. "See what happens? Say 'bath' and I become hysterical."

"I know what you mean." Using two hands, he put her away from him. "Here's the maid. You go first. Unless . . ." He held up two fingers and mimicked washing himself. The maid giggled and nodded yes. "There's another bathroom available to us," Hank said triumphantly. "We can be simultaneously clean."

Sylvia left him then. The maid offered to undress her, and Sylvia let her. She had never done such a thing before, but she suddenly felt weak and trembly. *It's shock,* a calm, nurselike interior voice told her, *a natural reaction to what you've been through.*

There seemed to be two Sylvias: this outside creature who couldn't manage buttons and a cool, detached observer who knew all the answers. But as she slid her body into the water, everything dropped away from her except the ecstasy of being lapped up to her chin by clean, flower-scented warm water.

She lay in the deep tub till her fingertips became soft and wrinkled, and she was pink all over. She was half asleep when the maid came with a blanket-sized white towel and held it up for her to step into.

The bath had drained her of all tension, even that of hunger. Her bed had been turned down, and a dainty batiste nightgown laid on top of it. It was too small for the senora. Were there De Cuyas daughters? She hoped there was a son too. The least she could do for the friendly cattle rancher was wish him a son. With that light, fugitive thought Sylvia drifted off into sleep.

The maid came and woke her up. She said "dinner" in English. Then she bowed her head and ran out as though she had worked some kind of spooky magic.

But it was dinner on the *second* day of their arrival,

Sylvia discovered when, dressed in the clothes laid out for her, she went to the *sala.*

Senor de Cuyas and Hank rose as she entered. "You've slept the clock around and then some," the rancher said.

"Did you get your jaguar?" Sylvia asked.

De Cuyas nodded. "His pelt will hang in my game room."

Sylvia turned to Hank. Like her, he was dressed in borrowed clothes—a white shirt open at the throat and tan slacks that ended above his ankle. He was clean-shaven and still a little gaunt and pale, but his eyes had lost their bruised, fatigued look.

"You look better," she said softly.

Hank grinned. "I slept a little, too, and Senora de Cuyas has been fattening me up."

"You've been so kind to us, Senora de Cuyas," Sylvia said. "Really, I can't thank you enough."

The plump woman with the pretty candy-box face showed small white teeth in a smile. "I don't know when I've seen such a bedraggled-looking pair. You had great stamina. Even Tomaso, the Indian who brought you here, was full of admiration for you, Senorita Sylvia."

"What will you have to drink?" De Cuyas asked courteously. He waved his hand at a low, polished table. "We have just about everything, I believe."

"Thank you, but I'm afraid I'd be drinking on a very, very empty stomach," Sylvia answered.

"Of course." Senora de Cuyas shot her husband a disapproving glance. "We'll go into dinner immediately. Perhaps you should eat lightly, my dear. When was the last time you ate?"

"Tomaso gave us manioc bread and water on the way here."

"Bread and water, prison fare," Juan de Cuyas said thoughtfully. "Hank has told me about your escape from Carlos Ronderos and Otto Lang. You're safe now.

Ronderos's influence doesn't extend this far. Even if it did, I wouldn't let myself be subject to it. And in the morning I will fly you to Santa Cruz, the closest point in Bolivia where you can get a plane for the United States."

"You're very kind," Sylvia said in a voice that sounded strangled. She choked down her still too-ready tears. To be safe and clean and fed. To be taken care of for a while. It was balm to her strained nerves, a replenishment of her emotional bank account.

She found that she wanted only small amounts of food, but that little was delicious. A light consomme, chicken cooked in a lemon sauce, a chilled white Soave, and a fruit dessert seemed the best meal she had ever had.

They returned to the *sala* for their coffee and liqueurs. It turned out that the De Cuyases' sophistication came from yearly trips to Paris and Madrid. The daughter whose clothes Sylvia was wearing was at a convent finishing school in St.-Cloud, outside Paris. They regretted that their son, also in school but in Spain, was shorter than Hank.

But these were the clothes they both would have to wear to Santa Cruz. Even after several washings the clothes they had arrived in were unwearable.

Senora de Cuyas put her finger delicately to her nose, thereby confirming what Sylvia had been afraid of. She and Hank had actually stunk.

The small glass of Grand Marnier that Sylvia drank gave her a pleasant, warm, buzzing feeling. At one moment she felt that she could stay up all night chatting with her charming host and hostess and resting her eyes contentedly on Hank. The next, she was drowsy again, fighting to keep her lids from closing over her eyes.

She caught Hank's worried look. For a moment she thought it was strange to be so tired so soon. Then the idea skidded away, out of reach of her mind. She wanted to say to Hank, "Don't worry, darling," but the words seemed remote, unreachable, so she tried a reassuring smile instead. She was dissatisfied with the results. The smile seemed to come off more like a drunken simper, but by then Senora de Cuyas had stood up and was extending a hand to her. "You still need sleep, my dear," she said authoritatively, maternally. "Tomorrow you will be as good as new."

The bed had been turned down for her again. The same batiste nightgown was ready. Later she couldn't remember putting it on. She seemed to fall immediately into a dense, sense-obliterating sleep.

She woke up to a figure standing in the darkness by her bed. She sensed that it was a man, that he was looking down at her, that it was his touch on her arm, flung outside the sheet, that had awakened her.

She raised her arms to him and whispered, "Hank."

When he didn't come to her, she thought he was angry. Had she disgraced herself somehow in the *sala?* It didn't seem likely. Hank would never react to anything so trivial.

As the figure continued to stand there, a growing realization began to mount inside Sylvia. "You're not Hank," she said. Her voice wavered a little, hovering between fear and bravado.

Suddenly the man's head was level with her breast. "I came to ask your forgiveness, Sylvia. I would never have harmed you. You must believe that. There is still a chance for us. I am no longer interested in Peter Burns or Weston or anyone but you. I will leave my country if that would please you."

Sylvia froze. Her body seemed to contract, with everything withdrawing into the center, where it was warm and safe and no evil could reach her.

She felt trapped by the sheer power of Carlos's persistence. Even myth was on his side. If he touched her, she thought she'd die of disgust. It must have been that nauseating to the princess to kiss the cold-skinned, slimy little frog, yet the frog-prince had won her in the end.

Carlos took both her hands in his. *I'll wash them when this is over,* Sylvia thought. *I'll scrape his touch off with a strong yellow soap that smells of lye.*

"You'll forgive me, won't you, Sylvia? You were always such an understanding person. That's what I liked about you. You'll forgive me and we'll go back to the way we were before. Say it."

Her tone was mechanical, listless. "Yes, Carlos, I forgive you."

"Not like that," he answered vehemently. "Say it as though you mean it."

She softened her voice, put a sentimental little tremolo in it. "I forgive you, Carlos."

"Thank you," Carlos said emotionally. "Without your forgiveness nothing would be possible."

He got to his feet. All his motions were rapid but controlled and silent. He opened the door, and two men came in. One was De Cuyas. They grabbed her with quick efficiency. De Cuyas pressed a soft cloth to her nose. Sylvia inhaled the sweet, heavy scent of chloroform, then clamped her nostrils and mouth shut to postpone passing out as long as possible.

Hank was in the next room. Sylvia opened her mouth to scream, but no sound came. Instead, she gulped in a huge breathful of the ether-smelling anesthetic. She could feel herself losing consciousness. One of the men —Carlos? De Cuyas?—picked her up in his arms. Her body was limp, a rag doll lifted into the air.

Forcing strength into her legs, commanding them to do the will of her expiring consciousness, she lashed out at the lamp by the bed. The sound of a crash, the explosion of a broken light bulb came to her from a distance, as though it had traveled light-years from a faraway star.

She was being raised high in the arms of an angry

chieftain, whose banners were blowing in the night wind like white ghosts trying to trap her in their folds. He dashed her to the ground, but somehow she knew it was not as a sacrifice to his savage gods but out of revenge for some unknown sin.

When she awakened, she was lying in her bed. Her head was clear, but her body ached everywhere. There was an insistent, throbbing pain in her left foot. She sat up and looked down at the fresh white bandage around it and the bloodstains on the sheet.

A group of people were standing to the left of the bed staring solemnly at her: Senor and Senora de Cuyas and an older man with the authoritative, professionally detached air of a doctor.

It was like Dorothy waking up in Kansas again. There was the Tin Woodman and the Scarecrow and the Cowardly Lion.

Suddenly she screamed, *"Hank! Hank!"*

"I'm here," he said quietly, firmly. Sylvia turned her head to the right, ignoring the sharp, jolting pain that seemed to pierce her skull. She flung her hand out to him, and he caught and held it. The wave of panic left her; her breathing slowed. She felt safe again.

She had to tell him, quickly. Before Carlos came back. Before they made another attempt to take her away.

But first she turned her head back slowly, enduring the pain once more, and looked Juan de Cuyas directly in the eye. "What happened?" she asked contemptuously, daring him to lie.

Senora de Cuyas, the plump, matronly wife, answered. "You must have had a bad dream, my dear, and thrashed around in bed. You knocked over a lamp and cut your foot. Then, we can only suppose, you fell out of bed."

Sylvia remembered. Her last willful act before losing consciousness had been striking the lamp with her foot. Then the vengeful chieftain had lifted her high in his arms and dashed her to the ground, specifically to the tiled floor of the bedroom.

"Where's Carlos?" she asked in a dull monotone.

Senora de Cuyas looked at her husband with raised eyebrows, furrowed brow, and troubled eyes, a silent movie scene captioned "The senorita is bewildered."

"There is no Carlos here," De Cuyas said gently, full of compassion for her plight.

"Carlos Ronderos," Sylvia insisted in a flat, positive tone.

De Cuyas shrugged. "I have already explained to you, I have nothing to do with Carlos Ronderos."

Now the worried, kindly doctor, lips pursed in careful consideration, eyes keenly assessing her condition, threw in his two cents. "Do you have these bad dreams—dreams in the course of which you become violent—often?"

"Every night," Sylvia said flippantly.

The doctor's eye slid to a table and the little black bag that rested on it. Sylvia was struck with terror. What if he gave her an injection, something that would knock her out as the chloroform had done? Hank was only one against a whole ranchful of enemies. These people could do whatever they wished with the two of them.

But why hadn't they already done so? And where was Carlos? Were they waiting for his orders? Was he getting things ready to kidnap her again, this time successfully? For that matter, why hadn't his previous attempt *been* successful?

She sank back on the pillow, too tired to think anymore. She could inventory her body pains better now. Her right shoulder seemed to have been wrenched, her chin was bruised, and her foot throbbed.

But her head was the worst. She put her hand to it.

"Do you want some medicine for your headache?" the doctor asked.

Sylvia laughed scornfully. She'd as soon swallow poison as accept medicine from the De Cuyases' doctor, if he even was one.

"Get out, all of you," Hank suddenly yelled. *"Pronto!* Now!" he barked.

Sylvia's eyes opened wide. What was he doing, giving the De Cuyases orders when he and Sylvia were practically prisoners in their house? Then, for the first time in her life, her jaw actually dropped open. All three were obeying Hank, falling all over themselves to get out of the room at his command.

Hank sat down on the side of the bed and leaned over her. "You'll be all right," he said earnestly. "You were banged around a bit, but nothing was broken. What happened?"

Sylvia told him about waking up and finding Carlos by the side of her bed, pleading for forgiveness, then about the entry of De Cuyas and another man, the chloroform, her kicking at the lamp, and the feeling that she was being thrown to the ground.

"The crash of the lamp woke me up," Hank said. "I ran out of my room and banged on your door and called you. Then I went back to my room and got a gizmo I use to unlock doors. You were on the floor. There was no one else in the room. The windows were open, the curtains waving in the breeze."

"The army's banners," Sylvia murmured.

"What?"

"Nothing. The last thing I saw before I lost consciousness were the curtains blowing. I thought they were the banners of an ancient army."

"Anyway, I didn't suspect foul play, although I should have." Hank's voice was bitter. "I thought maybe the strain we had been under finally got to you, that you had had a bad dream and fallen out of bed, knocking over the lamp as you went."

"In other words, I had a crazy fit. Thanks. Thanks a lot."

"Listen, I'm going to feel guilty for the rest of my life, thinking about what might have happened to you. To continue, I saw that your foot was bleeding and woke Senora de Cuyas up to help me take care of you. Then she and her husband called their doctor."

"Is he a real doctor?" Sylvia asked.

"Yeah. I gather he services all the ranches in the area. But I was present when he examined you, and so was Senora de Cuyas."

"How come *you* were giving them orders, Hank, when obviously we're practically prisoners here on the ranch? And why did they obey you?"

"Because I've got the drop on them, baby, the real old-fashioned d-r-o-p." Hank was beside himself with glee. "Senor de Cuyas is going to fly us to Santa Cruz tomorrow, and the senora is going to pack us a lunch."

"Stop being so mysterious." Sylvia put her hand to her head again. The throbbing pain made her irritable. "What do you have on them?"

Hank looked at her solicitously. "Do you want a cold cloth for that head?"

Sylvia rolled her eyes to indicate the last stages of frustration. "No! I want your story."

"Okay. Hold on to the side of the bed," Hank said exuberantly. "Here it is."

CHAPTER FIFTEEN

"I went poking around the outbuildings of the ranch night before last. I was curious about one in particular. The door was locked, and it looked like a small warehouse or storeroom. But other supplies and equipment weren't locked up, so I asked myself what was in that building that was so valuable."

Sylvia nodded, then regretted it. The movement caused a piercing pain in her head. "Naturally you had to find the answer," she said with an amused smile.

"Naturally. And guess what I found inside this building?"

"The Seven Dwarfs, polishing diamonds?"

"Making cocaine," Hank said softly. "Actually, there was no one there. But the building houses a perfect little processing lab for cocaine."

Sylvia arched one eyebrow into a question mark; then, speaking slowly, she traced out the logic of the operation. "De Cuyas flies it in from Bolivia, processes it on his ranch, then flies it out for shipment and sales, probably to the U.S. Right?"

"Right on the nail."

"But where do you come in? I mean, after you made the discovery, then what?"

"There's a shortwave set in the lab. De Cuyas and his contact and probably Carlos communicate that way." Hank put his hand in his pocket and pulled out a cassette. "I figured someone in the De Cuyas family would have a tape recorder. I searched the kids' rooms first and found one. Then I sent a message to the States on the shortwave and taped both it and the answer."

"Whom did you get?" Sylvia was excited. This was spy-thriller stuff. "The police? The FBI?"

Hank grinned. "I got a ham operator in Louisville, Kentucky. A high school science whiz who was home in bed with the flu.

"I told him about my terrific find—a cocaine laboratory in the Gran Chaco in Paraguay. He thought I was putting him on and kept saying things like 'Hey, man, you'd better get off that stuff. You got delusions of grandeur, you know that?' "

Sylvia threw caution to the winds and laughed. Then she winced. "Why does my head hurt so much?"

"You hit that tiled floor with a lot of impact. As I said, nothing was broken, but everything inside got jolted around."

"That makes sense," Sylvia said. "Did you tape this boy's remarks?"

Hank nodded. "With a lot of prompting till I got him saying things that sounded as though they might be coming from an official source. Fortunately he had a deep voice and sounded older."

"Then what did you do?"

"As soon as I discovered that De Cuyas was running drugs, I suspected a link to Carlos. Naturally I was afraid that De Cuyas, like Fowler, would want to do Carlos the favor of turning us over to him, so I played the tape for De Cuyas and told him the man I had contacted was in the international section of the Drug Enforcement Administration in Washington. I implied that I was an undercover DEA investigator. From then on I had him eating out of my hand."

"Not exactly," Sylvia reflected aloud. "He helped Carlos try to kidnap me."

"True, but as I see it, De Cuyas was between a rock and a hard place."

"My heart bleeds for him," Sylvia murmured.

Hank ignored her remark. "On the one hand," he continued, "De Cuyas thought the DEA knew exactly where I was, so he couldn't get rid of me. On the other, he couldn't afford not to do as Carlos asked because without Carlos he had no drug operation."

"After you had supposedly reported him to the DEA, he had no drug operation anyway, did he?" Sylvia asked logically.

"He probably figured he could finagle his way out of a crackdown, particularly if he had Carlos, with all his influence, on his side. What he couldn't afford to do was offend Carlos."

"So when Carlos flew here and asked De Cuyas to help kidnap me if I didn't go away with him willingly, De Cuyas said yes. He hid Carlos in one of the buildings on the ranch, and either he or his wife put knockout drops in my drink. But when I kicked over the lamp and you banged at my door, they didn't dare go through with the kidnapping."

"Right," Hank drawled.

"Where's Carlos now, do you think?"

"Gone back to San Lorenzo, I should imagine. While the doctor was examining you, I heard a small plane take off."

"Is there any chance of the law catching up with Carlos and the others—Otto Lang and Brute and De Cuyas—or at least of someone's exposing their vicious activities?"

"I'm going to see what I can do," Hank said dryly. He glanced out the window. The sky was beginning to brighten. "It'll be dawn soon. Let's get our pilot and have him fly us to Santa Cruz. I don't care if I never see this country again."

Hank avoided De Cuyas's outstretched hand when they landed in Santa Cruz. Sylvia fingered her blouse and said stiffly, "I'll send these clothes back to Senora de Cuyas as soon as I can." She walked away from the rancher's flowery protestations that she could keep them and he hoped there were no hard feelings.

"I can't wait to get them off me," Sylvia said as leaning on Hank, she limped across the tarmac to the terminal and a taxi. "What's De Cuyas going to do now, fly to some jungle airstrip and load his plane up with the raw materials for his cocaine lab?"

"I don't think so. He and Carlos will probably lie low for a while to see what our DEA does now that, as they think, it knows about them."

"Are you going to tell the DEA, Hank?"

"You bet. The war against drugs is international in scope, so they'd definitely be interested. But hey, let's forget about that bunch of crummy bastards for a while." He looked out the windows of the cab, then turned to Sylvia. "We're out," he said in an awed tone. "We're free. We made it, Sylvia, and we didn't leave any loose ends behind us either, anyone who'd have to pay the price for us."

He put his hand out and ran the back of it gently down her cheek. Her face was thin and pale, a little gaunt even. She was less pretty than he had ever seen her, but more beautiful, everything that was unessential to her stripped away by the suffering she had endured. It seemed to him that he had never loved her as much as he loved her at this instant, never desired her with the burning intensity he felt now.

Sylvia caught his hand and held it. She glanced out the window at the busy street and buildings, a movie theater, a park with swings. "I feel strange," she said with a little laugh, "as though I'm not quite ready to reenter the world yet."

"You're undergoing what people who have been through an intense experience—combat soldiers, prisoners of war—feel. You'll get over it."

"I suppose that's true," Sylvia said thoughtfully, turning back to him. "Right now you're the only person I want to see because you know what it was like back there."

Hank put his other hand on top of hers. "Will you marry me, Sylvia? I want you in my life always. I want to wake up in the morning and see you beside me, your golden hair spread out on the pillow, your lips turned up in a smile as though you had just had a happy dream. I want to listen to you laugh, the way your voice starts low and kind of bubbly, then rises and rises to a real, lusty laugh. I want to watch you move in that neat, graceful way you have." Hank lowered his voice. "I want to hold you in my arms and make love to you. Always."

Sylvia's green eyes were luminous with honesty and love. "Always, Hank. I'll always love you. I think I started loving you on Caldera Street. I thought you were . . . noble."

"I loved you from the moment I held you in my arms. I had to see you again. The thought that you might be friendly with Carlos drove me right up the wall."

Hank took her face between his hands then and tenderly pressed his lips to hers. The kiss was a slow fuse igniting their desire for each other. As the taxi stopped in front of their hotel, Sylvia pushed him gently away, but her heart was beating fast. She wanted Hank's love. She *needed* to be part of him again, to breathe in unison with him, to be so close that their bodies shared the same human smell.

The room clerk cast a worried look at them—Sylvia with her bruised face and bandaged foot, Hank in his ill-fitting clothes—but registered them anyway, with a raised-eyebrow "No baggage" to the bellhop as he handed the boy their key.

When they were alone in the room, Sylvia flung her arms wide. "It's luxurious!" she cried.

"It's only a bed, a bureau, and a couple of chairs," Hank said modestly as if he owned the place.

"But it's modern, and the bathroom has a shower—I peeked while you were tipping the bellhop—and it's ours. I like it. I think I'll stay," she added playfully.

"Not a chance. I'm booking us on the first flight to the States tomorrow."

He looked at her as she stood, her back against the wall, the lines of her body soft and yielding with the desire that heated her sea green eyes. All his longing for her blazed up inside him. His heart pounded against his ribs. His blood ran hot and heavy in his veins. Every muscle tautened and tightened in his urge to hold her, to feel that enchanting combination of delicacy and voluptuousness that was so particularly hers pressed against him.

Sylvia watched him come to her, his eyes opaque with desire. She felt herself flow into his arms as the river meets the sea. There was no seeking, looking, searching now. Their lips met and clung and separated in the sureness of their love. And met again.

Hank took her face between his palms and kissed it all over, pressing his lips gently to the too-sharp cheekbones, the mauve smudges of fatigue under her eyes, the bruise on the small, stubborn chin.

He passed his hands slowly down her sides. It seemed an eternity since he had touched her, had known her in this intimate, warm, close way. He shuddered with a sudden seizure of longing for her. Muttering, "I don't want you wearing their clothes," he ripped at the dress Senora de Cuyas had given her, and her lingerie followed. His hands pushed roughly against her breasts, the palm of his hand hard against their apple-smooth softness.

Sylvia felt faint and swayed a little. All the parts of her body had ached so with their need to be loved by him that she could hardly believe her desires were finally being met. She arched her back against the wall, giving herself to him, willing his mouth on her breasts, seeking its moist passage down her sleek belly, and its final heart-stopping caress where she most longed for him.

The blinds were down at the windows, the slats half open to keep out the sun, yet let in light. They made evenly spaced bars of darkness across Sylvia's love-flushed body. Hank traced the shadow that lay across her breasts with his lips, ending with a little love bite in the valley between the rose-tipped pink mounds.

"What are you doing?" Sylvia asked with a laugh.

"Untying the ribbon around your breasts."

"You're silly, you know that, Hank Weston?" She unbuttoned his shirt and eased it off him. "And you have far too many clothes on." She undid his belt, and Hank's breath came quickly as his excitement increased.

When he was as bare as she, Sylvia laughed, "You're all striped like a zebra too."

"It seems a little late to be teaching you the finer points of zoology, but a zebra's stripes go mostly up and down."

Sylvia wound her arms around his neck and looked with sparkling eyes into his face. "Well, I can't know everything, can I?"

Hank grinned down at her. His long, strong-fingered hands smoothed themselves along her shoulder blades and down the small of her back, sliding farther to grasp the soft, round buttocks.

Sylvia laid her cheek against Hank's virile chest and

sighed with the sheer happiness of being in his arms. She dug her fingers into the hard-hewn muscles of his back, reveling in the feel of his solid flesh.

Then they looked into each other's eyes, smiling proudly, happily. They clung, each to each, deliriously locking together in the thrilling seduction of flesh against flesh, their hot centers touching but not yet joined. The strong South American sun burst through the blinds into the room, lighting and heating their love to the searing intensity it had known on Caldera Street.

Hank lifted her in his arms and carried her to the bed. "I love you so much, Sylvia," he said, leaning over her. "I'm always thirsty for you, hungry for you, wanting to touch you, to love every part of you."

His lips roved her face, then descended to her throat and shoulders, nibbling, sucking, kissing. His hair-roughened chest teased her nipples into crimson crests, which he plucked lightly with his lips as if they were cherries. All the while her honeyed fingers, soft, feminine fingers, stroked him like the golden pollen-full wings of bees, caressing his hard belly and small hips and muscular inner thighs.

He girded her smooth little belly with his kisses and darted his tongue wickedly into her navel. As his kisses dropped lower, Sylvia gasped, and her body convulsed.

She cried out her need, and with a last whispered "I love you," Hank united them in a soaring, surging, joyously exultant act of love.

EPILOGUE

The New York Times, October 5

"Dance"

An extraordinary story was told last night backstage at Brooklyn College's Whitman Hall after the world premiere of the Goddard Dance Group's performance of "Affirmation." Sylvia Goddard, the founder of the company and choreographer of the highly successful, critically acclaimed work, explained that the idea for the dance came when she was forced to hide during a street sweep of so-called subversives in the Paraguayan city of San Lorenzo.

Miss Goddard went on to describe her daring escape with Henry Weston, to whom she is now married, from South American strong man Carlos Ronderos. In the course of their flight from Paraguay, which took them through jungles and across the desolate Gran Chaco, Miss Goddard and Mr. Weston were successively endangered by a Nazi war criminal resident in Paraguay and various members of Ronderos's drug ring.

Mr. Weston is presently writing a book with Peter

Burns, an American journalist who had been missing in Paraguay and whom Weston went to that country to find. Mr. Burns said last night that the book exposing the nefarious activities of Carlos Ronderos will be published next year.

Also present at the interview were Emily Adams and Elena Vanegas-Burns, former residents of San Lorenzo who helped Miss Goddard and Mr. Weston to escape. Mrs. Vanegas-Burns, a student of Miss Goddard's in Paraguay, danced the principal female role in "Affirmation" to enthusiastic applause. (A review of "Affirmation" and the other works performed by the Goddard Dance Group last night appears on Page 19.)